GW00836583

THORSTEIN OF THE MERE

THORSTEIN OF THE MERE;

A SAGA OF THE NORTHMEN

IN LAKELAND

BY

W. G. COLLINGWOOD, M.A., F.S.A.

Author of " Scandinavian Britain," etc.

A NEW EDITION, REVISED
1909

Reprinted
1990 by
LLANERCH ENTERPRISES
ISBN 0947992499

Kendal
Titus Wilson, Publisher
Highgate

" The public, a practical critic has remarked, flies from the very name of a Saga. If the public flies from Mr. Collingwood's *Thorstein of the Mere : a Saga of the Northmen in Lakeland*, the public will be the losers . . . It offers a distinct picture of the old life in the Lake country, when aboriginal Celts, Vikings, English, later Danes, and Scots of Scotland were striving for the mastery. . . On the whole, the book is not so much a Saga as a work in the manner of Bekker's *Charicles* applied to Northern conditions of existence. The story, when once we reach it, is really romantic ; indeed it is a form of the widely-diffused Jason Saga—the loves of the boy and the giant's daughter."—*Times.*

" Interesting, vivid, and convincing . . . Real living creations, whose fortunes deeply affect us. Amongst the other charms of this delightful book are its fine descriptions of scenery, especially mountain scenery. We know of no other work in prose in which the beautiful English Lake district is described with such poetical appreciation . . . Altogether this is one of the healthiest and most fascinating stories that it has been our good fortune to meet with for some time."—*Athenæum.*

HERE BEGINS THE STORY OF THORSTEIN OF THE MERE. CHAPTER I.—THE COMING OF THE NORTHMEN.

THERE was a man called Swein, who came into our country once upon a time, and built a house at Greenodd on the Leven. His father Biorn had been a land-holder in Norway, ploughing his own acres, and living in health and wealth, until King Harald Fairhair fell upon the people, and fought with them and made himself lord and master. Then, it is well known, good men of the old sort, who could not abide to see new laws made and old laws undone, took to their ships and sailed away west. Some of them landed in Iceland; some went to Orkney, and others wandered about the coasts of the Irish Sea to find a home; and wherever they could get shelter and safety, there they settled.

Biorn, with his people and his young child Swein, came to the South Isles, as they called them then—the Western Isles we call them nowadays. He lived as best he might, and died at last in battle, when Harald swept the Vikings from out of the seas between Lewis and Man. But Swein found friends and plenty of work; for there was always farming to do in spring and fighting in summer; and in the end he wedded well, and sat down under Bard Ottarson, who was then chief among the Northmen in the Isle of Man.

Unna was wife to Swein Biornson. She was the child of a Viking in the company of Olaf the White, the Norse king of Dublin, and her mother was Irish. She was akin to great folk, and Swein was the sort of man who could serve his friends; so that they were both well thought of in the island, and hoped for a safe home there. But before long came Ragnwald the Dane, of the sons of Ivar, he that was king in Waterford and in York afterwards; and he killed Bard and most of his people in a sea-fight.

Then Swein fled out of the battle hastily, and took his wife and whatever he could lay hands on, and steered for the far-away blue fells that showed under the morning sun, over against the cliffs of Man. For he knew that some of his kinsfolk had already found lodging on the coasts of Galloway and Cumberland and Wales, where the land was no man's land at that time ; and creeks and firths among the hills gave them sheltered hiding places, well out of sight when great fleets swept the high seas and ravaged the open shore.

When Black Combe grew tall on the sky-line, arose a stormy north-easter, and drove him down the Cumberland coast until he made Furness, the great foreland in the bay of Morecambe. When the wind fell, the tide flowed, and carried him up a broad firth like a gate into the hills. Up-ward he drifted, spying on all sides for a good landing spot ; and try as he might to the shoreward he ran upon sand, and never came nigh the soil. But in a while he turned round a green point, high and rocky and covered with trees, standing out into the deep channel. Behind it was a green field, even with the water, snug and sheltered among hanging woods. A great beck flowed through the field to meet the broad firth. There were no people to be seen, nor smoke of houses, nor cattle about in the good lea-land, and the channel of the river at last came in-shore. So he stayed there, and called that green point in his language Greenodd, and Greenodd it is called to this day.

CHAPTER II.—THE HOMESTEAD AT GREENODD.

ONCE upon an afternoon in summer time it was that our story begins, nine hundred winters and twenty and one since our Lord was born. Swein and his people had been but seven winters at Greenodd ; yet they had built a good house, and cleared land to farm it, and made the place look something like home.

So one afternoon before summer was over, Unna sat rocking her baby Thorstein to sleep, and sewing as she stirred the cradle with her foot, and singing as she sewed.

She wore a gown of ruddy colour, long sleeved; with a kerchief round her neck, and a housewife's apron; but because she was of high birth, she had a gold band like a crown round her head, and her yellow hair was tucked about it and fell away unbraided from under a white headrail. A silken pocket hung from her belt, and on her finger was a gold ring; but her jewels for the most part were locked away in a kist, against high-days and holidays. For this was a working day, and every one was busy.

Most folk were out of doors that time of year; only the mother was at home, minding the baby after her morning's turn round the farm; and to keep her company, an old nurse who, being a brisk body, was putting in a spell of work at a standing loom of the ancient make. She threw the shuttle slowly, and combed up the web but slackly, for the afternoon was warm, and the sun outside beat upon the roof of the house and made it hot. For the house was like one of our barns with its rafters and beams unceiled : and though it was heavily thatched, the air was hot within. It was somewhat gloomy too, in spite of the bright sheen that lay on field and fell. Though door and porch door stood open, the rest of the place was lit only by the smoke-hole in the roof. Through the hole a ray of sunlight shot across the hall, and caught on the chain of the hanging lamp, and lit up the thin smoke that rose in the midst. For the hearth fire was never let out if they could help. Even in summer it was needed morning and evening for their cooking, and bad to kindle from fire-stones and rotten sticks. So as wood and peat were plentiful, it was smothered between whiles just to keep it alight, and thus went on from year's end to year's end.

The hearth was in the middle of the floor, raised a little and paved with cobbles set in sammel clay. One could sit round it, working and tale-telling, and watching acorns and crab apples roast, and the boiling of their porridge in the great pot that hung by an iron crook and a chain from the house-beam over-head. And grand times they had of winter's evenings with their great fires of dry twigs—chats,

we call them—or else logs of which one end was out at the
door while the other was blazing under the black pot, slowly
burning away. They tell a tale of an old house where such
a log had been keeping the fire up for three days, when—
whoop! out flew an owl.

Up through the gloom and the little space of sun went the
thin blue smoke, like a stripe of rain from April clouds. At
the roof it was caught by the chimney flue, which was
covered like a belfry with a flagstone laid flat upon pillars,
but opening out beneath and crossed by the house-beam.
In the smoke hung the last hams and dried meat of the year
before. For at the back end of the year they always hung
their flesh meat against the winter, and Unna was too wise
a house-wife to let them eat all up before the next store was
laid in, however plentiful the season might be.

You must know this " firehouse " was the main hall and
living room of the homestead. Bedcupboards there were
alongside of it within the wall, and out-buildings; and a loft
among the beams, and an earth-house or cellar dug out
under the floor at one end of the hall. But the fire-house
was the House, as one may say; and in a homely spot like
this backwood bigging at Greenodd a thousand years since,
everything went forward in the firehouse; cooking and
eating, work and play, business and pleasure. This was
their hearth and home.

At one corner were its door and porch opening upon the
garth, and at the back part were out-buildings rising sharply
up the hill behind. At the ends of the hall under the gables
were great arks and kists against the wall, and at one end
the aforesaid loom : but along the side were hung the men's
weapons, spears and shields and coats of mail, and their
hunting and fishing tackle, well out of the way, over long
benches that lined the hall on either hand.

In the middle of the benches were two high seats, one on
this side and one on that, over against it. They were like
the great elbow-chairs or settles you see in old farm-houses ;
roomy enough for three, carved on their high backs, and

with carved heads to their posts in front. The children had a tale that one head was father and one was mother : older folk would say the figures stood for Odin and Freya. Anyway they were something more than just ornaments ; they gave a holiness to the place, and made the high seat of the master as it were a kind of temple-stall.

Before the benches on one side stood a long narrow table, all of oak, like the seats and the wainscotting and the rest, brown already with age and bright with rubbing : but on the other side the tables had been taken off their trestles and laid up to make more room, and because half their men were abroad with Swein at sea. On this side sat Unna in her own high seat with the cradle at her feet, and before her the hearth with its thin smoke going up, and the sun-ray striking through it, and blazing in the fern that was strewed on the floor. And when the sun-spot crept upon the cradle she stooped down and moved it a little backwards, so that the bright light should not wake the baby. And when he stirred she pushed the cradle with her foot and sang again while she sewed at his shirt. And the loom went clattering on with the steady noise that is good for babies' slumber. Nothing else was heard, except the birds singing in the green-wood around, and far-away clamour of people working in the fields.

When the baby was sound asleep again, Unna rose, and walked softly to see where his brothers might be : and her gown trailed on the ferny floor. She stood in the porch and called, but not too loudly, " Ho ! Orm ! Hundi ! where are you ? what are you doing ? "

But they were off. And so she sat down again and sewed till her eyelids were heavy with the warmth and the dimness of the place.

" Eh, barn," she said, " what makes one so drowsy ? sleep by day and starve at night, they used to say."

" Most like a stranger is coming," said the old woman from the loom.

For it was thought that a man's fetch went before and brought slumber.

" Few strangers here but bad ones," said Unna.

" May be it's the master and the men."

" Why, they are gone but these three weeks, and who knows when they may come back, and how ? And it's weary waiting, and a deal on one's hands : let alone the chances of raid and robbery."

" What, there's Raud thy brother and all," said the old woman sharply. " And folk must live. It would be ill liked if the master never brought home an armful of finery, or another hand or so for the farm, or a barrel of somewhat sharper than we can brew."

" Aye, it's a lone spot : not that I complain : for Raud is a handy lad. It will be a bad day when he takes land upbank, as he talks of doing."

" Nay, never heed his talk. He must light on some one fit first," answered the weaver : " and how will he do that hereaway, I'd like to know ? As for thy man, and my man, and the rest, they are men, with hands to their elbows and heads on their shoulders."

" Or had, you may say, to start with," said Unna with a sigh.

" Heads, aye, and know their ways about. Look at my old man. These forty winters he has come back to me the same as ever."

" Aye, he has a cat's life, has old Toli."

" Not so old as that comes to, neither," said the crone. " And thankful we should be for our good men and for a good roof over us. Eh, child, when I think on all we have come through."

" No fells, no dales," said she : " no loom, no clatter ; " but she hastened to add " I am out of sorts to-day. There's overmuch to be done before they come, to redd all up for the back end. There are his sarks which were put by at the washing, and I warrant never rightly smoothed. I wonder where the lasses have put the linen-glasses." And she got up and walked uneasily to the wardrobe kists.

" Nay, barn, let it be : it's none of thy job," said the old woman ; muttering to her loom, for there was nobody else to hear. " The mistress is queer and fidgetty to-day. One might think somewhat was going to happen."

The lasses were raking hay, and the round knobs of glass which they used to smooth linen were not where they should have been. Unna went again to the door. Over the water, and all round, wooded hills shook in the heat-haze. She shaded her eyes and looked once more for Orm and Hundi, but nought she spied. She came back and sat on a stool against her high-seat, and tried to sew. But the sun-spot crept on to her lap, like some little wounded animal, dragging itself painfully to refuge there. It shone through her work, and through her fingers, so that they seemed blood-red : and it dived into the red stone in her ring, and made it redder than blood : and it burned on the gold like the whole sun itself, a blaze of mystery, a dream of glory.

Clitter-clatter the loom went on. " Poor soul," said the old woman : " best thing she can do "—as she saw Unna's tired head sink back against the post of the high-seat, and her long white throat slide out of the white neckerchief, and her chin heaved up, like a blown wild rose leaf, warm in the reflected sunshine.

Then in the stillness the sun-spot dragged itself off her hand and off her lap, and tumbled to the floor again in one ronndel, just like a bubble that gathers !tself together in the dark pool under a waterfall, out of the shattering of the spray : a dream of death.

Clitter-clatter went on the loom nevertheless : and the birds sang still in the green world outside. The mother's dreams were soft and sweet, of life's love, and life's labour, that never fail nor come to bitterness; for these regard not glory, and fear not death.

CHAPTER III.—SWEIN'S HOME-COMING.

NOW we leave Mistress Unna and baby Thorstein asleep, to tell about Orm and Hundi and how they floated boats. Those boys had run off to the workshop where

smithying was done, and found a heap of chips and shavings,
and made each of them a boat, with a thin shaving for a sail :
like the lad Harald (Hardradi they called him later) when
Olaf the Saint asked him what were those chips and shavings.
" My war-ships," said he. Of course they must away to the
beck, as nobody was there to shout after them. So they ran
over the cobble-paved garth between the byres, and out at
the gate of the turf wall that stood round about the " town."
Then they were at the boat-landing, among planks and
rollers, ropes and chains, and the delicious smell of tar that
hung about the boat building sheds, and reeked in the hot
sunshine.

The shore was steep, and shelving into a dub just there :
so they ran downbank towards the flats that open out below
the point. Under the crags and fir-trees of the nab they had
to scramble over rocks and stones, and to splash through salt
pools left by the outgoing ·tide : but soon they came to a
stretch of rippled sand between fell and firth, and waded a
beck that flowed from the woods and wound northward along
their edge to join the Leven.

" Ha ! " said Orm, " now we are on my fairy island. It is
all gold, and yon side the beck runs down, and yon side the
beck runs up. Now we are on my holm, and I will fight thee
for thy boat."

So Orm beat Hundi, and ran off with both the boats and
pushed them from the shore until they sailed downbank with
the tide. There was no one to cry for, so Hundi held his
peace : he brushed his eyes with his hand and pattered on,
his bare feet crisping the soppy sand ripples, and leaving their
prints in a chain of little tarns. And when he came to the
next bend in the river, lo and behold his own boat came
straight to shore and into his hands, while the boat that Orm
had made was rocking in mid-channel with its sail draggled
in the water. Orm began to throw handfuls of sand over it,
to draw it in : and while they were intent upon this job and
keeping no look out, suddenly they heard shouts not far off,
and the clash of oars, and a great craft swung round into

that reach and bore straight down upon the chip boat. A moment they stood dumfoundered, and then turned and ran for the woods like young rabbits. For in those days it was no idle threat when mothers said to truant boys—" Mind you don't go out of sight, for fear a man catches you."

But just when the throb began to beat very hard in their throats, and they were stopped by the steep crumbling banks of the little beck that bounded the holm, they heard, like a shepherd calling sheep, " Ho, Orm! ho, Hundi! ho!" and they turned and looked: and then looked at one another with bright eyes and panting too much to laugh. They set off running back to the ship, which they knew well enough now. The rowers had eased and brought her close to the edge of the sandbank: and that could well be done, for she drew very little water and was nigh flat bottomed. Swein, with a brown square face, and bushy fair beard, and bright blue eyes laughing out of the locks of his tawny hair, came wading ashore. He caught up one child under each arm, waded out again, and hoisted them to hands aboard. Then catching at the gunwale near the steering oar, he raised himself half-length and vaulted over. The water dripped from his gartered hose and blue kirtle skirts : for his mail-coat was doffed, and he wore only a belted kirtle or blouse over his white linen sark.

" Eh, father, mother will snape thee for getting of thyself in a mess!" said Hundi compassionately. " But never heed her: I'll say it was to fetch us aboard."

" But my dragon is wrecked," grumbled Orm.

" And is that all you have to say to your old father when he comes home?"

" Nay," said Orm, looking round coolly, " what have ye brought me?"

" No great things, barn, this trip," said Swein, with half a smile, as he took the steering oar. " Now then, lads, all's well, by this token. The barnes say little, but there is enough of it, and enow of them. Forward all now ; a spurt to finish our day's work. Lift her ! here she goes. Lift her !"

A dozen of long blades, six aside, with a couple of men at each, churned the sandy shallows, as the boat swept round the curve and up stream. Long in the keel and low in the board she was, with swinging curves at stem and stern rising swan-like to the figure-head and the carved stern-post. But the ugly dragon mask was taken off the bows, now that they were so near home; for it was a belief among these people that the land-wights, good fairies and useful brownies, would be scared by such a sight, or at least take it in dudgeon, and depart. So the figure-head had a good face for home-waters, and a hideous one to put on when they got out to sea and to work among strangers. The gunwales were notched into dog-tooth markings and what old wives call box-pattern in their quiltings. The strong upstanding tholes were curiously carved with knots and worm-twists. Great oars were lashed to these tholes and the rowers stood to their work and pushed the handles. There was a step for a mast forward, but the mast and yard were lying along the gangway that ran between the ranks of rowers, from the decked forecastle to the quarter deck; and the sail, useless to-day, was wrapped about the spars. There was little else to be seen: the few bales or chests she might carry were stowed below, and her decks were clear, as if at any moment she might meet with an enemy. Over the gunwale hung the men's shields, a dozen aside, each by its strap from its own pin, and ready to be caught up in the twinkling of an eye. Black and gold they were painted for the most part, and if one was more black then the next was more golden, so they made a fine show from without.

Every man aboard was a sturdy fellow, who would go through with it, whatever he took in hand; bronzed with the sun and great-thewed with downright hard work. Some of them were Swein's own Northmen from the Isle of Man, old comrades and followers of former days: some were Welsh of the country, his bought servants, but trusty men under a good leader. They were all his house-mates, or lived in cots of their own hard by.

So now that they were near home they laid to with a will. The children played helping father with the steering sweep, which knocked them over every time it was put up or down. Swein gave the stroke, faster and faster as the landing place came in sight, with his " Lift her !" and they made her spin up the last reach. Round she went, and half-way up the bank ploughing the sand. Orm and Hundi tumbled on the deck laughing. Then out men leapt, and ran her up on her rollers above high-water mark, as they were used with these light flat-bottomed craft. The easier it was, for by now they were spied and recognised from the fields, and a dozen farm servants had run down to lend a hand.

You may be sure it was merry-night that evening at Greenodd, and Unna was wide awake and bustling to make amends for her laziness, as she called it. The servant lasses had a busy time, with the fire to stoke, and the supper to cook, and the tables to set. Meanwhile the men went to their bath in the bath-house, and shifted their sea-clothes. Long before the sun sank behind the high fell at the back of the house they were sitting at meat, cooled and ravenous, on the long hall-benches, behind heaps of barley cake and haverbread, and dried fish ; great bowls of broth and porridge into which many spoons were dipped at once : and platters of butter and cheese and curds, and trenchers piled with steaks, which they ate with their sheath-knives : and it may be said for them that if some eat foully with forks, others, to the manner bred, can eat fairly with fingers. As to drinking, the lasses had their work in running to and fro with ale and buttermilk, to slocken thirsty men who had rowed from Carnforth since breakfast on a broiling hot day.

CHAPTER IV.—ON THE HOWE.

SWEIN was in his own high seat, and while the din lasted ate like another, looking now and then but shyly through the hearth-smoke at Unn over against him. At last " Eat, Unna !" he cried, " and take thy supper. One

would think I was a merman, and stared at for a show,   Sup
thy porridge, lass, and be hearty."

- " I have supped," she said, " and supped well."

"Supped with her eyes," said old Toli, for here he was,
holding out his empty horn.   " A big supper, too, but a dry
one."

" I've seen her eat nought," said Swein.   " What has she
supped on ? "

" Thee," said Toli.   " Eh, Mistress ? "

But Unna, though she was used to the uncourtly ways of
her own folk and could laugh at a rough jest, was less at
ease than she had hoped to be.   When the meal began, she
had looked lovingly across at her man, making out his
features one by one through the dimness and the smoke,
watching for the open smile that he was used to give her, on
such nights as these of home-coming, when his first hunger
was stayed and the feasting was forward : the free smile and
friendly nod that signalled all's well.   But this time it was
long in coming : and she got only the half glances and the
rough and puzzling " Eat, child."   Her eyes filled with tears,
and her mind flew to chances of mishap.   There were all the
men back, and no wounds to be seen : the ship was safe :
what could it be?   Some woman in the case.   What else ?
And her quick wit, wrong for once, revealed to her, like a
lightning flash, a whole story of dismay.

Men were fed by now, and they drank healths, first to
Odin for the kinsfolk, and then to Niord and Frey for peace
and plenty.   When they were come to the cup for Bragi—he
was the god of talking and of tale-telling and song,—it was
Swein's old use and wont to begin the story of his doings and
travellings since the last farewell, and to hold them all till
midnight wrapt in the tale.   This time he put down the horn
untasted : and when they waited for him in wonder, suddenly
hushed, he thrust the table from him, and went forth.

Unna looked at Raud her brother who sat by her, signing
with her eyes as much as to say " What now ? " and the sign
he gave her was a nod toward the door.

" Aye, mistress," said Toli, " till him, and wheedle him
back. To think of folk leaving good ale for an idle whim."

" What then ? " she said, flashing back at him, while Raud
made room for her.

" Nought that matters : nay, never ask of me."

With a beating heart she went through the porch, and her
knees trembled as she passed. Swein was going slowly
through the garth, slackening his pace, though he neither
turned nor looked ; but yet it seemed as if he wanted to be
overtaken.

There is a steep path up the cliffs a little to the seaward of
the houses, mounting rapidly at first over the crags by rude
steps in the rock, and then through the great rough stems of
ancient fir-trees, and between thickets of blackberry-brambles,
until it comes out upon a clear space on the top. It is not
so far that one need halt to take breath by the way, and yet
lofty enough for the eye to sweep north, south, east and west,
down the firth and up the valley, and across to the far-away
fells.

This was Swein's howe, where he went daily and often-
times a day, to watch the bright line of the sea, if by chance
a sail might be made out, friend or foe or merchant vessel
cruising round the coast. There also he could overlook his
land ; for the acres of oats and barley and the hay-fields lay
close beneath, around the mouth of the Crake. His own
summer pastures were on the fells hard by, and his swine fed
in the woods around. He could see what was doing, and
what was left undone, from that howe : count men and beasts,
and hear the sounds of work going on in smithy or shed.
Here he would take counsel with himself about new dealings
with this man and that, and lay his plans and dream over his
enterprises. And when there was trouble or when things
went aslew, it was on this howe that he sat to wrestle with
his thoughts. And it was his mind when he should be dead
to be buried there and look out from his grave upon his
children and his home, and the kind land that had given him
a resting-place from his wanderings.

He sat down upon the turf seat on the top, and Unna, who had tripped lightly after him, sat down alongside. He rested both elbows on his knees as one ashamed to speak, but moved not away. What can it be? was her thought.

For now the sun was set in the gold half of the sky, and the other half was clear pansy coloured, with a round moon rising through the fringe of dusky woods. Below them the tide was flowing in, and the wash of it was heard in the stillness: the great rings and bows of the river in front swung about and along over the silvery flats, like the track of a skater on ice. And against the northern glow far away, sharp violet ridges of distant mountain stood around them, serene, above the tumbling forest and rich promontories of Crake and Leven.

Then she slid her arm over his shoulder, and her fingers twitched at the brooch that fastened his cloak; and it seemed that he was her man still. The moon had disentangled itself at last, and began to glimmer on the tide ripple. " Twilight brings talk," thought Unna, and waited for him to begin.

CHAPTER V.—THE KING'S MOTE.

" WELL, wife," said Swein at last, " I am trapped, seemingly. It is stand and deliver, is it? What, there is nothing so dreadful after all, turn and turn it over as one may. But that is yet to be judged: I suppose I must put my case, and tell my story.

" How we set off I need not tell. We came to Carnforth, and there we met most of our neighbours from the country-side. There was Arnolf out of Duddoner-dale, Raven and Ulfar, Orm and Hauk from Furness-way; and Arni was there on the spot, for he lives hard by, and it was his folk looked after the ships of us that came by water; and other friends from over the sands. We took counsel together, and agreed that being summoned to this meeting, be it peace or war, we should go: but that we should keep together and make one band, for it is ill dealing with folk that are neither kith nor kin.

" Thou knowest, Unn, that we reckoned this bit of land was no man's land until we came and took it. Northward beyond the fells the Welsh hold themselves under the rule of Donal mac Ædh, the Strathclyde king ; but never did I hear of his coming into these parts or having a power on Morecambe coasts. Across there in Cartmel they say they belong to the minster priests in York, and be no king's men at all : and beyond that again, if Ragnar Lodbrog's sons did ever take the land, neither English nor Dane in Kentdale or Lunesdale has paid shot to York for many a year. Less than fifty years ago, after Halfdan the Old sacked Carlisle and laid all these parts under him, and began to settle them from the eastward, then I grant you, this would be in the Danelaw. But now that there is is no law in York, but only these rascally bearsarks of Danes sacking and slaying up and down, why, look you, we owe them nothing, and need but keep together to be our own men like the Icelanders. And this talk we held to be but fair and good, and took hands all round upon it.

" So we got horses at the bank where the old road meets the sands, and came to a burg called Lancaster where we had to meet the main part of the host from the north. The burgers gave us what we wanted with little ado : a handful of chapmen and cowpers who trade with travellers on the great highway. But I thought they grinned a little when we talked of going against the Saxons.

" Well, in a day or so there is a great trumpetting and booming, and up marched men from Constantine the Scots king and his brother Donal of Strathclyde, and among them Ketel and others of our own men from Cumberland, and some from Galloway : and it was hail fellow with many an old friend.

" ' It seems we are but short-handed,' said I : ' or is the Saxon king of less account than we reckon for ? '

" With that they laughed outright, and the cat came out of the bag, tail and all : for they told us flatly that there was no fighting to be thought of : but only a great meeting of all the people in Britain under their kings and earls.

" ' And pray what king do you reckon us to be under ? ' said I to Ketel.

" ' Well,' said Ketel, ' Donal flatters himself because I have taken up my abode in his borders, that I am his man. I remember well, when I first met him, what a wagging of beards there was. Some were for hunting us out, at which the old whiteheads turned pale, though I made as if I understood none of their *dim saisnaeg*. By and by the whitest beard of all made a terrible long-winded speech, setting forth how, if they turned us out, there would be swarms more of us revenging ourselves upon them : and how there was land enough and to spare on the holms and flats by Dundraw : and how, when we Northmen were let alone we were decent merchants, buying goods and servants. He said we always had plenty of money and brought trade to the country-side : and he wound up in a flowery way—I could understand him well :—Look you, says he, waving his old skinny arms about. These white strangers (for they call us white, and the Danes black, and right they are to my thinking) these strangers, says he, will be a soft bolster to our heads. When hard knocks come, they will get them, and we shall feel the less.— So they blethered and clattered like crows, and in the end let us be : and here we are ! '

" ' Well, Ketel Bolster,' said I—eh, how they did laugh— ' If Donal suits thee for lord and master, he suits not me.' At which Ketel would at me, and I would have beaten him well, only they stood in and stopped us.

" Next day we trotted along the great high road. It's a strange thing, Unna, that folk ever took the trouble to heap hard stones together for nought but to walk on. But there it goes up hill and down dale, through bog and brink ; and everly built with cobbles, for all the world like a great long hearth spot, and as straight as an arrow-flight from day's end to day's end. They told me it was folk from Romeburg that built it ; though what they could have done it for, I know nought : unless it were a priest's trick to mark out the Church gate. Anyhow it was hard riding clitter-clatter on the cobbles all day long: I had rather have galloped over the green grass: but keep together was the word, for there were but few of us, and with such a pack of Welsh and Scots before and behind, one never knows what may happen.

"The next night we harboured at a spot they called Ribblechester, and the next at Manchester, which is a pretty place, and one would have thought a strong work enough to hold against any comers: but the Saxons took it last summer from those lubberly Danes. I fell in talk with the goodman where they lodged us, and it seemed that not only they in Manchester, but all the Danelaw, had got a thorough fright of the Marchmen and the Saxons, and they were hastening to this meeting like thralls to supper, each afraid to be last man in.

"'And who are *they*?' say I.

"'Why,' says he, 'everybody of account, but in especial the new king of York.'

"'New king?' say I.

"'Aye,' says he: 'Ragnwald Ivarson.'

"'What!' say I; 'Ragnwald, the rascal? He was at Waterford but a while since, and then in Scotland; what is he doing here?'

"'Why,' says he, 'where in the round world is thy den, man or mountain bear?'

"'Softly,' say I: 'Swain is my name and Bear's son is my breeding. Swain's fist or bear's paw, which wilt have?'

"'No offence, guest,' says he: 'But I thought every one knew that Ragnwald beat the Scots and Saxons at Tyne-moor—'

"'Well!' say I.

"'And marched into York.'

"'Marched into hell!' said I.

"'No such thing: there he is, and thou wilt see him at the king's mote, for he will be there to make his peace with Eadward and be confirmed in his kingdom.'

"'He shall see me,' said I, 'and get other peace than he wots of.'

" For Unna, never a day passes but I think of that fight off
Man, and our good Bard's ship going down with the Dane's
iron beak through her ribs.

" Well, this last day we rode over fells they called Peak to
Bakewell, and if it was forecast at Manchester, here was
sooth. Hardly were we within sight of the place, but a flock
of horsemen comes spurring out to meet us, and after some
parley makes a lane for us to pass through, one by one, like
sheep counted into a fold : and of each a jack-in-office asks
name and nation and so forth before he may go his ways.
And when we come among the houses, which were as thick
as trees in a wood, we must halt till we are told off to our
lodgings : and there we must bide till it please my lord the
Saxon king to see us. Not but that we were well bestowed
for bed and board : and to see the sights was something.
Houses, I say, for ever, and nigh upon all of them new built
or even in the building. Strangers from all parts of the land ;
why, from all the round world it seemed. And all day and
every day market in the lanes and open places, and wares to
be bought the like of which I never saw, not even on Dublin
strand when the fleet comes in. What little I had of silver
in my bag soon went : but it passed the time to chaffer and
turn the wares over. I got a bit of a scarf : the cowper said
it came from Micklegarth and maybe beyond : even he was
all the way from Londonburg. I paid a pretty penny for it,
and yet thought I was making a good bargain. Mayhappen
you will shake your head : but don it first. There are two or
three trifles beside in a kist the lads will bring up and we can
unpack to-morrow.

" All this while no Ragnwald was to be seen, and I began
to reckon nought of the Manchester man's tale. At last
comes jack-in-office, and bids us to the Saxon king : and in
we go : over a bridge and through a gate in the stout oaken
wall new cut : and there is a yard in the midst, full of his
housecarles, and one could not but see with half an eye
that they were big fellows and their weapons were of the
best.

" I need not tell thee, Unna, what a king's house is like : but this hall was a sight to see, for its bigness without, and within for its hangings and carvings and gold and silver : yet most of all for the king we have heard tell about sitting on his high seat, all gold, with his high crown and gold staff : and his earls and priests in gold cloaks and caps, holding their crooks like so many warlocks : and indeed who knows what spell they were casting over us ? Anyhow there were the Scots and Strathclyde Welsh, down on their knees, like men bewitched, and their hands in the king's hands, saying after one that stood by—' We take thee Eadward to be our father and lord, and father and lord of all our folk.' And then came Ealdred Eadulfson of Bamborough, with his English, and did likewise. And then came the earl of Lincoln and a scrow of Danes, and did likewise, only that they made oath on the ring, for they are not Christian men like those that went before. And with them Ragnwald.

" Unna, lass, I was mad wrath when I saw him, and I could have run upon him there : only Ulfar held me by one arm and Ketel by the other, and said ' Peace, man, at a mote ! ' And then stood one forth in the silence, and spoke, ' Forasmuch as you have commended you to our king Eadward, king of Angles and Saxons, and overlord of Cornwall and of Gwynedd and of all the Welsh, to be his men, each and all of you—'

" ' Nay, not I,' cried a voice : they said it was mine, though I knew not I spoke, for I was that angry. But you may guess if there was a haybay and swords drawn. They plucked me by the sleeve and shouted in my ears ' Peace, man, peace ! ' I tried to get at my sword, and looked for Ragnwald first. But the Saxon king sat still on his high seat, and waved his wand, and men were quiet again and I standing thrust out in the midst.

" ' Come hither, good friend,' he said, speaking very fair and slowly, so that I could understand him well, for the Saxon tongue is hard to hear at first : ' Come nigh and tell me what ails thee.'

"And I marched up to the high seat, and said I, 'Nothing but this, king; that I have sworn nought to thee: and I see my enemy standing there.'

"'Softly, good man,' says the king; 'this is a hallowed mote: if all foes here were to fight, we should eat each other up.' And he smiled, Unn, and I could not but laugh too, for I thought of yon Irish cats thy mother used to tell of.

"'And who is thy foe?' says Eadward.

"'Ragnwald Ivarson.'

"With that, out steps Ragnwald as proud as a peacock.

"'I never set eyes on the carle,' says he.

"'But I know thee, Ragnwald,' said I; 'and well I mind the day when thy ship ran Bard's down, seven years ago, off Man.'

"'And is that all?' said he.

"'Come,' said Eadward: 'this day we let bygones be bygones. Have I nothing against Ragnwald, thinkst thou? and were Bard Ottarson's folk sackless of scathe to me and mine? Who art thou, good fellow, and whence?'

"So I told him my name and where I lived: and the upshot of it was that Eadward says, 'Well, then, if I let thee dwell there in peace, wilt thou leave thy neighbours in peace?'

"What could one say but Aye?

"Now, all this while was the high priest muttering and making signs at me, and doubtless I was bewitched. For I looked in the king's eyes and clean forgot about Ragnwald, and all the mind I had to live and die my own man, and no king's man. The people in the hall seemed to be in a dream, and there were I and Eadward only. He reached out his hand to me, and my hand was in his, and the ring fell from his arm upon mine. 'Kneel, man, kneel!' cried the bystanders: but Eadward smiled, like one who has mated you at chess.

"'Take hands on a bargain,' he said: 'that is the Northman's way, is it not? Nay, then, keep the ring, friend Swein.'

"And there it is," said Swein, casting a gold armlet on the turf. "The bull's snout-ring, I call it: the thrall's collar."

"And is that the tale?" said Unna, stooping to pick it up. "Oh, man! serve the best and spurn the worst. I am weary of this wandering and warring; I would fain end our days as this day ends."

And the moon cast a great stream of light along the Leven.

"I thought there could be no welcome for a nithing like me."

"Welcome?" she said. "Thrice welcome for the best tale of these ten years: a thousand welcomes if the peace but hold good."

"Maybe through the winter," said Swein, as they rose to leave the howe. Then, as their feet brushed through the beaded dew, "I doubt if the oath will bind us long," said he. "Methought when he took mine, that I was holding a dead man's hand."

CHAPTER VI.—FURNESS FOLK A THOUSAND YEARS SINCE.

THREE winters wore and three summers came: and Eadward still ruled the land in peace. But about hay-harvest there were rumours, at which Swein nodded to his wife as one who says "You see I was right.'" And when hay-time was well passed, came people from over the fell bidding him to a meeting at Ulfar's town.

Now this Ulfar, of whom we spoke before, had land on the brink of the fells where they met the low country, about an hour's journey to the southward of Greenodd. He was an old man, and he had been a chieftain formerly, and was a man of worth even now, and a stickler for old times and the old laws.

Near his "town" (as we still call hereabouts any cluster of dwellings though it be nothing like a city) and between it and the waterside, there was a broad mound, not so high, but standing by itself: from which could be seen a great ring of

country all round : across the firth, Cark and Cartmel way,
and all the Sandgate, that is the road across the sands of
Leven, and whosoever was coming and going, for good or
ill : and then again westward to Pennington, where the
Pennings lived.

They were an ancient family of English kin long ago settled
there, and busied at whiles in getting red iron ore out of the
iron pits hard by, and smelting it and forging it.   They were
great smiths, and used charcoal in their furnaces or bloomeries
as we call these old works.   The charcoal was got from the
woods that in old times covered all the country : but by now
these Pennings and their people had cleared a deal of ground :
there was the Swartmoor between their town and the old
road, called so, maybe, from the burning that had gone to
clear it.   And so much iron they made that they were glad
to sell it to the merchants who came in ships up the firth.
When Ulfar came, at first they were angry, and fought with
him : but when they found that for all their smith's cunning
they could never give him the smith's stroke, as the saying
is, they came round to the mind of king Donal's counsellors
that Ketel told of.   They made peace with Ulfar, and found
that he was an honest man and abiding by his word.   When
he offered to take their ironmongery and sell it for them,
better than the cowpers who had come before, they were glad
of it, and did all the brisker business in his company : and in
the end they settled down into good neighbours and friends.

When the Northmen came into Furness, beside the
Pennings they found a few English and some Welsh here
and there.   There were Welsh in the low land over against
Walney, and Rhos they called the meadow-land thereabouts.
There were already villages between that and Dalton and up
to Broughton on the Duddon, and churches there, and priests,
no doubt ; but such as heard little of any English bishops, or
what we should call government whether of church or state.
Across at Cartmel the land and all the Welsh that were on it
had long ago been given to York Minster ; but Furness was
a bit of that broad debatable ground over which the tide of

invasion flowed from age to age and ebbed back again, just
like the sea upon Morecambe shores.   As time went on, here
a piece of sand was fully reclaimed, and there a piece of land
was swallowed up by the tide.   So also it is hopeless now to
seek any fixed boundaries of the people or of their language
a thousand years ago : we can only find here and there an
English or a Welsh name among the Norse.

But the Northmen sought the snuggest places for shelter
and for safety.   They always wanted a good landing spot for
their flat-bottomed boats, so that when summer came,
between sheep-shearing and corn harvest, they might use of
their spare time by pushing out to sea and doing a little quiet
trade, or may be at times you might call it "raid," up and
down the coasts of the Irish Sea.   And so they went on
farming and seafaring, turn about, and picked up a better
living the harder they worked at both.

Beside Ulfar there settled others of the Northmen along
the coast.   There would have been Raven at the south point
of Furness, from whom we call Rampside and Ramsey.
Beyond Barr-ey, that is Barley island, there is Orm's Gill,
and round about it the villages into which his folk spread ;
Hawcott, the high cottage ; Sowerby, the muddy farm ;
Sandscale, the shed by the sand ; and so forth.   Then up the
Duddon firth there is Roanhead, that is to say the headland
with the grove of trees, at one end of the road that goes from
Leven sands by Dalton into Cumberland.   Up the firth there
is Duddoner-holme, the island of the Duddon, a fine spot for a
stronghold ;   and opposite to it Mealholm, the sandy isle,
where in after times Millom castle was built ; and a little
higher beyond the Thwaites is the Wolveswater, or Ulfa,
flowing into the great river that encompasses the land of
Furness to the west and the north.

After a while, from these first settlements on the coast,
land was taken up inbank by the families and followers of the
first viking settlers.   Around Ulfar's town there were Rolf's
seat, and Asmund's lea, and Hauk's fields.   But in the lower
land of plain Furness there were homesteads and hamlets of

English at Urswick and Aldingham ; and these the first
comers of the Northmen do not seem to have taken by force
or destroyed, for the names given by the English still remained
to them.   In a while, it is true, they fell to Norse owners,
most likely by marriage and inheritance ; so that in 150 years'
time all the names of landholders in this part were names of
Vikings, and later still the language that was spoken in
Furness was still Norse, as the carved stone from the door of
the ancient church at Pennington tells us by its Runic
wording.

Of all the Northmen in Furness our tale tells that Ulfar
was the chief, both because he was a man of repute to begin
with, and an early comer, and because he had got wealth
from his trading and shipping iron to all parts.   Being, as we
said, a stickler for the old laws, Ulfar made a sacrificing place
on that mound near his town among the trees that grew upon
it.   He set up an altar to worship Thor in that grove, and
called it his Lund.   To the feasts of the Lund he bade his
neighbours ; and they were glad to come, not only for the
worship, and to be on good terms with the gods, but because
there was a chance of meeting one another, and talking over
their affairs.   When anyone had a quarrel with his neighbour
and there had been manslaughter or other misdoing, since
there was no king to do justice they brought the case to
Ulfar at one of these feasts, and he judged it according to the
use and wont of the Northmen ; so that Ulfar was called
their Godi, or chief and priest.   So many came and so long
they stayed, as folk who had a good way to travel and were
loth to return in a hurry, that around about the Lund they
built booths to lodge in, and set up tents.   Some brought
wares to sell, and others started games and wrestling-matches:
so that it was quite like a fair, at the great feasts after Yule
and after sheep-shearing, and after corn-harvest, the seasons
that stand for Ulverston fair to this day.

Well, as summer was passing on, Swein was bidden to a
feast, and took boat and landed at the Hummerside and went
up to the Lund.   There men were all talking of the new king,

and what should be done about him. For Eadward was now dead and Athelstan his son reigned in his stead; a stirring man, and not one to let the fire smoulder under his feet. Ragnwald also was dead, and in York the new king was another of the grandsons of Ivar, Sigtrygg, for some while king in Dublin, and known by the name of Sigtrygg the Crazy. The news was that he had marched out as soon as king Eadward was gone: but Athelstan was before-hand, and met him at Tamworth in the March, and there they made peace, and Athelstan gave Sigtrygg his sister Eathgita to wife, and confirmed him in his kingdom.

These great kings being at peace there was no longer any chance of a rising: not that it mattered much to the North-men hereabouts: but they were all good fighting men as well as good farmers and merchants. A summer without war was a season lost, to their way of thinking. So they went home again grumbling; and for a while nothing happened.

CHAPTER VII.—COWPERS' CRACKS.

EVENING it was, when the afternoons were already beginning to lengthen, but before the frost was over. Thorstein came running in at his bed-time, and " Mother, mother," says he, " the fell's afire! "

Sure enough there was a sight to make the boldest heart shake in its step like a ricketty mast. For it seemed that all the heavens were aflame; as though, beyond the high hills, woods and forests—nay, the very mountains themselves were blazing in a light lowe. And one while, great sheets of wavering flame turned blood-colour, and the sky between them was green, and the stars faded away. Then it throbbed, and shifted, and changed like clouds of sunset, though the sun was long down and there was no moon. Swein and Raud and the rest of them were aught but cowards: but when they turned in, they saw one another pale as grass in the firelight, and laughed but little that night. But what it might mean they disputed among themselves: and it was mostly thought there would be bloodshed wherever that blood in the sky had shone.

There was another evening soon after, when trading merchants came in a boat up the firth of the Leven. Such were never unwelcome in winter, when folk were at home and work was slack; there was time to rummage the wares and hear the news. These cowpers also found the coast a deal safer when no summer fighting was going on. As for storms, they were never out of sight of a shelter, creeping about the shore, picking up what they could, and always well entertained. They had come last from Cowprond, which was their "trading shore" and market-place with the Cartmel Welsh, where the old road met the Sandgate over the Leven. Greenodd was the only house up the firth, and it was not always that chapmen called there; and so they were made much of.

When they had got their packs up to the house, and when they had been served and suppered, out came news. For it seems that Sigtrygg had died, not long after that great fire-flaught in the heavens. "Aye," said the cowpers, "you may well cock your ears: others beside you guessed that great doings would happen. But listen now, Swein Biornson and all.

"Folk said there was foul play in that matter: and Sigtrygg's sons by the queen that was, the Irish-woman, charged it on the queen that is, the English-woman for whose sake the king had taken christening: but having won her, he went back on his word and took to sacrificing again. Upon which off she goes to her brother Athelstan, wed and yet unwed, as one may say. And then dies Sigtrygg. Athelstan, they say, knew as much about it as another: but that is only guess work, and neither here nor there. Anyhow he is a brisk lad and sprack, not the man to see his sister put upon, right or wrong. Away he marches with a great power to York; and no sooner is he in sight, but Sigtrygg's sons show him their heels, the best way they could: and that was out by the back door, and away up the big North road, across the fells, till they come to Penrith in Cumberland: and there we lose sight of them. But they do say that Guthferth Sigtryggson started on the North road to visit Constantine king of Scots, and get shelter with him if he could: and Olaf Cuaran said good-bye to his brother and went west, as if to seek his uncle Guthferth, who is king now in Dublin. The question is What next? for you may be sure they will not rest, and the Irish and Scots will be glad of a chance for a throw at the young king— the king of all England as he will reckon himself."

"And so that bad business at Bakewell comes to nothing?" said Swein. "I knew as much. But this lad Athelstan, by what you tell of him, must be a fine cockerel to crow so loud. And now I call to mind, he must have been the youngster that sat on the high-seat step at Bakewell: he with the bright eyes."

"Aye," said the chapman, "tall and slender: he would be some thirty winters old when you saw him: handsome and flaxenhaired: and ye will have noticed how his hair was all wreathed with gold threads. He's a real king to look at, though they say he is but the son of a shepherd lass whom Eadward his father lighted upon in his travels. And he is a good sort, they say, and has seen the world, and knows better than most kings how folk live. Why, he speaks our language like one of us, and has done a bit of seafaring. But for all that, he is a Saxon and he must stand by his own kin."

"Well, what are we to do? Knock him on the head?"

"To hold thy peace," said Unna, "is my advice: and watch the weather."

"A wise woman is my wife," said Swein, "and knows the weasel's trick. After all, we are free of our oath, and need not put our heads into the snare again."

"Laugh at the lightning when the storm has passed," said the chapman. "Athelstan with his power was at York awhile since, and may be in Lunesdale by now to foreset us."

"Let him come!" shouted Swein; "and hey for a gradely good stir-about, and pot luck for the sharpest claws!"

" Look you, master cowper, and all the rest," said Unna,
"if you set up for eggbattles and put my man on shouting, I
shall have those blessed barnes awake and on my hands all
night.   Swein Biornson is a good friend to all his friends but
himself alone.   We have seen a little fighting, to our sorrow :
and the talk of the trade hangs about the tongue, like smoke
in a half-burnt house.   But here we are, and here we stay if
we can.   As for Swein, his bark is worse than his bite.   He
shaped well for a good farmer in Man before Ragnwald
shifted us : and he shapes well for a good farmer now : and
pity it were if we be plucked up by the roots again.   These
great kings and their powers come not where nothing is to be
had but kale pottage and hard bats.   I'll uphold it, Athelstan
will be bound for the great burgs in the north, or connily on
his way home again.   And I should reckon it ill done of you
good fellows to go abroad stirring up useless riot, or coming
hither to entrap quiet folk into rash vows."

So the cowpers said they were but giving the news and
meant no harm : and that it never had been their way to go
talebearing and raising strife, nor never would be.   At which
Unna smiled, and got up to make them beds before the fire
on the benches of the hall.   When she saw them well furnished
with rugs to hap them and bolsters for their heads, she sent
her folk to their chambers; put her knitting away into a
basket ; lit a rushlight in an iron candlestick ; and bade them
good-night.

Child Thorstein was fast asleep on the farther side of the
bolster in their narrow lock-bed, with one sturdy dimpled
arm stretched upon the quilted coverlet.   Swein, sitting upon
a kist to unlace his shoes, looked sleepily at him, and then at
her, as she let a sheaf of yellow hair fall upon her white
night-sark : and the rushlight on the shelf shone down
through it, flickering in the draught from the little round window above : for the lock-bed was just like a berth aboard ship.

" Right thou art, Irish fairy," said he : " and always right.
But ah, you women, you never felt the heartiness of a good
fight."

"Nay, we are nought : that's well known," she laughed, drawing the curtain round the baby. "Bar the door, Norse bearsark."

CHAPTER VIII.—THE GIANT COMES IN.

RESTLESS they were that spring; and Unna was anxious and somewhat pettish when Swein talked over the chances of a war. For one good thing, however, he was eager to get forward with work at home, so that he might leave the place well redd up : and that pleased the mistress right well. So they put on until haytime, which is pretty early in the low fields by the waterside, and these were all they had under hay : for the summer-pastures on the fell were hardly stubbed, and far too stony for cutting with the ley.

They were all raking by the beck side, and the mistress was pouring ale to slocken them, and the boys were tumbling in the haycocks, when there was a terrible stir in the woods on the other bank. These woods were on a long hill that made a wall to the valley over against Greenodd : and the fields lay between, and the tide ran up the Crake to the point where the valley narrowed and the fields ended, and there was a wath or fording-place. Dogs barked, men shouted, and swine squealed. They could see by the shaking of the boughs that something was going forward : most like a wild-cat hunt, they said to one another, and left it to the swine-herds to deal with.

But presently there was a great splash in the ford, and out came an enormous man, half naked, with long red hair and red beard. He held one hand on high, carrying they could not see what. In his other hand was a huge ugly stock of tree. All the swineherds' dogs were after him, and the men too, for that matter : but he made no account of them, until one dog leaped at his legs as he came up the bank on the hither side. The big man turned and flicked him like a foot-ball, high in the air and splash in the water : and ran straight for Greenoodd garth.

Swein and his men ran up to meet him with their rakes
and forks, less afraid than puzzled.   The big man never
stayed until he came to the door, and then he thrust the
thing he was carrying into a chink of the posts, and began
talking in a strange tongue.   He was indeed a giant, head
and shoulders taller than any of the Greenodd men, but of
quite another make: crane-legged and clumsy handed and
jolter-headed ; unlike Swein, who was no little fellow, though
his strength was rather in the breadth of his shoulders and
the ropy sinews of his wrist and forearm, like a seafaring man
as he had been bred.   They could make nothing of the giant's
talk, but they saw that the thing he had brought was a burnt
splinter, and they knew that it was a war-arrow and token of
fighting : but whence or why they could not guess.   Presently
came Unna ; and listening to the man's talk, she smiled, and
began to answer him.   The creature made her a low court-
reverence, half haughty, half awkward, and spoke to her with
a strutting way about him, like a cock upon pattens, as one
may say.

When he had done, " Friends," she said, " this man's talk
is like the talk of our Irish : and I gather thus much of his
discourse, that he is the messenger of a war-rising in the
north : and bids you to a weapon-show beyond the fells, you
and all the country side, whoever will cast in his lot against
the Saxon king.   And you are to send on the arrow to our
next neighbours, and bid them likewise."

" Speer of him, Unna, where and when," said Swein.

So she asked him, and said his story was to the intent that
he would come again in ten days' time to lead them over the
fells by the bainest gate to the Scots king and the Welsh
king and all their friends : and she added that she was sorry ;
but she doubted nothing of the man's faith, for there was the
arrow.

Swein drew out the arrow, and gave it to one of his young
men, and bade him carry it to Ulfar by the fell-path.   The
red stranger watched him start, and saw him run up the fell
nimbly, and nodded his head : and then Unna signed that he

should come to the house for a bite and a sup, and sent the servants back to their haymaking. He ate like a wolf, until little was left for supper; and stared about him in great wonderment at the house and all that was in it, especially at the three boys, who gaped at him, while they kept hold of their mother's gown. At last he made another of his reverences, and a speech to Swein : walked swiftly through the fields : splashed across the ford : and so vanished into the woods.

Now when the arrow came to Ulfar he was right glad, and sent it on far and wide, and bade all his neighbours meet at Greenodd. So to Greenodd came two-score men with their war-weapons : and what the giant had left they ate. But it was a point of honour to give to all comers : and in summer especially there was plenty for the trouble of killing and cooking. They set up tents in the mown field to lodge them, and being all good neighbours there was no rough play to speak of. As for the errand upon which they were come, they held their meeting on the field over against Greenodd across the ford of Crake.

Then began they to ask after the red man their guide, for it was well known by this time that they were bidden to join Constantine the king of Scots and Owain the son of Donal, the new king of Cumberland and Strathclyde, and to march with all the north upon York by the great highway. But how to come upon that highway none of them knew, nor did they know the paths across the fells, for they had kept hitherto by the sea and hardly ventured inland where all was wild forest. As they stood in their assembly, some blaming Swein for putting trust in the red man, and some saying that he ought to have been kept by force and not let go, lo and behold the wood opened, and there he was beside them, true to his appointed time.

CHAPTER IX.—THEY TRAVEL THROUGH THE FELLS.

LITTLE farewell they made, and set out, some on horseback and some on foot, these two-score men. The giant striding along led them through wild woods up hill and

down dale. In the midst of the valleys and fells, they came
upon the traces of an ancient path overgrown with brambles,
and washed away wherever the becks crossed it. For a good
while it ran along between hill and plain : and then it entered
a narrow valley umbered with ancient trees, and wholly uninhabited. Then the path crossed the beck and crept up the
side of a hill to the right hand, until it got above the tops of
the trees and out on a heathy moor. From the brink of this
moor the travellers could see a delightful lake lying in the
valley beneath, among many little howes and hills, and all
smothered up in dark green forest. Between the hills on the
farther side there came peeps of blue water, here a little and
there a little ; to which the giant pointed, making signs with
his hands that these bits of blue were all one great long
winding mere. To which indeed they came, after travelling
down from the high place past an old ruin by a river side
where Hawkshead Hall stands now, and after toiling for
more than a step through the overgrown and deserted path-
ways. If it had not been for their guide one would never
have guessed that any pathway ran there at all, so hard to
follow out was that old track in the forest, and so lonely and
uncouth it seemed.

They stayed that night at the waterhead of this long mere,
upon a holm beside two rivers that joined and ran into it—
Breithá, the broad water, they called the one they first came
to, and Reythá, that is Trout-stream, the other, in which folk
say trout alone do breed. Upon this holm was an ancient
stronghold, built foursquare, and well-nigh even with the
water. The walls were in ruin, and the roofs of the houses
were fallen in. But it could be seen that this had been a fine
city once upon a time : for the houses were strongly built of
stone and tiles, and the defences were well planned, and
there were old docks and landing-places between sharp nabs
that ran into the lake. Among the ruins of the houses were
carven pillars and painted walls, so well done that it was a
wonder. But the place was overgrown with nettles, and
the fairest chambers were choked with briars. A few of the

old houses were patched up, and a handful of Welsh dwelt in them hugger-mugger. These Welsh our Northmen could understand a little, for they were used to the talk of their Welsh neighbours and servants. They got fire and a welcome, such as it was; for it seemed their coming was known, and more about them than would have been guessed. So they passed the night in the ruined burg by the waterhead of the great mere, among the rocky fells and forests.

Next morning their guide took them by a road along the valley until they came to another mere, a little one, under a great nab's scar: over whose axle they climbed about to another lake, not much larger, and with an island in the middle of it, and shores all overgrown with rushes and grass. The mountains around seemed to rise higher and wilder, and on one fell top was seen the likeness of a man crouching down, as if he would roll great rocks upon the road below. They looked at him again, but their guide took up a stone and pointed aloft, making signs that the man on the helm of the crag was no living wight, but a man of stone. And yet some of the Northmen were not sorry when they had passed to the other side of his crag, and saw him again in the mist as if he were asleep on his elbow. They were afraid of no mortal man, but they knew that this was a land of wonders and warlocks, and it could be seen that yon stone giant had heard them coming and had stirred in his sleep.

Not the least wonder was that road, running through wild forests, up and down rocks and hills, always straight forward, and paved with cobble-stones; no little broken path like the one that brought them to the water-head. Swein likened it to the Manchester road, and wondered if the Roman folk had been here too, where no churches were, and whether they had made that stone image on the fell for their god. And in this mood they climbed over a high hause where the mountains were at their wildest and rough screes fell down from the rocks on either hand through the ragged trees. And soon they had an adventure.

For on coming down from that pass, they found a stronghold of Welshmen that was called the city of Helvellyn. It was built on a rock above the swampy flats at the head of another lake, and fenced round about with a great wall of huge stones. On one side was the mire, and on the other side rough rocky ground and a waterfall running down from the high mountains. The road came up to it, and turned sharp round to encompass it and to come in at the gate; and then, after passing through the houses, ran out again; and so to the cliffs overhanging the lake. A big man came out to meet them, swaggering, and dressed in strange ancient armour of iron fitted to his body like an iron skin. All the same he seemed very filthy, and sodden with drink. He gave them to wit in Welsh that he was governor of this border-land for the Cumbrian king, and seemingly a greater man than the king himself. "For," said he, "Owain and his father, son of Æth, are no Romans, like the old Donal that went before them. But I," said he, "am of Roman blood, and my name is Elphin map Rhydderch map Caradoc: and I let no man nor woman pass without tribute."

"Ah!" said Swein, "here we have one of the folk who made this road. I guessed they were of the trolls' kin. Look you friends, no iron will bite upon him."

And since the fellow would not let them pass, Swein with little ado smote out his fist, as it might be to try what would happen: and the brainpan of Elphin was cracked against his own stone door post. Their guide gazed awhile upon him, and turned him over with his foot, saying nought but "Aigh!"

At this place they stayed awhile, and the people brought them honeymead to drink: and it seemed as though Swein was made much of, and pointed out by the women and children, who came thronging to the door of the house where he sat: and at their departure a crowd followed them along the road, beckoning with their hands and making merriment. Swein thought they were glad to be quit of the long-named carle, Roman or no Roman.

Then the road took them on the edge of wonderful great cliffs by the brink of a long mere. Halfway along the mere was a narrow place, and a wath, near which were houses, poor enough, of men who seemed to be the giant's kin, and there our travellers stayed for the night. Next morning they crossed the wath, and at the foot of the lake they came to a place where four dales met among high mountains and crags. And here there was a sweet spot alone in the wilderness, with cleared meadow-land and a little brook coming down from Helvellyn through the leas, to meet the great river that ran from the lake, and turning sharply round went by a deep valley. Afterwards they called this river Gretá, which is as much as to say the Stony water; and there is none indeed that has a rougher bed. They took notice of this dale because of its sweetness in the midst of wild rocks and forests, and because it is not often one sees four dales meeting in one spot like the rays of the sign of Thor.

But their path led them onward through the deep dale of the Gretá, with crags on one hand and a roaring river or spreading swamps on the other, until they came to a wide valley, and on the other side of it, at the foot of the mountain Blencathra, their path struck a great road which led them eastward. By nightfall they came to another of those ancient foursquare strongholds: and hard by, across a little dell, the army of the Welsh lay at Penrhydderch.

Owain the king received them well, and thanked them for their coming, and promised them the foremost place when they should meet the Saxons. In his tent they met Ketel Bolster, as Swein had called him, and the Northmen from the holm on the Solway, and they fell in talk together. But before they had spoken many words, men came running in through the lanes of tents, crying out "They are here!" Owain bade them have peace: and took Swein and his chief men, and went out to the brow of the hill. There in the twilight they saw the valley beyond thronged with a great multitude, and knew, by the lights that started up from point to point, that Athelstan with all his power was camping in the fields of Dacor.

CHAPTER X.—DACOR.

DACOR was then, as it is now, the name of a village in a pleasant vale, on the border between the plain country of Cumberland and the hills of Lakeland. Among the mountains at that time were dwelling only wild Welsh, and still wilder fell-folk of Gaelic kin and tongue. But in the plain country were many homesteads of English and Danes, dotted here and there beside the old high-road. The Danes were new comers, who had crossed the waterparting, the Keel of England one may say, as they talked of the Keel of Norway. But the English were old inhabitants since the days of Ecgfrith and other great kings, whose heirs ruled at Bamborough, though in diminished splendour, until Athelstan took their realm to himself.

They were Christian people, and had priests and monks among them. One of their churches was at Dacor ; and near by, a monastery. A church is there yet on the spot : as for the monastery nobody knows where it stood ; but it was doubtless in that valley with the lovely winding beck and among the acres of corn and pleasant meadowlands which the monks had cleared and tilled, bordering on the wild home of rocks and wolves. The Welsh of Penrith and Penruddock and Blencow lived thus alongside of Danes and English : not always quiet neighbours perhaps, but yet on some terms of neighbourhood : and if not good subjects to Owain king of Cumbria, still reckoned within his borders.

So when Athelstan had news about the plots of Owain and Constantine to put back Sigtrygg's sons on their father's throne, he marched from York by the old high-road straight over the Keel : and in three days he was here at Dacor guesting with the monks. And his foes, who had come south too late to carry the war into the country of York, found nothing left for them to do but to agree with him as best they might.

Athelstan the king sat in Dacor hall, and the kings of the north swore to him as they had sworn to his father Eadward : and they gave their hostages into his hands, and renounced their dealings with idolaters, namely those heathen Danes, the sons of Sigtrygg. "For," said Athelstan, " it is a shame if we, being Christian men and ruling Christian men, suffer these unbaptized pagans to ravage a Christian land, to burn the churches, and slay the monks, and rob the holy women our sisters. And if we three but stand together, we might clear the whole island of such knaves, and keep it clear for ourselves and our people, in peace and plenty."

To such at that while Owain and Constantine were well agreed, and all the readier because Athelstan's host was bigger than both of theirs.

Now Constantine had with him a young son of his, yet unchristened; and Athelstan, willing to knit himself closer to his new friends, said that he would stand godfather to the child: for in those days it was thought nearer than kinship by blood to be god-sib, or bound by holy water and the vows of baptism. So they brought the young child to Dacor church, and baptized him, and Athelstan stood his godfather.

When he was out of the water, and dressed in white, with white linen wrapped about his head, said the priest, " Here is water, king, as the Scripture says: what should hinder these from being baptized ? " and he pointed to the Northmen who were standing without, and neither signed themselves with the cross nor bent the knee at prayer, but stared in through the church porch at the gilded imagery, and at the glass windows that Bishop Wilfrith's artificers had put up there in ancient times.

With that there was some shrinking back among those who had been most eager to look on ; and Athelstan turned and fixed his gaze upon Swein, and spoke in the Northmen's tongue, for he knew it well.

" What sayest thou, friend ?   Wilt thou set the good example ? "

" King," answered he, " I am a primesigned man and no church robber."

(For it must be known that many of the heathen were, as one may say, half-baptized: not that they meant to change.

their faith, but in order to have dealings in trade and other-wise with Christians, who might have no communion with the unbelievers).

"And," added Swein, "I have a mind to stay as I am."

"But if I bid thee?" said the young king.

"Eadward thy father asked no such thing of me, when I took him for father and lord two years ago."

"Why, brother, I seem to have some inkling of thy face. Wast thou not the brawler of Bakewell?"

With that they laughed and Swein reddened, and replied somewhat angrily, "Saving a king's presence, I was no brawler, nor did Eadward call me so, to my face."

"Nor behind thy back, believe me, good man. For I tell truth when I say that after all were gone, and we were together at supper, my father said this to me: Boy, he said, we have done a good day's work;—and I remember well how he cracked a great nut when he said it. But, said he, the best touch of my kingcraft, for many a year, has been the winning of that stout franklin and his fellows. And he charged me to leave no stone unturned to get the love of you Northmen, such as had settled peaceably upon our borders, and were busied in tilling lands hitherto waste, and in the carrying trade about our coasts. Now, what shall I give thee, since thou dost refuse the best gifts in my keeping?"

"King," said Swein, "they say we Northmen are greedy of gold, and of blood, and of plunder alone. But by this I know that thou art wiser than other men, and bearest a grey head on those young shoulders. Truth it is when thou sayest that we are busied in tilling waste places, and in sea-trading; and this no man can gainsay. And indeed if at times we are ready to fight, and to fight our best, it is but to keep the homes we have made with our own hands, and to give them into the safe keeping of our sons."

Then Athelstan thought awhile and said "It has been in my mind now these many days that it would be a wise law, if every such brave seafaring merchant who has made three voyages with his own goods in his own ship, should be called

Thane of England. Will that cap fit, friend?"

'Well, king," answered Swein, "many a voyage have I made with my own bulk in my own ship, cheaping a little and —"

"And taking what came in thy way?" broke in the king with a smile.

"That's as you may call it," said Swein.

"Well, for the law the Witan must look to it: and for thee, friend, come to me once again when thy mind is made up, after talk with the priest here, and with the good monks hard by."

The priest was glad to talk with Swein, and so were the monks, for that matter; and they went near to tearing him in pieces between them.

First he must away to see the monastery: and in it was a carved shrine of gold and enamel, curiously worked, and holding their treasure. Swein looked for a crown of jewels at the least: but lo and behold it was only a lock of hair. But they said that this lock of hair was from the head of Cuthbert the great saint of their faith: they told Swein of the wonderful things which that lock of hair could do: how it had healed a young man who was diseased in his eyes, and such like, as was writ in the book of venerable Beda. Swein wondered at the casket, but he took little heed of the relic, saying he thanked them, and he would come back to them when his eyes ached, if no wise wife at home could cure him.

So, finding him a hardened sinner, the monks turned him over to one who served the church at Dacor and was the priest of whom Athelstan spoke. He led him back to the chapel door, for he might bring him no farther, and bidding him look in, began to expound the mysteries of the cross and of the creed. It was no news to Swein Biornson, for many's the time he had heard such things before in Ireland, being indeed, as we have said, a half-baptized man already. But like many another in those days—and these—he would say to himself "Who knows?" and halting between two opinions, find much that was good in both.

Indeed it was of one near akin to him and little older in years that it was said, " He was a Christian but prayed to Thor when he was at sea or in a tight place," as many men do even now.

Well, the priest preached to him, and he listened. He told of the life of Christ and His death and resurrection; of His love and law; of His Godhead and glory; and then of holy church, and the authority of it, and the mysteries of it, and the miracles of it, and the might of it : and long he spoke earnestly entreating his guest : until Swein laid his hand on the frail shoulder of the priest, and said gravely :—

" Young man, these two-score years I have followed the gods of my fathers : and one while they have been good to me, and another while they have been evilminded. Now I will not lightly take a new god at the bidding of yonder king : nay, not to be Thane or Earl. Nor do I wholly understand all thy words, though meseems they are good words, and spoken from a good heart. But this I say, that no priest nor church shall ever be the worse for me or mine : and when my day of need comes, if thy God will help me, he shall be my God."

He took the priest's hand, and went his way. But the priest knelt there, weeping passionately and praying, " Oh God, give me that man's soul. Nay, not unto me, oh Lord, but unto Thy name be the glory."

CHAPTER XI.—THE GIANT'S BOON.

HAYMAKING was begun when our Northmen started on their journey to Dacor : and it was not yet finished when they came back, as empty-handed as they went. When they were once again in the hall at home, and the red man had brought them safe and sound through flood and fell, Swein said to his wife, " Now that this man our guide has taken us in good faith through strange places, and brought us home again, though little we have got by our travelling unless it be gain to be no worse off than we were, but the more assured of peace and quietness : I would not send him away without thanks, but I would give him a gift, even if it be a good weapon, or as many sheep as he can drive. Ask him then to make his choice, and he shall not find us stingy."

Unna agreed very readily to this: and when she had set it forth, the red man was silent for a time, looking round as if to choose something out of the house. At last he stood up, and made a long speech in his own tongue, waving his arms and shaking his head. While he spoke, they saw her grow pale as grass, and the tears came into her eyes.

"Swein," she said, "and friends all, here is a hard thing for us to answer: and indeed I know not myself what to do. For the man says that he has enough and to spare of all the goods he needs; and that he is a chief among his own people, so that he may not take a hired man's wages for service done rather to his king than to strangers. But if I understand aright he says that he saw at Dacor how men had respect to thee, Swein Biornson: and that even the great king of the Saxons spoke with thee friendly, as with a great chief. And moreover I gather from his words that he has some foresight from his own dreams or from a wise man's, that you strangers are to be mighty in this land, and that nothing will stand against you in the end: and that you will wipe his people from the face of the earth, and take from them the homes of their fathers. Now he says he would be thy friend and brother; and for a pledge of our peace, he would have nothing else but the fostering of one of our sons."

With that they all cried out astonished, and Swein laughing a little and harshly, said, "Tell him that we do not give our lads to giants and wild men of the woods nowadays, even if Signy gave her child to Sigmund once on a time, as the old song says."

"Nay," she said, "I will not anger him, or he will do us a bad turn one of these days."

"Tell him that we humbly thank his lordship for the honour, and one day we will wait on his lordship at his lordship's palace."

But the red man, though he could make nothing of the

words, knew very well from the horse-laugh and the rough
gesture of Swein that he was despised and his offer scorned:
and before Unna could speak, he dashed his great club on
the ground so that it tore a hole in the paving, and made the
cobbles fly. Then turning round, he went swiftly and disappeared into the woods as before.

They looked at one another as if mischief should come
next, but Swein said, " Take courage, wife, and never fear
that I will give up child of ours to such a foster-father: and
you, friends all, be on your guard, and keep a watch on the
ford and the woods, so that we be not taken unawares. As
for you, barnes, let me not say it twice: stay with your
mother, and never wander away out of her sight, or the sight
of the good fellows who have charge of you."

Days passed, and months: and all that winter nothing was
seen or heard of the red man: until it became a jest among
them. For when any of the boys were unruly, they would
say to snape him, " Folk would think the giant had thy
fostering."

But what with fear of this wood-man, and what with lack
of neighbours, Orm and Hundi and Thorstein grew up in
their father's house, and were not put out to foster parents
like many children of that day. For all that, they were not
brought up in idleness, to be spoiled lads and good for nought;
since, although there was plenty of servants, it was the way
of these people to do their own work, and to show their
mastery in craft of hand as well as in cunning of head.

There was a smithy on the farm; for how else could they
shoe their nags or fettle their weapons? and Swein was proud
to be called master smith of them all, and would spend many
a winter day at the anvil, forging the iron they brought in
their boats from the Pennings' people. So the boys picked up
something of the craft, maybe not so workmanlike as others,
and yet serviceably for the needs of people whose things were
less for show than for use. Their fine jewellery and gold-
smith's work they had from abroad: but even so there was
always some conceit of daintiness or quaintness in the way

they turned out their homely jobs, because their time was before them, and they liked smithying, and lingered over it as a pastime : curling the horns of a door-latch or a candle-stick into ringlets with the tongs : twisting the bar of a horse-bit into a screw, and engraving a blade with devices or punching it into patterns. And if there is little of their work left to show, who knows, as one said who was learned in such matters, that the old carving-knife in the homestead is not the ancestral sword ground down, and so forth ? In ancient graves and hidden hoards we do now and then find the smith's work of this heathen age, in the parts bordering upon the Lakeland mountains.

Beside smithying there was always wood-work to be done, for their houses were wooden, and many things for which we use potter's wares, they made of wood : as cups and platters and all sorts of vessels. In the winter evenings especially this work went on round the hearth, while the women spun and wove. The lads were not long at whittling sticks before they were set to make arrows and shafts for weapons and tools, and it was a proud day when they made their first piggin with hoops and staves complete. And from that they got to carving, since these people were as nice about their wood-work as their iron, and could not abide a blank kist-panel or door-post, after they had once got roof raised and land stubbed.

Moreover on these winter evenings there was story-telling and singing of ballads, which let the lads into some knowledge of olden times, of the kings and the gods, and especially adventures in strange lands. Add to this that their mother, half Irish as she was, and the Welsh thralls with whom they consorted, as children will with servants, taught them something of other tongues than their own. And Unna showed them their letters, drawing the runestaves with a charred stick on a board for them to carve. As to book-learning, they got on very well without it.

CHAPTER XII.—RAIDS.

SPRINGTIME was now come, and the children of
Greenodd went with their playmates from the thralls'
cottages to roam the woods. For then were the hollows
among the knolls by Crake side all carpeted with golden lilies
and dim white wind-flowers. And when the time of these
was over, bluebells, sweet scented, and growing as thick as
grass, covered the glades. Thorstein, who was now six years
old, and some of his playfairs were in the woods one day ;
and their game was to make a queen of the prettiest girl,
dressing a bower for her and crowning her with bluebells.
In the midst of it who should come suddenly upon them but
a wild red man, bellowing, they said, like a bull, and shaking
his great club as if he meant to kill them all. But he only
caught the biggest and best looking of the boys, and dragged
him off. When the boy bealed and screamed, the robber
nipped him round the throat, and soon stopped his noise.
The children ran home with their knees trembling, and said
that a giant had got their playfellow to eat him. But whatever he did with him he did not eat him ; for the next morning
before the men could start to lait the lad, he came down the
beck with his head broken.

Said Swein, "No use to shut the door when the roof has
fallen in." Then he sent a good gift to the thrall whose child
was lost, telling him to wipe his eyes with it : and forbade the
youngsters wandering in woods or out of sight. So all was
quiet for a time, and if there were uneasiness about robbers,
it was no more than what everyone felt everywhere in those
days, when by sea and shore men carried their lives in their
hands, and trusted to luck to keep their women and children
from bloodshed and slavery.

In the next winter there was much snow, and the distant
mountains were curd-white, both at Yule and for many a
week after. Even the moorlands were covered and the
forests were choked : and when great storms blew, the mealy
snow would drift in streaming clouds, and fill all the hollow
places and the gills : so that many wild beasts were buried in

the drifts, and many came down into the valleys, where the snow lay not so thick and melted away between whiles. Sheep and cattle needed double care; for though most of the stock was killed and hung in smoke, some beasts always had to be kept, and fed with the hay of the summer, and holly boughs, which the shepherds cut and let them pick up when they took them out from the byres and folds. Even so there was always danger of drifts, and the burying of whole flocks in the snow: and then they had to dig them out, which was a great labour to the men, but a fine playtime for Thorstein and his brothers. For to the boys the snow was like fairy-land, and rare enough to be something of a marvel to children in sheltered Greenodd by the sea. What storms they feel come mostly from the warm south-west, and if the wind blows from the north-east it brings sunshine, with blue sky and black frost that vanishes away before noon.

One day Thorstein went with the shepherds and their lads to an uplying fold to serve the sheep, and found the snow much trampled, as though wild beasts had been there, for all there was a high turf dike around it, with a sharp fence on the top such as no wolves were like to climb. So the shepherd began counting out the flock, in their way which Thorstein learnt from him :—" Un, dau, tri, y-pedwar, y-pump : chwech, y-saith, y-wyth, naw, deg." And we may say that our old folk still use this way of reckoning little changed but to make the words easier with rhyme, as :—" Yan, tyan, teddera, meddera, pimp; haata, slaata, sour, down, dick :—" and so forth.

When he had counted a score he marked it off on his fingers, or scored a notch on a stick, and began again. And so counting he found that two sheep were gone : and worse than that, they saw, by the blood on the snow and by the footprints, that thieves had cut their throats and carried them off. So away they went to track the thieves at once, which was easy enough because of the snow. Before long, stopping to listen, they heard a crackling of branches ahead, and shouted, and put Thorstein in the rear, and pressed forward.

Then were seen through the leafless trees three men, or not men but giants they seemed, long and gaunt and red-haired. One had a sheep on his shoulders, and another had a sheep on his shoulders, not a little encumbered as they pushed their ways through the underwood and thick tangle.

The shepherds had gone .too far to go back; and beside that, they were armed, while the thieves had only their .cudgels. But when it came to blows, such was the tangle in the wood that they were soon scattered: one was stuck in a thicket, and another floored with a broken arm; and the robbers were off and away. So when they came to collect their forces there was one wanting, a shepherd's son. They shouted and searched the wood as well as they might, for it was beginning to grow dark. In the end they were forced to return home without him, and their sheep were gone and all.

When they brought Thorstein to the house and told their tale, Swein listened with a very long face, and saw to their hurts: for it was the chief's business to be surgeon, both to handle wounds until the blood stopped, and to set broken limbs and bind them. It was the lady's to make drinks of herbs for medicine. Some good drink Unna gave them, and they went home: but Swein and she talked late that night after Thorstein was asleep.

The next day Swein himself, with a band of men well armed, set off early, and soon found the place where the fight had been. Thenceforward by the broken branches, for it had snowed and the tracks were covered, they followed the robbers up the fell and towards the moors. But when they came out of the wood upon the heather, what should they see but the boy who had been carried off, lying on the ground, and dead. It was plain that the robbers had knocked him on the head: though why they should take him all that way, and wherefore they should kill him at the last, nobody could tell. Swein gave a good gift to the shepherd whose son had been killed, saying that he could get no other atonement at the time: but that one day he would gather his neighbours together and clear the fells of such vermin. And he said no more of the matter, unless it were of nights to the mistress.

CHAPTER XIII.—OF THE ALTHING IN CUMBER-LAND.

ALL that year king Constantine and king Owain were quiet, and held to the peace of Dacor. But king Guthferth Ivarson of Dublin, to whom Olaf Cuaran Sigtryggson had fled, was not in the treaty, and thought himself in no way bound to refrain from attacking the realms of Britain, but quite otherwise. For it was an old use and wont of the heathen vikings to plunder Christians whenever they got the chance: and there was now not only the open door to York, but friends within, the party of Sigtrygg's sons, were bidding him to come over.

So king Guthferth and his nephew Olaf Cuaran and their host crossed the sea, and landed, as our story has it, at Ellenburg by the mouth of the river Ellen in Cumberland, where now stands Maryport, and before those times stood some old Roman city. Thence there was the good road that the Romans had made, straight through the fells and between the two waters of Bassenthwaite and Derwent, and so to Penrith, and over the Keel. In a week or so they were again in York: but not for long. For as soon as Athelstan heard of it he went northward, and drove them home by the way they came. There was a deal of confused fighting, of which folk never will know, and maybe never did know, the rights. And sorely he blamed Owain for giving the Danes passage through his kingdom. But Owain came off this time with the excuse that in Strathclyde he had enough on his hands, and could not be answerable for vikings who forced their way through the extremest borders of his dominion. Yet when the same thing happened again and again and every time the viking host left behind it stragglers and settlers to hold strong places and good lands on the Cumberland coasts, as a flood tide leaves its wreckage on the shore, then the English king was forced to take harder measures with the Cumbrians, as the tale tells in the end.

Meanwhile Athelstan held counsel about that borderland which lay around Morecambe Bay, where our Northmen

lived. Neither Swein nor any of his neighbours had come in
to him, ready to be baptized and to take his service: or maybe
he might have set one of them over these parts as Thane or
Earl, to rule the country in his name. On the other hand,
the land of Cartmel was already in the holding of the priests
at York, and they no doubt were instant in their claims to
take under them the whole of which they held a part. So
Athelstan, for the good of his soul, and for the souls of the
Northmen who should be brought into the fold, and for the
better ruling of these outlying borders, gave to the priests of
York Minster all Amoundernesss—that is, Lancaster and the
Fylde, and the land round about.

After a while came the summoner from York church, to
take tithe and tax from the Northmen, as he was wont to do
from the Cartmel people. But they made short work of him,
before ever he got so far as Greenodd: and when next there
was a meeting loud talk was held about the matter. Even
Swein Biornson, though he had loved Athelstan when he saw
him at Dacor, was angry with him now, for giving away what
was not his own to give, and lands that he never had so
much as set eyes on.

Then stood up one and said, " News, friends! I have been
lately seafaring by way of the South-isles and thereabouts:
and wherever I came the talk was that Olaf Cuaran had fled
to Scotland, and that Constantine the king had received him
as guest: and more than that, had given him his daughter to
wife. Now, what think you of that, friends?"

There was a great hubbub when this came out, for not a
man of them but knew what it meant, and they were glad to
think that if they themselves had a quarrel with Athelstan,
friends would be easy to find. For by giving his daughter to
Olaf the heathen, Constantine had already broken the peace
of Dacor.

Well, some were for war, and some for waiting; and they
talked it over this way and that, until Swein bade them have
peace. " For," said he, " I know this Athelstan, that he is a
brisk man and full of good counsel: and I know the Saxons

that they are not to be despised. If we alone set ourselves up to make war we shall be fools : for they have men enough to sweep us off the face of the earth, as a thrall sweeps out a byre with a besom. But if Constantine and Owain and our kinsmen in the north are agreed, and come together to invade the south country, well and good. My rede is to lie still and watch the weather."

Now Mistress Unna was all this while in the house, cooking the supper for Swein and the chief men of the Thing, and little did she know that all the Northmen were being ruled by her counsels.

"To lie still and watch the weather," says Swein, and nodded his head and looked wisely round. "But," says he, "pity we sit so far away from those kinsmen of ours across the fells in the north : better it were for us if we could take counsel with them now and then, and shape our plans together. For when we were called to Bakewell, I mind me that we knew nothing of what was forward. We went out for war, and found the rest of them jogging along as to a quiet and peaceable Thing-mote. And then again when we went to Dacor we knew nothing, and were but made fools of, and much better had stayed at home. Now if we fixed some place of meeting with Ketel and the others in the north, we should learn the news of those kings from time to time, and talk over the affairs of our whole kindred, as we do here among ourselves."

Then stood out one and said, " Swein Biornson and all, I have a friend from over the seas, new come from Iceland. Now in Iceland, mayhappen you know, there are many of our kindred who live as we do upon the lands they have taken, and owe no more than we owe to any man, least of all to kings in other parts. For their worship and sacrifices they have temple-steads as we have, here and there : and for the punishment of evil doers and the atonement of quarrels, the godi of each temple-stead sees to it. But it appears that of late things have come to such a pass, that manslayers who have been outlawed from one country-side have fled to

another, and have been kept there as guiltless men, and
thence have returned to do what harm they might on their
old neighbours. And so there has been fighting and unpeace
stirred up, and the authority of the godi set at nought, as if
there were no law in the land. Therefore all the men of
Iceland have taken counsel together, and hallowed one
Thing-stead in the midst of the land; and at mid-summer
they are to meet there, the chiefs all and all the free men,
under one law-speaker. And if any man has a grievance
that cannot be settled at a Thing by his own godi, there at
the Althing it will be judged by Raven Ketelson, the law-
speaker over all. And there also they are to fix the feasts
and seasons for the year that is to be: and if any new law or
custom is to be made, there will they make it: so that the
whole land may be under one law, and be of one mind, and
at peace within itself. Now it seems to me that if the Icelanders, being men famous for their wisdom, have taken this
counsel, we too should do well to take the counsel of Swein
Biornson, and join with our brethren of the north across the
fells in such a spot as we may find convenient, mid-way
between them and us; to talk over our common matters, and
especially how we may ward the land we have made our
own, against all its foes and ours."

With that they took their weapons and shouted "Aye" to this
advice: and Swein said " Friends, since we have agreed that
there should be this Althing established, it remains only to
mark the place of it, and to bid our brethren in the north to
meet us there. This place here we find good for a meeting
because it is mid-most of all our land to the south of the wild
fells: and he who comes from Lunesdale on the east has no
longer journey than he who comes from Eskdale on the west:
and to Kentdale and to Duddoner-dale the ways are equal:
and across the bay it is not far to go, whether by the sands
or by the sea. Now, when we were coming home from
Dacor, we started in the company of Ketel and his men, and
when we parted from him they had still a day and a half to
go before they were home, while we had two days and a half:

though doubtless on kenned roads, and if we had nothing to carry nor any hindrance by the way, we might make short work of it. But I say that if we went a two days' journey from here, and if they came a two days' journey from their home, and met upon the great road that leads through the heart of the fell country, that meeting-place should be our Thing-stead. And I think it would not be far from a little dale you remember well, near the foot of the mere with the wath in it, and at a spot where four dales met. A fair place it was, with a likely howe and a conny bit of flat that offered well for a Thing-field, and everything else fit for our purpose."

So, to make matters short, they sent the arrow, by which men were bid to a meeting, round the sea-coast until it came to Ketel's holm on the Solway and up the firth of Eden. The Northmen thereaway met together and agreed on their part to set off on the day appointed : Swein and his neighbours set off on the same day : and their two companies fell in with one another by Thirlmere, which they thenceforward called Brackmere, from the Thing-brekka or hill of assembly, which they hallowed at Legburthwaite, as we still call the place, forgetting maybe that we say Law-burg-field, being the midmost spot in all Lakeland from Solway to Walney. And having hallowed the place and held their meeting, they made their tryst for next midsummer, and went their ways home.

Lucky it was for our Northmen that they took Unna's counsel, and listened to Swein when he told them of the briskness of Athelstan. For Constantine, who had received Olaf Cuaran and given him his daughter, before ever he could draw his host together to invade England, while he was yet preparing for war, saw the ships of Athelstan bear down upon his coast ; and fleeing inland, whom should he meet but Athelstan himself with an army, come through Strathclyde to avenge the peace of Dacor. And great mischief was done before the English went home with pledges of a new peace wrung from the Scots, who for their part had no mind to keep it, any more than their oaths of seven years ago, and only waited for the day when they might take their revenge.

But if the York priests complained of their new liege-men, and told Athelstan on his way home how their summoner had been treated; and if Athelstan laughed and bade them study to be quiet, as the epistle says, and mind their own business, it is no more than was likely. For he had enough to do without taking his host across the Keel to gather tithes from the Northmen.

———

CHAPTER XIV.—THE FINDING OF THURSTON-WATER.

NOW the story leaves those mighty kings and their wars, to tell of Thorstein Sweinson, and how he went up the river Crake, and how he found the great water at the river-head: the same that old folk call Thurston-water, and we mostly call Coniston lake, from the name of our village hard by it.

In the year after the ravaging of Scotland, Thorstein was thirteen winters old, and a grown lad: sturdy at all games of strength, and skilful enough in all kinds of work that a lad was set to do. He could catch a nag on the fell, and ride it home through the heather; make an arrow, and shoot it to the mark: handle the smith's tools or the woodwright's: swim and row, wrestle and race with his brothers, and often beat them, and always beat the thralls' boys. Most of all he took pleasure in going about with the herds, to look after the beasts and the sheep on the summer-hills: and when they were once out and away, he would egg them on to take him farther, to see the little dells and winding valleys on either side of the Crake, as if he might find there something of the great world which he had heard about and longed to wander through.

It was nigh upon seven years since the wild men of the fells had made their last raid and carried off the thrall's son: but still Swein would often warn his boys to keep within sight of home, and bid them stay by their mother if he himself were abroad. But he might as well have warned the smoke not to go out of the chimney; for northern blood stirred in the lads, and Thorstein often looked down the firth to seaward, and wished he were big enough to go viking in a ship of his own. Orm said he would go with him if it were trading he meant: and thought that they might make a deal of money by selling the thralls' children. Upon which Thorstein hit him in the face, and said, "Thou shan't get our little May-queen for one." And he spoke no more of his plans to Orm.

Hundi was a better friend to Thorstein, and they talked a deal together of the travels they should take and the deeds they should do. There were those great mountains in the far distance, always beckoning to them ; peopled with giants and fairies,—had not their father often told them of the stone man that kept the road beyond Grasmere ? and had they not the dim remembrance, not easily let die, of the red giant ? They knew by hearsay of wide lakes among the fells, lying all alone for the first adventurer to take and hold. The beck that flowed through their fields, and the greater Leven that they could see from the howe or from Legbarrow winding far away among the hills, came down, so the Welshmen said, out of waters full of fish and haunted by fowl in countless flocks. And as they sat on the rocks at Crakemouth when the tide was low, moulding clay arrows in the rune-shaped clifts and chinks of the smooth rock, they wondered what troll or fairy had been there with chisel and mallet, and what more marvellous marvel there might be to find in the unknown wilds beyond. Crake, the rocky river, came down night and day, sometimes fierce and swollen, sometimes faint and shrunken, but always singing over its rocks the same song of enticement. " If we could only track the beck," they said, " and find the great water, and take the-fish and fowl, and build a house by the shore and make a boat ! "

So at last the wish grew into a plan, and the plan into a purpose. When nobody was looking they were to slip away : follow the Crake to its mere, take the land about it, and make a backwood bigging of their own. They filled a bag with meal, took their knives in their belts, and set off one morning early, as though they were going for a day with the shepherds. Where the fields ended, they took the path to the outlying folds : and when they were near the folds, they turned through the woods to the river, so that they might not be seen, and scrambled for a great way up the stony channel. It was only half filled, because, as often happens in those parts, the spring had been dry, and the rainy weather was yet to come on, after the days began to shorten.

For a while it was easy work: there is a flat shore on the left hand, and they could run over the shingle even where the water went swiftly and fell in eddies and foam over rock-ridges. But soon the hills on either side close in: the banks are steep: the river foams beneath thick trees which spread their branches, making the squirrel's bridge overhead. Thus it is even nowadays, but in old times at many places great firs had fallen right across the deep channel, or huge oaks had lost their hold of the rocky bank from very weight of age, and had rolled into the torrent, to be weirs and dams that held the water and flooded the banks: so that what with the swamp, wherever there was a bit of flat shore, and what with the rock walls, or the slippery sodden tufts of moss and fern, wherever the gill-banks were brant, the lads made but little way. And whoever has stood upon Spark Brig and looked up-bank and down-bank, and dreamt over a time when all the mills and houses were unbuilt, and the land uncleared, and nothing but wild timber, dank and dense, filled the dale, with the logs that rotted where they fell, and the brambles and creepers that matted the growing trunks together: and wild bulls and wild boars, wolves and cats, hag-worms and lizards, tenanted the place :—he will know what the adventure of those two boys was like. And whoever has fought his way up one of our moorland gills where the land is still rough, will know how they stumbled over the shallows, and scrambled over the boulders, and waded the mires, and swam the dubs, as they came through the jaws of Crake, and out into the easier ground by the eyot beneath Lowick Green, as it is now. There, if the river was less rough, the trees were still thick and the banks steep: and on the right hánd the fells seemed to come nearer: and standing out through the black fir-trees high over head, white brows of crag seemed to frown and nod above them, as they sat on a great stone in mid-stream to take their breath.

The kingfishers flitted past, blue flashes in the green gloom. Where a ray of sunshine came in through the vault of trees overhead and pierced the brown water, they could see, beneath the mossy rocks fringed with fern, little dippers running over the bottom among the trout, and as free as if they were on dry land, for all the rushing of the water. Now and again a wild animal ran down to drink, and started back crashing into the wood : but there was no sign of houses, nor of men dwelling in this uncouth wilderness.

They toiled on afresh, mounting the stream where it breaks over long-drawn ledges, around a rocky eyot at a sharp bend, and through a swampy tarn (as it was then) till they came to the spot where Lowick bridge now stands. It was high noon. They sat down on the steep bank above the swamp; and taking handfuls of the meal from their bag, soaked it with the clear fresh water and made their dinner. When it was done, said Hundi, "Well, old forge-ahead, how much farther? For my part I call the shepherds' tales all Welsh lies. There is no great water that we can see, only this dirty puddle : and we shall have work enough to get home before supper-time, down the screes we have climbed and this waste of rubbish."

"Nay," said Thorstein, "the beck must come from some-where, and I mean to see the end of it."

"What, and sleep in a tree like a squirrel?"

"Why not, if I must, thou slug-a-bed? The nights are short and warm enough."

"Well then," said Hundi, "I will sit on the howe over there, and wait until the conquering hero comes back. I'll count six score, and then."

"And then go home like a wise lad to thy mother, and say Thorstein is coming to-morrow with news, and a great fish out of Thorstein's mere; for it will be none of Hundi's."

"Hundi's howe is here, Thorstein's mere is nowhere." And indeed afterwards the story says that Hundi lived hard by, and was in the end buried on that howe : but that is still to tell. Said he, "A wilful beast must gang his own gate, and I'll not mar sport, nor splash thy mere to frighten thy whales. Come, Thorstein, don't be a fool. Turn back with me now, or rue it!"

"Neither, dear lad: and don't anger me, but hie thy ways home, and bid them not worry.   Happen I'll light on my journey's end sooner than we think for."

"Happen thou'll light on mischief sooner than thou think'st for.   Come along, I say."

"Go along, I say.   We can't miss the road, for its down-bank for thee and up-bank for me to the end."

"Nay, that's an ill speech," said Hundi, "for parting."

"Well then, home for thee, and away in the wide world for me, for evermore.   Will that suit?"

"Nor that either.   I wish thee luck, and thy big fish: and I'll foreset the scolding that awaits thee: and have thy breakfast kept warm: for yon bag of meal will be gone before to-morrow, if I know aught."

"Good lad, then; we part friends:" and Hundi turned and slid down the bank and splashed down stream: for he was always an easy-going lad.

But Thorstein toiled on as before, and found his work no less, at first: for he had to win his way up Lowick force and through the swamps at its head.   But then he saw, at last, rising above the trees, a crest and a cone, of high rugged fells, distant indeed, but not a mere blue line as he had seen them from the heights of Greenodd.   The afternoon sun threw its lights and shadows on the great scars of Dowcrags, and the rocks of the Coniston fells stood out bold in the blue air.

The lad's heart leapt up, and he shouted as he plunged again in the rapids that swirled beneath the wild steeps on his right, and the long dark slopes of Blawith, the Blue-wood, on the other hand.   By and by he was lost again in the crooked ravine where the Nibthwaite Mills now stand, where the water narrowed to half its former breadth, and slid over ranks of rock, sloping downwards like carven tables, or a giant's stairway, sunken and aslew.   But at the head of every force, there were the great fells again in sight, and every time nearer and clearer, grander and more wonderful. At last he came to a sweet round tarn.   It was bedded in the woods, and the likeness of every several branch lay upon the water. Thorstein shouted: but then he stayed. Was this the mere he had come so far to seek? and no more than this?

He pressed forward, round the miry edges of the tarn, and stumbled through the narrows of Arklid. Hitherto the stream had been ever narrower, and, but for a few ledges and flats, ever steeper: but here it suddenly became both still and deep, and opened out into breadth. Thorstein's heart beat hard when the wood thinned, and the waterway broadened, and the world grew brighter, and lo, beyond, a great gleam of blue, and a blaze of golden sky.

Close beside him, seal-bushes fringed the shilloe banks, bulrushes stood in their ranks right out into the shallows, and purple flags and white and yellow water-lilies lay along the edges of the lake. On either hand, seaming the deep forest that clothed the sides of the valley, sharp craggy spurs came down, as it were gateposts to the hall of hills; and broke at their bases into long nabs, rounded here and rocky there, running far out into the mere and tufted to the water-edge with dark oaks and dark firs. And between there were blue nooks of ripple reflecting the evening sky, and the wild ducks and teal swam through the ripple, and the gulls floated above it: and in lound spots a hundred rings showed how the fish were rising.

Thorstein climbed a howe on the left: and as he climbed, the lake opened up before him. Beyond the nearer woods there was the deep of blue, and the lonely island in the midst of it: and from his feet, away into the uttermost distance, the huge fells, tossing like the breakers on a stormy beach, and rolling away and afar like the heaving waves of the sea. And over them late sunset brooded in the north, with bars of level cloud, purple and gold, and fading rose-flecks over-head.

Unwearied in his exultation, the lad ran down to the shore again, and stripping off hood and kirtle, hose and shoes, all stained and ragged with scrambling through brake and briar, he waded out into deep water, plunged beneath, and swam

sturdily through the calmness. Then he flagged at last, and
crept ashore; he donned his clothes, and looked about him
for a safe night-lair; smiling as he thought of Hundi's horror
at sleeping like a squirrel. He crept into the boughs of a
great spreading oak, and its thick leaves sheltered him like a
thatched roof and hid him like the hangings of a shut-bed.
The level clouds drew together; the purple colour darkened
into black; and a line of dusky light alone lingered in the
North over Helvellyn, while he slept, dreamless.

CHAP. XV.—THE GIANT GETS HIS FOSTERLING.

THORSTEIN slept on in the tree long after the day had
dawned through those level clouds : for at mid-summer
in Lakeland it is never black night; the sun only dives, as it
were, behind a fell or two, and up again ; and you can follow
its track by the light that travels round the north, like the
ripples which betray a diver in shoal water. But this dawning
was a dull one, for those level clouds had lowered, and
thickened, and turned to rain : and wind came up from the
seaward, as the gulls had foretold. And yet it mattered
little to the lad in his oak-tree lair, except that no loud singing
of birds awoke him, and the dimness of the light let him sleep
on, when he should have been well on his way homeward.
For as to the plan of taking land and building a house and a
boat, that was out of his mind now that Hundi was gone.
To take land, one must go round it with fire, and have
witnesses to the deed. Some other day he would come back,
now that he knew the road. And it was lonely waking there
in the damp mist, hungry and stiff, with all that waste of
wilderness to tread before ever he saw home again.

Back along the bank of Crake and round the little tarn
went Thorstein until he heard, in the woods on his right
hand, shouting, and the voices of men. At once his heart
came into his mouth and he stood stock-still to listen. Could
it be Hundi come back, and the Greenodd folk in search of
him ? What if they should go forward and find his mere,
and he away and out of it all ? What of the chance of a

good bag of meal or a barley cake somewhere about them? For he was both clemmed and starved. So he crept through the wood, and now and again the noise came louder. He followed it, slowly forcing his way among the deep fern and the brambles under the great trees. The voices were heard more plainly now, singing and shouting in a strange manner. It was not Hundi and the Greenodd folk: but who? Thorstein was drawn by a great desire to know this secret of the woods, and to add one more marvel to the story he should tell at supper.

On the top of a little howe, clear of trees, but rocky and ferny like the wildest moorland, sat huge men, red-haired and red-bearded, crane-legged and clumsy handed and jolter-headed, clothed rudely in skins, and devouring great ugly gobbets of flesh from a roebuck they had killed, and seemed to eat with little or no cooking. Thorstein gazed at them openmouthed and astonished: it was like a dream of the wonders he had pictured to himself, but never fully hoped to set eyes on.

The branch he held by, snapped: and forthwith there was a terrible shout, and a crash on his head, and he seemed as in a dream to be falling down a dark pit.

Then it was all light, grey light, and no green gloom of the woods; and beneath him the red ling-blossom fled away, as he was carried by someone or something swiftly over the wide moor. He began to know that he was weary and in a great pain of his head; and at every stride of his bearer he was jerked so that it hurt him. He kicked and struggled; the huge red man put him into the middle of a deep heather-tuft, and set himself down to look at the lad, as a cat watches a mouse.

Then Thorstein rose on his knees and tried to scramble away, but the giant man just reached out and gave him a great batt with his hand, that sent him heels over head, scratching his face in the heather. Then the same thing happened again; and the third time Thorstein plucked himself together and flew at the giant, snatching out his knife, and

minded in his rage to stick it in anywhere or anyhow. But
the giant never moved off the stone where he sat: he just
caught the knife in one hand, and with the other crushed the
lad down. He looked at the knife long and curiously, then he
nodded and laughed to himself. Then he looked at Thorstein
where he lay on his back, kicking up the ling-blossoms: and
then he waved the knife as if to draw it over Thorstein's
throat. Thorstein shut his eyes and his mouth as tightly as
he could.

The cold knife cut his neck a little, and the blood came;
Thorstein waited to be killed. The rain pattered on his eyelids, and when he opened them again half blinded, but not
with tears, the giant was looking at the knife-handle and the
marks on its blade: and nodding to himself. Then he picked
up the lad under one arm, and strode off through the heather.

CHAPTER XVI.—THE FELL-FOLK'S HOME.

BEYOND the heather was the giant's home, on the fell
between Blawith and Broughton. On one hand were
the waste wet mosses of the moor, and on the other hand,
far below, the great flats of Woodlands, surrounded by
the tossing rocky range of Dunnerdale fells, from Brimfell
on the right hand away down to Black Comb and the glittering
sea.

In a high place like this, people might live for many a long
year unseen and unknown of their neighbours in the dales:
and if they were hunters and robbers, no doubt they could
pick up a living of a sort even now: but in old times when
the land was waste, it was as good a place as could be for
the home of wild half-savage fell-folk. The ground is not so
high as to be bitterly cold in winter, and at a time when there
were trees in plenty where now is only fern or heather, they
could find shelter. Down in the valley at that time every
thing was smothered up in wild wood, or uninhabitable for
swamps and dampness, except where the ground had been
cleared and drained by the hand of man. But high on the
moors the ground drained itself more or less: so that both

for health and wealth it was the moor that was the chosen
home of the earliest dwellers among the mountains: and their
children lived on in the old places, even after new comers
had begun to make their farms and villages where we see
them nowadays.

Upon these moors, here and there you can find the walls of
their buildings, and even in little corners what may be
chambers, or store-houses, or fire-spots, or what not, curiously
built of great stones: but all quite different from the farm-
buildings of our own people, and plainly the relics of an earlier
race.   Within these homesteads there are heaps that are
round and hollow in the midst, with a gap for a doorway,
and edged with stone within and without.   Though the top
of it is fallen in, one can see that such a ruin might have
been a hut shaped like a beehive, and roofed over like those
Pict-houses they tell of in other parts: high enough inside
for a man to stand up in, and big enough for him to lie at
length.   When we dig into them, we find potsherds, and
bones of their feasts, the charred stones and ashes of their
fires, and now and then a scrap of iron or bronze, on the
paving or along the skirting of the dry-stone wall.   Also,
hard by, one may light upon plenty of graves where the fell-
folk doubtless lie buried.   Indeed, upon Blawith moor, under
the Knott, there is a great barrow in which folk digging found
burnt bones, and you can see the tall stone that stood at the
head still standing there.   They call this place the Giant's
Grave: and old neighbours tell that it is the burial place of
the last of the giants who dwelt in that moorland village, and
that he was shot with an arrow on that very fell side, and so
was killed, and his race ended.

So, when the big red man strode off through the heather
and the ragged birches of the moor with Thorstein under his
arm, such was the spot he came to.   He marched in at the
gate of the intake, and up to the homestead through cattle-
folds with little cows of the old Northern breed and rough
mountain goats, grazing between the walls: and through
patches of kale and rye by the side of a tarn lying blue and

clear in the midst of the place. There in the evening sunshine, among the huts, would be a dozen or so of women and children, dirty and half-naked, both the old hags and the little goblins. They had four posts set upright in the earth, and a skin stretched over them in which was seething upon a fire of sticks a mess of flesh in its own broth. Some were making ready for the evening's feast, and some were cobbling skins together: but for the most part they were a set of idle do-noughts, to reckon by the filth and hugger-mugger in which they lived.

They raised a screech when Thorstein was brought in and cast on the ground, and set upon him to stare at him and pull him about; until what with the raggedness of his torn clothes and their handling he was mother-naked, and not a little ashamed of his plight, and of his white skin. Not that the fell-folk were blackamoors; but they were sunburnt with going unclad, and grimy with dirt. So there he sat, part covered with litter and bracken which he pulled over himself: and he brazened it out as well as he could.

CHAPTER XVII.—THORSTEIN'S BONDAGE.

IN a while the rest of the men came up, not all as huge as the giant who had caught him, but all long fellows, gaunt with fell-running and hard fare. They began their feast, dipping bowls and spoons into the skin over the fire, and drinking out of horns and cups until they were merry. Then one of the youngsters spied Thorstein where he sat, and threw at him the bone he had been gnawing. Thorstein warded it off with his hand, and others that were thrown: but whenever they hit him there was a horse-laugh. When all the bones were gnawed and thrown, one of them picked up a dart, which he threw at the lad: and it would have made an end of him, but Thorstein dodged it: at which they all cried " Oigh ! " and seemed to wonder at his address.

Last of all one of the men, seemingly enraged at his luck or cunning leaped up and ran at him with a cudgel, a thick stick with a stone hammer-head at the end of it. Thorstein

had been through too much to cry out now: but what was
his surprise when one of the children, a great girl with long
red hair over her bare shoulders, ran in and flung her arms
round him, half smothering him with her mane and the
closeness of her embrace.

Then there was gabbling in a strange tongue while she
kept him tight and seemed to forbid the giant lad to touch
him: and the chief of them all spoke long, waving his arms
and nodding his head, as who should say " Let the boy be,
and we will keep him for our thrall." He seemed to show
how he had threatened the lad with his own knife, and held
up the knife, and pointed away over the fells: from which
Thorstein gathered that they knew whence he had come and
somewhat of who he was: and for the first time a gleam of
hope shone into his heart.

In the end they gave him some of their meat, which he
loathed and could not swallow: and pushed him into the
stone hut, the best that there was, though even this could
not be entered except by creeping: and they signed that he
should lie down and go to sleep. But little sleep came to
him: the place was filthy, and he was among unfriends: his
head ached and all his bones were sore. So he watched
them as they came in one by one, and stripped, for the hut
was as hot as an oven: and they lay down, as it seemed, in a
heap, like snakes in an old tree root.

At last all was quiet without, and within they were snoring.
The air was thick and foul: Thorstein could not breathe.
It was fun to sleep in a tree with squirrels, but this was
sleeping in a pighull among swine. He dragged himself like
a worm, a little nearer the doorhole and then lay still. After
a while he dragged himself a little nearer: and lay still again,
with his heart beating so loud, he feared it would awaken
them all.

Out into the fresh air Thorstein crept in the end: and it
was like a draught of cool ale after haymaking to taste the
night wind. He stepped warily between the huts, straining
his eyes in the gloom lest he should run against anything, for

the night was cloudy and there were no stars, not even the dawn-streak in the north. He groped his way like a white ghost to the first wall, and began to climb it ; but just as he reached the coping, down it came with a rumble and a thud, and the stones fell on his feet and crushed them, so that he could not stir for the pain. And straightway he was in the grip of the giant again, who belaboured him with a dart, as if he had been a dog. The pain of his crushed feet and sickness was such that Thorstein felt little of the giant's blows, though every time the dart-head touched him, it cut into the bare flesh.

But when he woke up at last, it was in the nasty hut, and every one was gone except the child who had flown at him before ; and she was nursing his head and weeping over him. She looked so ugly, thought the boy, as he opened his eyes, with her face all blubbered and red, and the tears making dirty water-courses down her freckles, and dripping off her chin, and upon her rough red hair that hung all about. But when he came to himself, she called out shrilly, and an old woman brought milk in a pan and put it to the lad's mouth : and when he drank, the child let go his head to clap her hands and laugh. It hurt Thorstein to drop his head, but he thought she was less ugly when she laughed, and threw back her hair : and he saw that her eyes were blue, and her teeth shone. And it rested Thorstein when she took up his head again, and smiled and stroked him.

To make a short story, he lay there for days and nights, and sometimes slept, and often raved, and only now and then knew that the child was holding him and giving him drink from the milk-pan. Whether it was dark or light when he awoke from wild ugly dreams of swamps and snakes, and things chasing him through the brambles, and high endless walls to climb, and torrents of stones rolling down with him into the snakes again : whenever he came to his senses there she was, and no other pillow he had. In the end, the fever left him. As for his wounds they let the bark harden, and Thorstein had a whole skin before ever he was strong enough to stand up in it.

But when he could look about him, the child seemed to be eager in giving him what pleasure she could. She brought out a little kist that held her treasures : there were shining beads, and pennies of silver and gold with holes to hang them by, and a gold thing like a Thor's hammer, but Thorstein guessed it must be a cross: for the child set it up and knelt down before it and prayed, looking sometimes at it and sometimes at him. Thorstein knew that his own people set little store by Christians, because they were not so good at fighting as the Northmen, and because they could be over-reached by their chapmen, so they said : and he thought that all strange uncouth folk were Christians, as a matter of course : and so the wonder was less that giants and troll-kin in filthy huts should be of that faith.

But when he slept again after this awakening, he dreamed that he was at home, and his mother was kissing him good night, and stooping above him through the hangings of his own shut-bed : but her hair seemed to be all red like fern on the fells after early frost when the summer is over.

CHAPTER XVIII.—RAINEACH.

SO Thorstein was healed of his sickness ; but not until the summer was far spent, and not until he had begun, little by little, to learn words of the fell-folk's language. For whatever the child did for him or showed him she was not silent about it, but chattered the while, and often said its name loud and plain ; and when he said it after her, she laughed and nodded. When she brought him milk she would say " Bainne :" and sometimes when he was thirsty the little roguish creature would wait awhile, as he clacked his tongue and licked his lips, until he would say " Bainne :" and then she laughed and brought the milk-pot. And Thorstein soon learnt with such teaching, and never thought of being shy as children are when they are taught a strange tongue. Nor was it quite strange to him : for his mother had told him a few words of her mother's language, which was Erse, and not unlike the words of these people, only spoken a little otherwise. So when he one day saw a ring in the child's treasure-ark, and came out with " Fainne," and saying " Meur" put it upon her finger, she was astonished, and the rest of them laughed.

Now that he offered no longer to run away, they treated him well after their fashion. He got the cream of the milk, as if he had heen a chief's son at fostering : although the cream was always sour from keeping in foul crocks of rough clay ; and indeed they liked it so, as though new cream were tasteless. There was always plenty of flesh meat, of roe-deer and hares and other savoury sorts, good enough, said he to himself, if one doesn't watch the cooking. As the saw says " What the eye never sees, the heart never grieves after," so their clarty ways vexed him less and less, as the days wore, and as Greenodd began to be like a dream on the other side of awakening.

Lying in the hut, or sitting out in the sun wrapped in a deer-skin, Thorstein watched the people, and when they were not so new to him they seemed less strange and uncouth. Even when the men came in, whereas at first he crept as far out of the way as he could, at last he was drawn to look on at the game they brought, red-deer and roe-deer, wild boar and hares, all manner of moor-fowl and mere-fowl, and wonderful fish, spotted trout, and silver and golden char, whose pink flesh is the delicatest of all eating. Thorstein had seen some little sport at Greenodd, but it was plain that here the great lake was a teeming fish-pond and the great fells one deer-park, and that these red men were the cunningest of hunters and fishers, if their farming was nought.

Nor were they rough with him now. Once, when a huge youngster began to tease him with some more horse-play, the giant carle who was father and chief of them all, laid open the lout's head for him. And if once he had thought that they had no manners, and their customs were beastly, now he began to find that they were cunning in their own craft, eloquent in their own tongue, kind to their own kin, and proud of their own havings. It was not always growls and blows: many a time the little wench would play with her ugly father, and cuddle him prettily, and he would pet her as if, said Thorstein to himself, they were no Christian savages, but decent Thor-fearing folk. And if he had looked down upon them as the dirt beneath his feet, he now gathered that they reckoned less of him than he thought for, and kept him at arm's length while they treated him well, just as a boy treats a squirrel he has caught, stroking it while he holds it hard, for fear it should bite.

So the summer wore and the autumn came, and Thorstein was kept within walls or close at hand. He spent his time with the women for the most part, helping them in their work, but much as he liked. They let him stack wood for fires: sew and fashion such garments as they made from skins, or from cloth that they got by barter for pelts among the Welsh. Sometimes he was let milk the cows and goats, and take them to pasture; but then there was always somebody to watch that he should not run away. Other whiles he tried his hand at woodwork: but it was long before they let him handle a knife, and when they did, sharp eyes were upon him all the time. But they seemed mighty pleased when he turned out little stools and boxes, pegged together with wooden nails, or bits of hooper's work that would hold water. And as he began to be useful, so he got on famously with them and felt homelike.

The child who had nursed him gave him to understand that her name was Raineach, that is Fern: and indeed she was not unlike the bracken when it is red in autumn, and she was slender and strong and wild as its tall fronds that smother up the hollows among the boulders on the moors. She was maybe a year or so younger than Thorstein, but as tall as he. Her father, the giant as we may call him, was a head and shoulders taller than even a tall fellow among the Northmen, and far away bigger than the Welsh. Big as he was, it was easy to see that she ruled him, as he ruled the rest—all except Thorstein who by now seemed to belong to her. And Thorstein by this time was little loath to have it so. When-

ever his mind went to Greenodd it took Raineach there too,
and he could see her in his dreams in their hall, sharing his
trencher and cup, and friendly with Hundi, and tormented
by Orm.   So he put off the escape that sometimes he planned,
until he might persuade her to run with him.

But when at last he had words enough to open out his
mind, and to tell her of his longing for home, she was
astonished and grieved, and gave him to know that she
thought him a very lucky lad to be living in such good
company and so well off as he was.   For many days she was
cool with him and said little : which angered him, so that he
would say nothing to her.

But once when they were out with the goats together, and
she was groping in a blackberry bush, a wild cat sprang
straight out at her, like a shot from a sling : and fixed teeth
and claws all together in her shoulder.   Thorstein had the
creature throttled in an instant, but great work it was to get
it off, and to kill it, bang as he might with his thick stick.
And then he got her home, and the women put herbs on the
bite to take the poison out, and to stop the blood.   So it was
Thorstein's turn to be nurse for a while, and his sulkiness
melted away : all the more that she gave a fine story of his
bravery.

Which when the giant heard, he said the little fellow was
good enough now to go out with the men.   And after that,
for many a weary day and through many a terrible night,
trotted he behind long-shanks and his lads by moor and mire,
chasing the red deer and the roe, and snaring the fowl of
wild-wood and water.   And one while he got good words for
his work ; and other whiles, for all he could do, it was nought
but ill luck, and an empty belly, and blows to his back.   But
to such doings one hardens when limbs are young, and each
time the weariness and the danger are forgotten.   Hunger
and cold, and rough companionship, and the squalor of the
huts became too common to be feared any more.   And as
the months passed, the boy waxed and throve in the keen air
of the fells.   He grew cunning to track the slot, keen of eye

and deft of hand, like any savage of them all: and Raineach was proud of her foster-brother.

CHAPTER XIX.—THE THREE TASKS.

WHEN Thorstein had found his tongue and could talk to the fell-folk in their own speech, he would often tell Raineach about Greenodd and his home.

Sometimes in the winter weather, as they were crouching by the open-air fire in sleet and wind to dress their meals, or cowering in the foul huts from the storms that swept the moor, there would come before him, like a dream, the bonny eld-house and its beloved rafters, and the bright things gleaming on the wainscot, and the lasses in their neat kirtles a-spinning or a-sewing; his mother with her needle, and his father with woodsmith's tools, and all so cosy and well-to-do as they worked and sang in the warm fireshine.

Then he would whisper to the giant's lass, as they huddled together in the muck, and the men growled or snored,—for there was little to do in the winter up there but sleep it out like bears,—and he would say, "Raineach, I see them, I see them! There's our great dog asleep with his nose on the edge of the hearth, and father is kicking the logs together, and he pats the dog and says to mother, 'Where's poor old Stein now? I wonder if he's all right somewhere, or tanning his hide in a cold peat-pit.' Mother shakes her head at Hundi and says, 'Eh, lad, it was a bad day thou tookest him off: the elder should have been the wiser.' For I'll uphold it, Hundi has led a hound's life ever since. But I can see mother working flowers on a kirtle, and she has been working at it every day this back-end: blue flowers, Raineach, and gold leaves on a brave red stuff: eh, if you saw what I see, you would see some bonny things and all.

"And the chapmen will be coming about, with packs full of wares from all the round world, and they'll be feasting them. And at Yule, what doings! Pies, lass, as big as ant-hills: and butter to thy haver-bread, and honey in thy porridge: and laiks in the afternoons, when the tables are cleared and folk pull skins across the fire, and one side lets go and down they tumble: and one is blindfolded and hunts the others: and I'd show thee a safe place, Raineach, so that they couldn't catch thee. How thou'd laugh, and how they'd laugh: and how we'd sing and tell stories, and get eh, that frightened, and then mother would say ' Barnes to bed,' and we'd pull the clothes over our heads while we heard their goings-on. Grand it would be if I could get thee there to peep in on them all."

With such talk, Raineach, who had looked on Thorstein as a poor savage at first, came to feel a great longing to see what wonderful things might be yonder across the fells: and once even asked her father whether they could not pay a visit to Thorstein's folk at Greenodd. She said they would come back again, never fear: and maybe bring some of the things Thorstein told her of. He laughed at first; then he growled, and shook his fist at the lad, and bade him say no more to the child. And for a good while they found it hard to come together: there was always something for her to do, and something for him elsewhere: and life was worse than before.

At last when spring came, Thorstein plucked up his courage and said boldly that he wanted to go home.

" Well, my little man," says the giant, " here we have nursed thee for a summer and a winter, and given our best: and what," says he, " shall we get for a parting gift ? for it is little we have got as yet."

Thorstein said that his father would be sure to give something.

" Nay," says the carle, " I know him and his gifts."

Thorstein reddened and bit his lips.

" Now," says the giant, " do this for me, and I'll let thee go: keep my cattle this twelvemonth, and see them well served: but if one be missing thy head shall pay for it."

So the lad became herdboy to the fell-folk: and well he knew his job, for he had been among the beasts at home, and was used to all that belonged to cattle. But these were well-nigh wild, and bad, bad to manage. Often they would break bounds, and give him a rough job to hunt them out of the mires and woods, where wolves might get them before ever they had time to be lost. And many a night it was only by the help of the lass that he could gather them together and drive them into the fold for the milking : and sometimes it seemed that an unfriendly hand would loose them, and give him a sad scare. But Raineach managed so that in a while the rest of the folk were ashamed or afraid to meddle. And they throve that summer, and after the slaughtering at the back end of it, Thorstein kept as many as would make up his count for the spring : and was diligent in serving them with everything he could lay hands on. So the end of it was that when winter was near spent he delivered over his full tale to the carle, and bade him farewell.

"Not so fast, my little fellow," said the giant. "I reckon nought of this. Here are all my beasts again, no doubt : but what more ? We are no better off than we were."

"What then ? " cried the lad, aghast.

"This," said the carle. "Seest yonder tarn ? When it is as yellow with corn as it is blue to-day, we will talk more of this matter : but if I hear another word, it will be the word for knocking thy brains out with this club of mine." And he dashed about him with his great oaken cudgel in a way that was grewsome.

So Thorstein was angry and mad angry ; and in his anger set himself to bale the water out of the tarn the giant had pointed to,—one of a many there were in those days about the spot, though now they are all peated up. Then Raineach came and stood by ; and when she saw the water trickling back into the pool, and the rain beating into it, and the sweat running off the lad's face, she laughed. He asked her what she was laughing at : and she said, "At thee." Then he threw at her the crock that he was baling with, and bade her begone for a heartless wretch. But she drew back, and it fell on a stone and was broken : at which she laughed the more. Then he sat down and wept. And she came to him in the rain and comforted him, and called him a fool, which is often the best comfort from one that can help.

" Look," she said, " silly lad, how the water runs out of the broken pot. Break the tarn, and it will be dry."

" Nay, I know that well enough," said he.

" Well, do it," said she.

" But how ? " said he.

Then she showed him that the rock ran in ridges, and that he might dig the earth away between the ridges and make a beck. So he dug the earth and made a beck : but still there was water in the tarn.

" Who is the fool, now ? " said he.

" Not I," said she : " throw upon the tarn all the earth out of the digging, and fill it up."

Thorstein thought she was a clever lass, and threw all the stones he could find, and a deal of earth upon them into the tarn ; and if it was somewhat miry, it was no tarn any longer. But now he was let down for seed to sow : and beg as he might, they said they had but enough for themselves. Then after some days of bitter words and nights of useless thinking, came Raineach with a bag full of corn. She would not tell whence it came, but it was good seed corn : and Thorstein sowed it, and watched it morn and eve, and built a fence around to keep man and beast out of it. And glad he was when it showed above the brown earth, and fain when the ears began to turn yellow : and bade the giant see to it, and let him go forthwith. But all he got was a growl and a roar.

" Where did that corn come from ? "

" Not from thee," says Thorstein.

" Thief ! " says the giant.

" Liar ! " says Thorstein : and they were both as angry as they might be. But the giant would not kill him, and best knew the reason why. For he meant to keep the lad against a time when there should be trouble with the Northmen, and then give him over as a ransom. So he was in no hurry to let his prisoner go.

" Look you here," says the red man at last : " those great firs yonder where the crows build,—they must be cut down and made into a house for me, before ever I let thee go."

" Ask another to do the job," said Thorstein.

" Never another will I ask," said the giant : "folk that can make corn grow in tarns, can make firs into houses."

So Thorstein toiled at one of the least of the trees with his knife and a little hatchet, the best he could find : but he could only notch it round, and it stood as straight as ever. Then Raineach came and laughed at him again, and bade him go to sleep till she helped him : but she would not say how or when. And in a while she disappeared altogether.

One day when nobody was nigh, the men all away hunting, and Thorstein bewailing himself, he looked at the firwood from afar, and thought one of the tree tops shook more than the wind used to shake it. By and by it fell, and he heard a crash in the wood. He ran down to the spot, and there was a great tree on the ground, and chips of new-cut wood all about it : but never a soul to be seen. Then the lass came laughing, and saying it was magic, and the good folk would have none of his spying ; and so she took him by the shoulders and pushed him out of the wood. Magic or no magic, she managed that on certain days the men were out early and home late, and none of them noticed that the fir tops were gone : and Thorstein was hugely puzzled. At last he went to the spot by stealth, and saw strange men working there : they looked like Welsh, and he guessed they might be from the brough across the flats. They had many of the trees down, and sawed, and squared into timbers, that men might carry on their shoulders. Raineach was not there ; but round the neck of the foreman of them, as it seemed, was her gold cross hanging. Then the lad knew how she had helped him : and right proud he was of her and her favours, and told her as much.

So when the winter was on them, one day comes Thorstein up with a plank on his shoulder, and " Where is thy house to stand ? " says he.

" What ! " cries the giant, " who felled my trees ? "

" They are felled," says the lad.

" Not by thee."

" That's neither here nor there," says Thorstein : " where is the house to stand ? "

The giant was not ill pleased to think he was to have a house like the Northmen, and so he let things be : and Raineach made the lads of the fell-folk help, in that they dragged up the big timbers right merrily, and Thorstein was master of the works. And if his building was not great nor very workmanlike, it was game to him when the studs were sunk in the ground, and beams hoisted and fixed with pegs, and rafters began to show the shape of the roof. And all this was done with the tools left in the wood by the strangers, of whom nothing could be heard. Most folk said it was fairies.

CHAPTER XX.—OVER THE FELLS.

BEFORE the building was done, that is to say in the early spring when Thorstein had been now three winters among the red folk, there was once more rumour of war throughout all the north, and the sound of it came even to these wildernesses, so far as they were apart from the dwellings and intercourse of men. For the red giant, being in this respect like Swein Biornson, was a borderer and a dweller on no man's land, that is to say he had no laws nor kings of his own kind over him, and was bound to no government of lawmakers. And yet he was akin to other Gaels dwelling up and down these parts : who, though they were at ancient feud with their Welsh neighbours, yet could let sleeping dogs lie when it served their turn, and play at give and take, or even do good work for Owain the king of Cumbria. For since these hardy hunters and fell-runners knew the lie of the land better than settled ploughmen or townsfolk, in many ways they were useful, as in guiding the Northmen to Dacor, and in spying upon them often, when little they knew what eyes were gleaming through the green leafage. Add to this that the king's service was not unprofitable ; and poor folk must live, however proud they be.

So when war was talked of, the news came to their ears somehow, handed on from one to another of the woodlanders,

or picked up at market; for there were times when they came
in to sell their furs to the Welsh or English at burgs and
trading places on the outskirts of the mountains, as at
Broughton, Ravenglass, or Cartmel.

This time it seemed certain that the north was going to
rise against the south in good earnest.   Constantine and Olaf
Cuaran, Owain and the new Dublin king Olaf Guthferthson
had made common cause.   Says the giant to Thorstein,
" Thy folk will be gathering at their meeting-place in the
mountains, and that is hard by our meeting-place too.
Thither I am going, and if thou hast a mind to see thy
father—"

" Say no more," cried Thorstein : and they made ready for
the journey.

In those days, to one who knew the country, the best roads
were not the roads we travel, but the tops and ridges of
the fells.   The valleys were all umbered up with trees, or
choked with swamps ; and what with wild beasts and what
with wild folk, travelling was no child's play.   But in the
waste wildernesses of high moorland, on the tall rock-ranges
that joined peak to peak like bridges in the air, foe in shape
of mankind was hardly to be found.   It was rough work over
snow in winter and through moss and mire in summer-time,
and a stranger would easily be lost and never seen again :
but these hunters were at home anywhere between Skiddaw
and Blackcomb.

The giant, with Thorstein and a few of the lads that
followed him, were not far on their way, when there was a
stir in the woods behind them, and presently through the
coppice came a slim running figure, in brogues and tightly
knit plaid and deer skin, and a great bush of red hair streaming
behind.

" How now, Raineach ? " says her father : " what folly is
this ?   We want no wenches on this journey."

With that she pouted, and when he bade her turn back,
she began to weep, and sat down on a stone to lament.
Thorstein was vexed to see her cry, and would have stayed

by her to comfort her: for indeed it had been a sore parting but a little while before. Then the giant took him by the elbow and shoved him along the road, telling him not to be a fool, or never a sight of his father would he get.

Well, they went along for a space: and as they climbed one height of the many on that moorland around what we call Beacon tarn, where the lad used to fish with the lass: and while he was thinking that after all they were happy days he was leaving behind: just then, one of them cried out that that there was a stir again in the birch boughs on the height they had left: and a red spot flitted over the heather from cover to cover. The red giant bade the man shoot an arrow to scare their follower: and the man shot, but took good care to aim wide.

They pushed on, until they were out of their own grounds, so to say, and nearing Coniston, and as the travellers came towards the place, along the brow between Banniside and the lake, there was a shout in the rear, and a scream, which they could not but understand. So they ran back on their traces, and soon saw Raineach fighting and kicking in the grip of a rough fellow, who made off when he saw the big men. It was little use to scold her, and too late to carry her back home. Her father said no more when she came up with them, and only strode on with his best foot foremost, so that it was all she could do to trot after and keep in sight, for many a weary hour.

From Coniston they slanted up great crags by a narrow footway until they got to the top of the high waterfall we call the White Lady, because she comes and goes like a wraith. Thence they found their way over the bogs to Weatherlam cove and the head of Micklegill that runs down into Tilberthwaite. Then away they went up and down over the rough fells, until they found lodging for the night in a lone dell Langdale-way, with some kindred fell-folk who had their huts there. The children were right glad to rest their swollen and battered feet on a heather-heap all night, whether asleep or awake, while the men talked loud round the fire.

Come morning it was up and away over wilder ground than ever, climbing by the ledges of rock to the bogs that make as it were a thatched roof above the walls of those great mountain houses, whose streets are the dales, and whose gables are the peaks. All day long it was wading work through the mosses, or clambering over the screes, up and down long slopes that seemed in the passing clouds and showers to lead nowhither but into the rain and the mist. In the afternoon they were aware of a great valley beneath them. They had come so to say to the eaves of the house of mountains and yet could not look over, nor see what was going on below. But they were above the dale through which the great Roman road goes, where lies the city of Helvellyn and the lake of Thirlmere and the Northmen's Law-burg-thwaite.

At the city of Helvellyn, as they reckoned, there would be some force posted to defend the border and the main road to the south, for it would be a likely point of attack. With this point guarded, and the coast road, and the Maiden Way that comes through the Westmorland fells, king Owain would be safe, and free to throw his whole power upon York by the great way over the Keel. And it was thought that the king himself might soon be there, to speak about the defences with the people of the place, and with the Northmen whose Althing would soon be held hard by.

But the red giant had no mind to put his daughter in the way of Owain's soldiers, any more than to leave her in the clutches of the ruffian on Banniside : neither would he give Thorstein the chance of getting away before his time. So he avoided the Welsh burg at Wythburn, the city of which we spoke, and led them down upon a dwelling of his kindred, such as dwelt here along the brink overlooking Thirlmere, on the Benn as we still call it in their language,—the great mountain between Armboth and Thirlmere water-foot.

CHAPTER XXI.—ALUINN.

DOWN came they through the bracken, which was just beginning to shoot among the boulders of the moor, and were stopped by a group of men who seemed to have sprung out of the ground; and indeed for colour and rough aspect they seemed to be part and parcel of it, as paddocks match mud and caterpillars mimic twigs. A shout in the fell-folk's tongue put all to rights without fighting; and then they saw two low houses on the slope of the moor, built of great stones and roofed over with peat. They passed by these to the head of a gill that ran sharp down between cut rocks, and then they found more of these houses, all low and foursquare in the plan, better built than their own dwellings, but squalid enough. There were people about, who welcomed them when they knew who the visitors were, and came out of the huts, unkempt and fierce as themselves, and yet as proud in their mountain fastness.

It was built on a nab between two ravines, and the only path ran steeply down to the wath across Thirlmere. From this spot one could see the length of the lake and all its rugged shores, cleft into scars and steeps, and whatever was not rock or water was green leafage. Over against them was the great wall of Helvellyn, rising high, and seemingly sheer and unattainable in the clouds of heaven. Such steepness and such dizzy terror of falling the children had never known, as when they came to the utmost of the houses, which stood on the axle of the nab. There on either hand and in front the ground fell suddenly away, as when one stands on a high tower, and men are like mice underneath one's feet.

A woman kept house in this place, not old, but no longer young; tall, and sinewy in her arms, with beautiful fair hair, but a harsh face, and a harsh voice. She welcomed the red man, and said little to the children, but did them no harm, and gave them a better supper than they were used to have. For though the cot was rude, she seemed to have plenty, and there were neighbours, and the road was below, by which a sort of marketing could now and then be done if one had the means; whereas at Raineach's home neither love nor money could get what was never there to be got.

When they had eaten, out they crept as children do, to see the new place they had come to: and looked over the brink into the gill with its soft moss and purple butterwort cushioning all the rough hard rocks, and sweet-fern fringing the fountains that sprayed into dimpling basins among the stone, or slid down black slopes under a roof of silky-barked birch and white-flowering rowan. Here and there ancient gnarled hawthorn-trees clung to the crags: one especially was thick with may-blossom, as if it were loaded with snow: its rich almond scent hung about the place, coming and going like a breath.

The children scrambled down the steep side to get at its boughs from above, for it grew close to the slope, like a flower in a girl's bosom. But when they broke a hole as it were in the white thatch, what should they see but the loveliest lady in the world sitting among the twisted boughs, and the finest prince in the world, as it seemed to them, standing below, reaching out his arms to her, and speaking passionately, with his eyes afire and bonny smooth cheeks aglow. But when he saw the strange little faces thrust through the blossom-roof, with wide opened mouths and staring eyes like goblins, he slid away with a start, down the forest slope, like a snake in the whins, so that they could just see the flash of his mail and the glint of red and blue in the leafage as he disappeared. And when they looked again for the lovely lady, she was gone.

They were too astonished to say a word, but Thorstein held Raineach's hand, and they climbed back to the cot, and crept in, bidden to sleep by the woman of the place. It was not long before something bright was at the door; and in came the lovely girl they had seen, with grey eyes wide open as if she saw wonders, and a smile that stirred their heart-strings, and all her golden hair flaming about her green gown.

The woman—they could only be mother and daughter—looked at her quickly; and looked at her again: and even

the red giant, who had not yet gone away, bent his brows
upon her in amazement.   Then he made one of those clumsy
reverences of his, for he had at whiles a sort of half forgotten
courtesy about him, like a man whose has seen better days.
"So this is thy lovely daughter," said he.   "When I saw
Elphin map Rhydderch, the worthy lord warden of the march,
roll in the dust, little did I think what sweet flower would
have sprung from such a dunghill."

"Peace," said the woman.   "And thou, Aluinn, what
news?"

"News?" said the beautiful girl.   "Grand news!   Nay,
what news should there be?"

"Fool," said the mother.   "Greet thy kinsman, and give
word of thine errand."

She kissed the big red man on the beard, and stood
thinking: and said, "Ah, the king's men have come, if that
be all."

"Well?"

"Oh, a good troop; maybe three score, maybe six score."

"And the king?"

"Oh, aye, the king, I suppose, and the young king, I
suppose: and all as it should be.   But oh mother, the hawthorn is sweet to-night, and the birds are wild with their
singing, and I was fain to bide out in the gill.   It was bad of
me, for I should have been here serving the company.   Is
our good kinsman suppered?   Where are his folk?   What
can I do to help thee?" and she began as if to busy herself
with the housekeeping.

"Peace, child," said the mother.   "Thy kinsman is served,
and for his folk, they are bestowed.   Two of them, hush, they
are asleep."

But Thorstein and Raineach, vaguely bethinking them of
manners little learned on the open fell, sat up on the
heather heap in the corner which was their bed.   Aluinn
started at the two goblin faces, the red head and the tow
head, unkempt and uncouth, rising in the dark corner: and
she screamed and laughed wildly.

" What's to do with the silly thing now ? " cried the woman, and shook her: but all she got was a flood of tears.

The red man was mightily aggrieved that his children should be taken for goblins, and all manner of talk was held, as Aluinn came to her right mind: and said she was sick, and lay down in her bed. And so they all rested, uneasily enough, for that night.

In the morning she was quite another lass, and chattering like a jay. Raineach her young kinswoman was made much of, and if she stared shyly at the wonderful beauty for half a day, she was won over into companionship by the afternoon. The lad was ill at ease: he could not tell why, though nobody spoke him aught but fair. His keeper was away to the king's army: and now and again there were sounds of stirring below, as if horns were blown far down through the forest, and men shouted.

Thorstein moped about, staring at the great mountains half hidden by rain and mist, while the two lasses foregathered. He came in and helped his hostess with her tasks, but she looked at him askance. He had never felt more a stranger, even in his first days among the fell-folk. At bed-time, the beautiful Aluinn turned to him and waved her hand. " Lads lie there: " she said. " Raineach is my bed-fellow."

Thorstein crept into the place she pointed at. It was a little tiny shed at the end of the hut: a sort of kist of stone walling, just high enough to crawl into, and long enough to lie in: a dog-kennel or fowl-house it might have been. But the heather was soft within, and he crept out and gathered more, and piled it around him.

Early in the morning he was awakened. Raineach's face was at his feet, peeping in through the door-hole. " Heigh ! " she said, whispering loudly and eagerly. " Thorstein, listen ! I know it all. The bonny man is the king's son. Wake, Thorstein ! Aluinn wears his gold collar round her neck: I saw it when she doffed her clothes. And she gave him her ring. Thou wilt give me a gold collar, Thorstein ? Wake up, lad ! And thy father killed her father, think of that !

He was a wicked man, and they were glad. But Domhnall
is a lovely man. And if thy father hadn't killed her father,
she would be a lady at the Castle down there. Domhnall is
the king's son, Thorstein: and Aluinn will be queen, Thorstein.
Oh poor Thorstein, they said thou wast a wolf's cub: but I
said nay. Now, thou must have a red coat, and I would
have thine eyes shine like—"

"Go away!" growled the lad from his lair.

CHAPTER XXII.—THORSTEIN SEES HIS FATHER.

NOW all this while Thorstein was eager for a sight of
his father : why else was he here ? And all the more
because his heart was sore against Raineach who could so
lightly leave him for her fine friend. He bethought him,
little as he knew of love-making, that he must cap yon
glittering Welshman, or else be cast off as a good-for-nought
and a lout. There was only one way of doing this : namely
to get back among his own people, and let it be seen what
like they were, and what like was he when his hand was in
its glove again.

Over yonder he knew was the Althing-stead, somewhere
across the water. Run he could and swim : why not away ?
So he slipped off and slid down the gill, steep and steeper
down the great crags beneath the fell-folk's houses, and buried
deep and dark in trees that covered the brink on both hands
with well-nigh impassable thickets. Down the cliff he went,
holding by tuft and ledge, and at last let himself go, sliding
down the scree with a fall that brought him to the water's
edge.

It was a black basin of rock into which the white foam
tumbled through the ferns, a secret place among rowan and
hawthorn. In the splashing water lay great rocks, some as
it were bits of carven pillars six sided, and others whose
fragments were bright with red and green colours, and
curiously inlaid with patterns of white and black that looked
like lace work. They seemed to be the precious stones folk
put in rings and brooches, only larger and more precious in

every way. He picked them out of the water, and broke them smaller to get the glowing bits out, thinking what fine jewellery he had lit upon: there would be enough for more than Raineach could wear, aye, and for every one he knew: and maybe gold might be found where jewels were, if he could but lay hand upon it.

He hunted stones up and down Cockrigg gill until he was wearied, not to say bruised and bleeding with his scrambling among the sharp rocks and with many a fall in dub and force. So he lay down, wet as he was, beside his heaped treasure, and slept. But when he awoke, the bright colours on the stones had all faded: they shone only while they were lying in the water, and against the black and grey of the wild rocks in the gill. The white hawthorn and the purple butterwort were brighter by far, and faded not so soon as the fairy colours of these stones.

Then he bethought him to explore the gill and find his way down to the lake: for every beck comes to dale at last. But this was no beck like the streams of the lower moorlands. It was all fierce forces with rocks on either hand, and when the ground was ever so little passable the trees had got a hold of it, and hedged it up. And yet he won down, and lighted upon the road that led to the wath. Then came folk. Thorstein went back into the wood, for he dared not risk being seen in broad daylight. He forced his way up the brow of the fell aslant through the wood, and struck a path that brought him to the houses above.

So the long day wore, and the gloaming came late as it does in Lakeland in midsummer: but it came: and the lasses were abroad, and the woman throng with her house-keeping in the cot. He slipped away down the gill again and found the big road, and stood awhile wondering whether he should swim the lake or go boldly by the general fording-place. Then there was a noise of horses and men. He climbed a hammer, a jutting rock that overhung the road, and lay down flat upon it to see and not be seen.

The troop of wayfarers came on in silence, as wearied men

who had travelled far between morning and this late twilight-time, on wearied beasts,—ponies we should call them rather than horses : for the nags they rode in those days were tiny compared with the great chargers of the knights in after ages. It was grey mirk by now. and only when they came close beneath him did Thorstein know them for Northmen. But even so their mailcoats and their fighting helms of iron, with great leather flaps, disguised them. He crept nearer to the edge to look over. A stone fell from under him and one of them passing beneath looked up sharply. " Father, father ! " cried the lad ; but at that very instant was gripped from behind, and throttled fiercely, and dragged up into the wood : with two great hands round his neck, and a knee in his back to hold him down, quick or dead.

Beneath, upon the road, there was a scurrying to and fro, as Swein Biornson swore it was his lad's voice, and he would know it anywhere.

" Nay, man, it was but an owl," said some : and others upheld that it was some trick to draw them into ambushment : or maybe a troll of that hag-ridden wilderness. Swein climbed the hammer, where nothing was to be seen or heard but the roar of the beck in the gill, and a grisly moaning in the wood, that might be wind in the trees, or wood-sprites, or what not. So they went forward, none the slower for this adventure : and the sound of them died in distant pattering.

" Ha, my little wolf-cub," said the giant, loosing his grip of Thorstein's throat : " so thou hast eyes for thy father, and none for thy foster-father. Well, what was my promise ? That thou shouldst see him : and thou hast seen him. Good : we are quits. Now no more straying of nights, dog. Get to thy kennel." And he drove him through the woods with many a stripe, and kicked him into his lair, and rolled a big stone against the hole of it.

CHAPTER XXIII.—DOMHNALL.

SO there we leave Thorstein to bite his hands and weep for that slip between cup and lip, the bitterest he had known. The giant came into the cot, and what should he see but Raineach, giggling and wide-eyed over a silken scarf that a gay spark, he knew him well, was tying round her bare shoulders: and the house-mistress smiling and becking and bowing like a fool. Aluinn was not there: but they seemed merry, and the wild lass looked quite bonny in the firelight.

"What, goodfellow giant!" said Domhnall, with somewhat shame-faced bravery, as he scowled in at them; "here we are all as merry as hares by moonlight; and upon my honour, I make my best bow to the father of such a bright little thing."

"See what he has given me," said Raineach with childish pride.

"She'll be back before long," said the mother. "I warrant, now I know of it, Aluinn just slipped away to look for some-body. But take something, sir. It's little we fell-folk have to offer the likes of you: though fair's the day that brought you: and it's a poor place for a king's son, if the last drop of Roman blood runs in the veins of our Aluinn."

"It's the sweetest spot in the world, mother," said Domh-nall: "and no finer greeting can I give you when we take our Aluinn to court, and all the lords of the land have to bow down before her."

Then Aluinn burst in, breathless and haggard and panting. She flew at her lover and held him tight, taking no heed of them all.

"What now?" cried they, and the young man unwound her arms from his neck, and held her off a little.

They learnt bit by bit that she had strayed out to look for him, and away on the road toward the wath. She had hidden while a troop of men rode past,—Northmen they would be, going to their meeting place. She had heard them splash over the ford, and then it was dark and she turned homewards. But suddenly she saw a light, as if some wayfarer were camping in the wood by the lake-side. It brightened and spread, until she thought the forest was on fire. But no sound of crackling branches or hissing flame could she hear. The blaze grew broader : sparks flew on high, and all round it seemed one great flickering. Then she was terrified and fled by the well-known wood-paths, daring no more to look behind her.

The men went out to a little spying-place on the uttermost brink of the nab, but fire there was none. The glow of the Northmen's Thing-stead was hidden behind Great Howe, and the Welsh city was away beyond the crags.

"Why, pretty one," said Domhnall, coming in, "what fancies are these? The heather's afire I know, for all the country is up : but that is the only blaze, and black night it is between here and Helvellyn."

"But I saw it," said the lass shuddering.

"It was only a glint of moonshine : come, little silly, let us be merry again."

"Nay," said her mother thoughtfully, and stood up, tall and strange. "She saw it. I have seen it. Twice before I have seen it, and well I know the sight. Once for death : and again for death : and the third time."

"Come, good mother," said he, "never seek to scare us. King's sons and queens that are to be, give no heed to old wives' soothsayings. Aluinn, smile now, and drink. It will do thee good, and me too."

"Peace, young man," said the mother. "Are not all thy men now bound for battle, and unappeasable war with the great king? Which of them all, think'st thou, which of them that drink to-night and shout drunkenly round their fires, will come unscathed out of the fire of the fight, to march hitherward again in triumph to the homes of their fathers and their children? Nay, I tell you, not a man of them all. And which of them will lie in agony on the desolate heath far away in Saxon-land, till the ravens pluck out their eyes, and the wolves tear the hearts out of their riven harness? Aye,

by that token, many and many a one. I see them there, the
proudest, the mightiest, the bravest : I see them in their
blood : and I see the handful that flee over heath and hill, in
their shame and their sorrow, terror-stricken before the sword
of England and trembling beneath the spear of the stranger,
fleeing to their lairs in the mountains and to all the wild-wood
fastnesses; and I hear the wail of the mourner, and the
scream of the captive, and the curse of the mother that bore
the coward and the coward's son."

"Ah, my life, go not out to this battle," cried Aluinn,
clinging to him. "Stay by us in peace : and if evil must
come, let it roll over thy head, lying hidden here in safety."

"What!" said Domhnall, "shirk the play for a girl's
vision and a woman's fears ? "

"King," said the red giant, " for thou, lord, may'st be king
before this moon has waned,—these are no idle counsels. A
brave heart is the praise of youth, but a seeing eye is the
glory of a king. Hear me. Life is good to us in the woods :
is it not good to thee in the city and in the court ? And if
blood must be shed, why should the blood of father and son
redden one field together ? Stay by us here, and claim from
king Owain the wardenship of these marches. It is a post
of honour. And so we shall keep the seed corn while we
spend the reapings of the harvest."

Thus they talked until morning, and it was resolved that
Domhnall, nothing loath, for the sake of Aluinn if not to save
his own skin, should withhold himself from the battle. The
red man, because he knew the land, and was cunning as a spy,
got the ear of King Owain next day; and saying nothing of
the vision, bade the king go in peace, and begged that Domhnall might be left with the defenders of the border, to keep
them in heart, and to be king of the land in his father's room,
to do justice upon the upstarts and peacebreakers, who
always showed their heads when the king's back was turned.
Such advice was held to be good, and the army went on its
way to fight Athelstan at Brunanburg.

CHAPTER XXIV.—THE GIANT'S CASTLE.

CLEAN gone were the Welshmen at last, and the Northmen with them; and then came the giant and dragged
poor Thorstein out of his lair, where he had lain a night and
a day with little ease: and took his daughter with them: and
over the mosses they travelled, no long way, to the stronghold
where the fell-folk were used to retire in times of war and
trouble. All along the Benn their houses were scattered, but
on the side away from Thirlmere there is a deep valley. No
wilder might be in any part, and scarcely in any land inhabited, than this that opens at Shoulthwaite. On either
side high cliffs, brant and broken, rise above the sheets of
ruin, which fall from them among scanty leafage of battered
forest-trees. In one place the crags frown over the gill as
they frown nowhere else in our fells, overhanging their bases,
as if they would topple down with a breath. The gill is steep
and rocky; the chasm that cleaves its sides, one long waterfall from top to bottom, comes down from the high moors and
desolate bogs to the low-lying valley and inhabited plain
between the Benn and Blencathra.

There in the midst of this trough runs out a tongue of land,
steep on either side: and the tip of it rises abrupt into a tall
rocky island, precipitous all round, and approachable only
by a narrow neck that joins it to the mountain.

Across this neck great trenches had been dug in ancient
times, deep and wide, and curving round the castle rock, like
the new moon lying about the old. So huge they are that
they remain there to this day. And if the first is climbed
there is the second; and if the second is climbed there is the
third, twice as high; and no way to circumvent it or avoid it
if one would get up to the stronghold in the midst. And
then there is the hollow in the rock where a few houses might
be built, as the forecourt of the castle or its outer bailey,
defended on two sides by the sheer precipice, and on the
third by the trenches: but on the fourth side rises still higher
the uttermost rock, a tower unapproachable save by a narrow
path like a ledge in the side of it, so that one only at once

can enter ; and one man above with a good spear could easily
defend it, thrusting each new comer over in turn, and down
into the gulf below, like sheep one by one thrust into the pool
at a sheep-washing. Then on the very top is a plain place, a
rocky platform, whence the eye searches all that valley and
views the great vale and the roads below, and Blencathra
and Skiddaw rising beyond them, and the mountain tops of
Helvellyn above the nearer crags, and Ullscarth over the
moor. By a steep path one could come upon the road
leading from Thirlmere out to the plain and round to the old
fort at the foot of Derwentwater : and from spying-places
could be watched everything that passed, and all that was
doing below. So that this was the safest place for refuge,
and the most dangerous to the neighbourhood that could be
found : a stronghold seemingly impregnable before the days
of gunshot, and still among the wonders of the fells.

Here it was, our story says, that the giant kept ward on
the passes with his men, and held Thorstein in a prison from
which there was little escape. But so long as Raineach was
there, life was not bitter nor unbearable : for she was all the
world to him now.

And yet there was little to give them pleasure in the
horrible black rocks and roaring gill, and the loneliness and
deathliness of all around. Never was the place without a
guard upon the gateway, so that none might go out or come
in. And indeed, what with wild beasts and the terrible
country round about, to say nothing of a time of war when
every kind of evil-doer is abroad, there was little to tempt
them forth, so long as they had a roof over their heads, if it
were no better than a pighull ; and a wall between them and
the world, even though it were a prison-wall.

The summer sultriness thickened day upon day, until
Blencathra was but a film of grey, hung like a cobweb in the
sky : and the beck began to dwindle, and its roar died into a
murmur beneath the bulwarks of the hold. Then followed
the stillness and the heaviness that makes one weary in the
hour before a storm bursts. But if the sky was threatening

and if the air was full of dread, in their hearts was a still greater unease while they waited evening after evening for the news that must by now be on its way to them,—the fulfilment of Aluinn's sight-seeing and the sooth-saying of her mother.

One night the men came back and called for drink ; and Raineach brought them a jar of strong mead. The red man drank and bade Thorstein out of his sight. The lad crept into one of the ruined chambers,—low bields they were, like dog-kennels against the wall, in the lap, so to say, of that Castle-crag : and he lay there long, waiting for the thunder to begin. But all he heard was the sound of loud voices, and furious talking, and Raineach's shrill tongue scolding, begging, threatening : and at last a smothered scream, as if some evil had happened. His heart went quite cold, and he crept out to die with her. She was there beside him, sobbing and shuddering : but she put her hand upon his mouth, and drew him into the chamber.

"He has beaten me," she whispered : "and he will kill thee. He says the wolf-cub is a burden, now the wolves are slaughtered. And he will kill me too, if I stand in his way. He is wild. Oh, Thorstein, listen ! he is coming !"

There were shuffling footsteps without : the giant, drunken with strong drink, was groping towards them in the darkness. His hand pressed the broken thatch of the shed where they lay, and the underside of it cracked away and dropped on them. But he could not find the door. After a while he growled and muttered, and sank into slumber.

"Thorstein," said she, "let us away while he sleeps. Oh save me, lad, and save thyself out of this den !"

Then Thorstein, terrified as he was, tried to soothe her : and in a while the quietness gave them courage to look forth.

CHAPTER XXV.—HOW THEY FLED.

DAWN was at hand, and things began to loom through the blackness of mirk night. The giant snored on where he fell ; but the gate-guards lay in their places, whether sleeping or waking the children could not know; and none could open the gate without stirring them.

Thorstein looked over the bulwarks and into the gill. Black it was down yonder; even the waterfall, into which he was used to throw stones for pastime, on the fell-side over against them, had dwindled so that the white of it hardly showed. Beneath him the rock went sheer down for a space; and underneath, he knew that there were tufts of heather and saplings growing out of the scree-side that sloped from the crag. He stole breathless to one of the chambers where some little store of bedding and apparel lay, and brought out a bundle of girdle-thongs and such like, and began to tie them into a line. But they were scantly enough to loop round a big stone, and to reach thence to the wall edge and a very little way overboard. He went back for an armful of skins: but how to rip them up into thongs without a knife?

Then Raineach crept up to the giant, and loosed his sword in the sheath: and as she rattled it, he gave a great groan: and she let go. But he sank into sleep again, and she drew it out. They cut the skins into strips, and knotted their line in haste, with trembling hands, and threw it over the wall.

Raineach sat on the edge, and clinging tight to the line, slid down hand under hand, fending herself off the crag with her feet, until they touched the rough scree-slope. Down came Thorstein, with the sword thrust naked through his girdle behind. Her heart beat lest the line should break, or the stones come away from the wall-coping upon them both: but at last he stood beside her, and they stumbled down the long slide of ruin to the gill. There was just light enough for them to cross it without being carried down the stream; and they scrambled up the other side on the grassy bank of the waterfall as steep as a hill-side can be, all under those terrible hanging crags, in the glimmering dawn and the thunder-mist.

Then there was a roar and a crash, and splinters of stone flew about them. They saw a head over the bulwarks against the sky, and long arms whirling as they took aim again. She

screamed and they ran up-bank on hands and knees while
the stones flew, and the curses and threats with them. But
they never looked behind again until they were a good step
out of the deepest of the ravine, and well up towards the
moor, where the ground was not so dangerously steep ; none
the worse yet except for cutting their shins on the scree, and
tearing their faces in the blackthorn bushes.

They stopped for breath, and a last sight of their prison :
but they stopped only a moment, for the gate was opened and
folk were running after them in the grey mist across the
tongue of land. So they plunged into the birches and the
bogs, and crept through the underwood, and waded through
the tottermoss, startling the hag-worms beneath and the wild
fowl above, as they beat their way up and ahead, hoping only
to be lost and out of sight.

Then they came to a high ridge, with piked rocks standing
on it, from which they could see that their homeward course
was plain, over a great swamp and a bleak tarn, and along
the green mountains beyond it. But from their rock they
could track the giant not so far behind, making his way
through the wood, which was harder for him to force than for
the lithe light bodies that could slip between its boughs, and
over its half-dried, cracking mire-holes in which his bulk and
weight stuck and sank continually. And yet he went at it
with main strength, swinging his club and hewing a passage.

Down from their peak they flitted, and up he came from
the other side, shadowy against the lurid sunrise. With a
shout he strode over the edge, taking great steps against the
sky, while they were lost in the maze of oozy rills, too broad
for them to jump, and too deep and too treacherous to wade.
While they looked wildly for their crossings, he leapt the
ditches and gained on them, until at last he whirled his club
round his head, and it flew hurtling through the air. They
fell flat in the mire, and it skimmed close over them. Then
they struggled to their feet and ran neck and neck for Blea
tarn. Thorstein plunged in, dragging her after him, and
struck out for the other side, sorely weighed down by her

head on his shoulder, and well nigh choked by her grip round his neck; for she was no swimmer, and gasped and struggled in the black water. He landed her, though, upon a shoal, and up the bank they fled, on firmer ground now, and with a clear way before them and treeless, over stones and grass, forward and upward to Ullscarth.

But a terrible roar came up from the tarn; and they looked back, and saw the giant near the middle of it, fighting with the black water, and lashing it into foaming waves that circled and spread until all the mere was in a turmoil. And then his head went under: but he rose again, flapping and battling like a wounded heron. Then he sank again, and once more came to the surface, drifting like a log in an eddy. And then the water closed over him, black and calm, and the pattern of the mountain tops began to take shape where he had been. The children stood fixed to the spot. A stream of bubbles rose, and burst; and the reflections joined again, Raineach turned suddenly on Thorstein and dealt him a blow that felled him to the ground: she burst into a passion of weeping, as she flung herself beside him. "Thou hast killed my father," she wailed: "I hate thee, I hate thee!"

Thorstein was in no mood to say good or bad to her, so utterly weary was he: least of all to make love-speeches. He lay awhile, and the tarn-water ran from him upon the grass.

"Listen, Raineach," he said at last: "I hear the shouts of the men that follow us afar."

"Oh, lad," she cried, "dear lad, take me with thee."

So they climbed the ridge, and held by it on the farther side, hidden from their pursuers, and saw them no more.

But now the day had broken, a dismal day of thunder-mist and gathering storm. The highest tops were lost, not in their homely cloud-caps, but fading away into black vapour; and through the rents in it the sun shot beams of coppery and swarthy sheen, down into the smoky dells and tumbling precipices, that seemed to ditch their moorland road on either hand. The long rise and fall of Ullscarth before them looked like a vast bridge in the air, and leading no-whither but into darkness. Far to the right, gaps in the gloom showed awful edges of mountain, rolling and plunging along the skyline, as wheels that moved, great toppling balls advancing slowly over hill and dale, wayward and unescapable. Nigher at hand were huge monsters, misshapen and grey and foul to see; many headed things, with eyes and crests and spiny backs, crouching along the naked ground, among white and bleaching bones in the black soil. And when the children came nearer, hoping to slip by, for there was no other way, these things became great boulders, as it might be images of unknown dragons of dreamland, or they were weird tussocks of grass on black and embattled towers and pinnacles of crumbling peat, that took the shape of laidly worms and all the terrors of winter-night tales.

They won their way over the bridge in air, down through the silky green mosses and heatherless moor-grasses, to Greenup raise: for they dared not try the valleys on either hand in fear of losing the only way they knew, the safe and solitary ridge that must bring them southward and homeward. But the darkness deepened, and then came a flash and an instant crack and roar that sent them speeding upward in panic. Then the storm began, flash upon flash of blue light, terrifying, as they scudded through the din and rattle of hail, blindly seeking shelter: and dashed into a nook of white shattered rocks, an island on the great heaving billow of moor. As they crushed themselves into the bield, some ugly beast with a snarl and white teeth pushed out, and fled past them into the storm. And there they cruddled, in shelter at last: and such was their weariness and the heaviness of the air, that they knew no more until they awoke wondering.

For the sky was violet-blue above them, and the sun was going down among torn flitters of cloud-wreck. All around, the mountains were hard-edged and dark purple, with streaks and stripes and slashes of dim white from the hail and sudden cold. The children crept out, shivering and tottering.

" Oh, Thorstein," sobbed the lass, " I can go no farther: let us lie down and die here."

But he comforted her, and bade her lean on him, and led her up the moor, slowly and painfully toiling, until step by step they gained a rocky pike among white tables of stone and strange pillars and domes and curving hollows, like the icebergs they tell of in the far northern seas. And looking homeward in the twilight from that tower, they saw a deep dark valley below, a gleam of water and a rising shadow of mountain beside it, that wiped off the stars from the southern sky. Aye, and Thorstein greeted as he held the poor lass up to look at the strip of light in the distance. " It is my mere, it is our own mere, Raineach. I know it ! "

How they came down Langdale side in the darkness they could never tell. From ledge to ledge, among the hammers and knots of rock, clambering and groping for foothold and handhold, sliding sometimes down the screes and losing one another in the deep fern : but still descending, even when they were swept down the mazes of the black gills and the torrent beds roaring from the rain-storm : light-headed with hunger, and reckless from fatigue, they reached the valley.

Guided by a red spot of firelight they came upon the huts of the poor folk who had harboured them on their outward journey : and there they found food and a respite from their travelling ; and made a ready tale how the men had gone to the war and sent them home. For if they had let it be known that the giant was dead, it was odds but the fell-folk would have been rough and mishandled them. But for pity's sake they were good, and made them welcome, and wondered how they had come through the storm unscathed. They housed them, and fed them, as long as they would bide, and then set them a good step on their way, until they struck the path over Hawkshead moor and down Rusland pool to the Leven.

As they came within sight of Leven firth and the well known hills, wooded softly and winsome after the horrible ruggedness of the mountains, Thorstein laughed and sang and shouted for joy, and stepped briskly forward. " Come along, lass," he cried, " come along with thee ! Yonder is Legbarrow, and the sands of Leven : a bit more and we shall see Greenodd. Home, lass, home! Step out. Why, what ails thee, silly?"

"Oh, Thorstein, I dare not. My heart is like water within me, and my head works sore."

"Aye, poor thing, little tired thing. I'll help thee along. See: yonder is our howe: and the smoke from Greenodd. See the bonny fields and flocks in them; and ah! they have built a new cottage by the ford, and sown a bit of the intake on the fell. There's Greenodd, Raineach: there it is; our own house!"

"Nay, Thorstein, I can go no fárther. My feet are broken, and my knees are trembling. Oh let me be, and leave me."

"Why, lass, it is but a step. Well, then: well, then: bide here if thou must, and look for me back in a hop, skip and jump to lait thee."

She saw him trip off with no more farewell; and then she dragged herself up into a wild apple tree, and it began to grow dark: and she waited for him, sick at heart. Then the night fell, and still she waited for him.

CHAPTER XXVI.—THE ARVALE FOR SWEIN
BIORNSON.

GRAND doings were at Greenodd house. There was a
table set out before the door and drinking horns upon
it, and a vat of ale in the porch. Rosy-cheeked lasses, in
their feast-day kirtles and kerchiefs, served all comers by way
of a welcome and a foretaste of the supper. For this day
was the Arvale made for Swein Biornson who had fallen at
the battle of Brunanburg.

It was their custom to bid to the funeral feast all their
neighbours and friends, not only that they might do honour
to the dead, but also that they might bear witness to the
incoming of his heirs according to law and the wonted order
of kinship. This they called Arv-ale, which is as much as to
say Inheritance-ale: as they said Bride-ale for the wedding-
feast. And still in these parts the name is given to cakes
they make at funerals, which they call Arval-cakes.

Now when Thorstein came up to the door, guests were in
the act of arriving : namely a good neighbour whom he knew
for Master Asmund, whose land was Asmundar-lea, away
over the back fell : he had come now and then to feasts and
meetings at Greenodd. He was finely dressed in a new kirtle
and hose of the best homespun : he wore a broad felt hood, and
leather riding-boots with bright spurs to them : and when he
lit down from his horse, he stood in the porch with a season-
able sadness, and drank his ale to the good luck of the house,
and hemmed, and sighed, and wiped his beard, and walked
in.

With him was a bright little slip of a lass, who must be
his daughter, for one could see that her nag was well groomed
and well fed : and though she was covered from head to foot
with a great hooded riding-cloak of dark blue and somewhat
splashed with mud, such a merry grey eye looked out from
the hood and such a dainty foot stood in Thorstein's hand as
he helped her from the saddle,—for he happened to be the
nighest,—that there was no doubt of it, who she was. She
just put the horn to her lips, cast her eye round with a little

grimace, and mimicking the grave gait of her father, stepped in after him.

Thorstein looked at the servant-lasses, but they were strange to him. He saw that a feast was forward, and guessed well enough the reason why: for the fell-folk had already heard tidings of a great defeat, and he knew his father had passed him, that night of evil luck, on the way to the battle. He could put two and two together now. And as he stood in the porch, glad to be home again, it came over him suddenly that this was no more his father's house, and that his three-years'-long desire was unfulfilled after all : and the tears came into his eyes.

Just then stood forth a couple of finely dressed young men, returned to the porch after bestowing neighbour Asmund and his daughter within.

"Now, my good fellow," said Orm roughly, "no loitering here with the lasses and the ale. The thralls' quarters are yonder."

"Hold hard," said Hundi. "This is none of Asmund's folk. He is more like a wild lad from the fells, with his long naked sword. Nay now, he is a queer one. What is thine errand, friend ? "

Thorstein said nothing. Words failed him. To think his own brothers knew him no more !

But just then the mother came out, wet-eyed, but bustling over her guests, and anxious that all should be rightly seen to. Nay, never ask if she mistook him, or bade him begone.

Well, the guests had come and the supper was ready. The hall was hung with its finest tapestries, and the floor new strewn with fern. After a fashion that was sometimes followed thenadays, men and women were paired off to eat together. Unna sat in her own high-seat, with Asmund as honoured guest beside her. On her left hand was Raud her brother, who had taken land just across the water at Roudsey. One place was empty, the high-seat of the master of the house : but in all others men and women sat according to their rank, for the women's thwart-bench was not yet come

into fashion, but if for weddings. As it fell out, Thorstein
was given for his partner the young lass Asmund's daughter,
Asdis by name. Folk nodded and patted the table with hard
fingers when they two sat down, as if to say "Welcome
back!" and as though they would add, "Well matched, lad
and lass!" For Asdis came out of her cloak like a butterfly
from its shell; and Thorstein, when his mother had bathed
him and trimmed his hair and dressed him—and little else
she did before supper-time from the moment she set eyes on
him—why then he was quite another lad, and they all said
as much. Hundi was quite friendly, and Orm was civil
enough; though he whispered to Hundi "Why couldn't the
fellow have come to-morrow?"

"Eh?" said Hundi, bluntly. "Why to-morrow?"

"Only that half is more than a third, thickhead."

Then Hundi went over to Thorstein and kissed him, and
gave him a good slap on the back, saying "How about that
whale, lad?" At which they all laughed, for they knew the
story well: but sobered themselves of a sudden and fell to
business, namely their supper. Asdis, the roguish lass, ate
off Thorstein's plate and drank out of his cup, for at feasts
when guests outnumbered the household goods, that was
their way. And between the mouthfuls she chattered in a
low voice, for it was not seemly to speak loud at a feast for
the dead.

"So, neighbour Thorstein Sweinson, ye've been seeing the
world?"

"Aye."

"You don't say so. Hark to him. Happen you've been
faring to Micklegarth, and aboon?"

"Nay."

"What then? Not over seas? Well, maybe over the
fells and far away?"

"Aye."

"And clean forgotten thy mother tongue; or more like
grown a peacock, that has never a word for such as us?"

"Nay."

" I thought as much. Tell, me, neighbour, didst thou see a ragged lad in the porch this afternoon ? "

" Nay."

" Good. Then I'll tell thee. He was a scarecrow, he was. Who'd have thought of a prince in disguise ? "

And so she went on teasing and bantering him, while he could not but spy at her, round the corners of his eyes, so pretty she was in her low-cut kirtle and gold necklace on a white smooth neck, with the locks of her unbraided yellow hair brushing his sleeve, and the dimples in her little soft knuckles coming and going, as she handled and turned the cup before him. She was so dainty that he was fairly abashed, and never knew how to answer her, and hardly dared touch the trencher with his rough paws. There she was laughing softly, and joking in a whisper, with her apple-blossom chin over his shoulder ; and folk staring at him too, till he was fit to sink under the table. Then he drank up all the ale, and held out the cup for more, and drank that : and then he felt more blate than ever, and sat stock still, for fear he should do something foolish. For ale-drinking was strange to him ; he got little stronger than milk on the fell, at the best of times.

When they had eaten, healths were drunk ; a cup to Thor, and a cup to each of the gods. At each health they all rapped the tables and shouted. Then one stood up and hemmed and coughed,—it was Master Asmund their neighbour ; and he spoke in a loud sing-song voice :—

" Friends all, and neighbours, here we are met together under this kindly roof-tree on a joyful errand—nay, what say I ? Joyful is the day that brings the wanderer to his home " (at which they shouted " Hear him ! welcome Thorstein Sweinson ! ") " And joyful it is to find a hearty welcome from our worthy hostess, even in the midst of her great sorrow " (" Well said," they cried all.) " And right and meet it is to come together to cheer the widow and the orphan, and to speak a word of praise for him that is gone." (" Speak on ! " they cried.) " Aye, friends and neighbours,

he was a good man, was Swein Biornson. When I bethink
me of the days he used to come home, ten and twelve winters
it is and more, from summer-leading, before ever this new
order of things began, when there was none of the nonsense
that's talked nowadays about folk-right and king's law and
the like : I say when I bethink me of our good neighbour that
was, and him coming home by harvest time as regular as the
swallows in spring, with a shipload of fine wares that had
cost him many a hard knock in the gathering, and many a
long cruise on strange coasts, and through stormy seas : I
can see him once again in his seat over yonder, at the feast
he used to give for his home-coming and the harvest of the
sea, and well I mind his hearty voice; ' Take thy time,
neighbour; make thy choice,' he would say : for he had a
gift in the heap for every guest, and a good word with it.
And when I look round on the land he stubbed, bonny corn-
riggs and lea land it is now, and few of ye can call to mind
as well as I the rough spot this used to be, before ever he set
to work upon it : when I come over the fell and look down
on this fine house he raised—fit up it is with every comfort,
and nothing awanting to suit his lady, highborn as she may
be, what with householding gear and servants out-doors and
in, dairy fit for a king's daughter and byres of the best, and
all the stock so well managed,—for there's a deal more in
managing, mind you, than some folk allow, that are always
blaming their luck for every beast they lose, and every load
of hay that they let rot in the rain : I say he was a grand
man, and long will it be or we see the like of him again. It
is not his friends only that say so, mind you : they tell me the
very king of England himself offered our neighbour to make
him a thane, and set him over the country-side to take scat
of the folk : but ' Nay,' says Swein Biornson as proud as a
prince, ' Nor thane of thine nor thrall of thine will I be,' says
he to the king. ' I am a free statesman, and a good neighbour to all,' said he : ' and ye kings may lait your tools
otherwheres.'   That was a grand speech, friends : and many's
the grand word we have had from him over yonder at our

meetings, and many a time folk have been ruled by his rede. For look you friends, there was never a man of us but kenned right well that Swein Biornson spoke his mind, and every word came out of a good heart, and honest; though maybe we could not all of us go as far as he did, in some matters. And now," said Asmund, bringing his speech to an end, "He is gone, and we shall see him no more. Over the fells in the great battle-play, hewing down his foes as a lad haggs weeds with his wand, leaping through the spears of the Saxons and shouting to the cowards who dared not follow him : the kemp and captain of the little band that backed him, until the Saxons faltered and fled, so they tell the tale that saw it. Aye, and if Owain and Constantine and Olaf the Red had but found a handful such as he, there would have been another tale to tell of the doings at Brunanburg. But it pleased the Allfather to send for him, and take him to himself. Right glad we should have been to have laid our neighbour in his own howe, to overlook the lands he has won and the house he has planted ; but afar on the Winheath he lies, and Odin has spared him the sorrow of a straw-death. Let us be glad, friends, and rejoice for him : for the deeds he has done in his life, and for the glory he has gathered in his death. Drink with me this cup to him : drink to Swein Biornson."

Standing up, they drank in silence : and in silence they sat down again. Then Orm Sweinson, as being the eldest son of his father, stood in his place to drink the Bragi-cup. It was their custom at Arvales to leave the dead man's high-seat empty until his health had been drunk, and honoured with some fitting speech or vow made by him who should be the chief heir to the name of the dead :. and not until then might he sit in the empty high-seat, and by that token take the rule over the house of his father.

So Orm's cup was filled, and he rose and came into the middle of the hall, and stood with one foot on the stone curb of the hearth. "I drink," he cried aloud, "this cup to Bragi ; and I vow hereby to do vengeance for the dead, and justice to the living." Then they cried out that he had vowed well ;

could say no less and need say no more : and they made room
for him to take his place upon his father's seat, as master of
the house thenceforward.

Then far into the night they sat to drink, and each man
told his tale of him that was gone, or sang a song in honour
of him. But long before they were done with their feast,
Thorstein's eyes were closed, for he was heavy with travelling,
and with the joy and sorrow of home-coming, and maybe also
with the strong ale he had drunk. So he slept where he sat,
long after Asdis, pouting and vexed, had gone off to the
chamber with the rest of the women-kind.

Thus ended the first day of the Arvale for Swein Biornson.
And all the while, in the dark night, Raineach clung to the
branches of the wild apple tree by Crakeford, weary and
hungry and sick at heart, and listening for Thorstein. And
when she slept for very weariness, she dreamed that he was
dragging her among proud strangers who scorned her : and
then that he was saying " Off, off, ugly paddock." And she
awoke weeping, and listened for him, in the patter of the rain
upon the drenched leaves in the dawning.

CHAPTER XXVII.—SWEIN BIORNSON'S HEIRS.

MORNING came and they were stirring. Thorstein
found it hard to awake ; but as he rubbed his eyes
and shook himself, there came over him the thought of Raineach and how he had left her : and he was bitterly ashamed.
He ran to his mother, and " Mother," said he, " I have been
both knave and fool."

" What now, barn ? " said she.

" Mother," said he, " I had a gold ring in my hand, and I
dropped it in the ale vat."

" Never heed it, barn," said she : " thou wilt have gold
rings enough, and that thou wilt see before to-day is done.
And thy old one will land up when the ale is drunk."

" Mother," he said, " there was a young lass with me as I
came along the road : and I left her hard by Crakeford ; for
she was weary, she said, and would come no farther."

" A lass, barn ? What, thou art young to lead lasses up
and down.   But lads will be men nowadays, no sooner than
they are out of swaddling clothes.   And what sort of a lass
may she be ? "

" She's a good lass, mother, and a kind one to me : and I'd
liefer by far lose ring or ring-finger."

" What then, lad ? I'll say nay to nothing, now I have thee
home : but be guided.   Here we are all throng as throng can
be, and folk to break their fast : and men-folk are aye fractious
on the morrow of a feast until they be served.   And there's
the settlement to follow, and a gey work it will be to get
through unless Orm be more reasonable than I fear.   Let
me send one of our men to lait thy lass, and bestow her in
one of the thralls' cots until we get these guests off our
hands : or if thy mind is to fetch her here upon us all, maybe
Asdis Asmund's daughter will give her a share of her bed.
That's a bonny lass, Thorstein."

" Nay, mother," answered he, stuttering, " I doubt Asdis
will give us no thanks for thrusting a stranger upon her : and
Raineach—"

" What ? " said his mother : " is it an Irish woman ? "

" Never mind what, mother, now : but I say she will be
better suited elsewhere than here, until this turmoil is over,
and then."

The first thing was their breakfast, which was a great meal
with the North-folk then-a-days, and the set-out was well nigh
as big as at supper time.   Next thing was the settlement,
and division of the dead man's goods ; to be done before the
neighbours, fair and square and above-board : for in those
days they had no lawyers and writings and such-like, either
for the making of laws or for the conveying of property, and
all was done by word of mouth and deed of hand in the
presence of witnesses, whose testimony was the only token of
the continuance of a custom or the assurance of ownership.

After question asked and answered about debts the dead
man might owe, and after sundry to whom he had lent money
or goods had repaid them in bags of silver or ells of cloth

they came to the division of the estate.   It was their use for
the widow to take one part in three, both of the land and
goods.   After some talk, they climbed the howe and parcelled
out the whole landtake of Swein Biornson, both wild-wood
and cleared land: and coming down from the howe they all
walked over the grounds as they had measured them out from
above, beating the boundaries, and planting staves or stones
from point to point along.   And this side of the line, upbank
towards Greenodd, was to be Unna's, and the other side was
to be for the rest of the heirs.

Of furniture and movable things, ornaments and apparel
and household gear, they carried out a third part and stood
them in a heap in one of the sheds, until it should be settled
where Unna would bestow herself and her goods.   Then she
chose out her third part of the thralls, both men and maids,
and set them aside.   And by that time the morning was spent,
and the mid-day drinking was served to them in the disordered
garth.   But to the younger folk all this was a holiday-making,
and it was merriment to see arks opened and goods shifted,
and the thralls set out in a line and chosen: and to hear the
maids say "Oh mistress, take me!" and to one and another
the mistress replying "Nay, lass; I know thee too well."

So then they talked about what should be done as between
the three lads; until one said, "It has been done before,
neighbours, and it is often a good custom, for the first-born
to get house and land, and for the younger to take the
movable goods.   Now here we have three lads: and if we
set all that remains in three shares, namely house and land
and farming-stock to one share: and the ship and all that
belongs to it, boats and boat-sheds, tools and tackle and
such-like, to another share: and lastly if we reckon up silver
and gold, apparel and furniture and such chattels to the third
share: then I say we shall not be far from a fair parting of
the estate.   And I say that if Orm Sweinson takes the house
and farm, he will do well: and if Hundi takes the ship and
goes abroad, he is like to thrive: and if Thorstein the child
gets the money and movables, he will be well set up."

At this Orm boggled somewhat, for said he, " An empty house is cold cheer." But Thorstein answered " Why, brother, we can mend that. Give me and my goods house-room, and I will give thee the help of me and mine." And so said Unn, for she was loath to leave the old spot, and Orm knew right well what a manager she was. And so they settled it, without more ado, and went down to the field for a game of wrestling.

There they played until supper time, and Thorstein acquitted himself right well, though he was far from full grown. But his life on the fells had hardened him, so that Hundi Snail, as they called him because he was easy and fat, went down under the youngster : and even Orm was thrown twice out of thrice ; at which he was vexed, though he said little. So to set matters right Unna bade them in to supper : and as they went up to supper said Asmund to Thorstein, " A word with thee, my lad."

" Say on, master," says he.

" Look you now," says Asmund. " Thou hast been these three winters away, and no doubt we shall hear of thy doings. But one thing I see, and that is, thou hast not lost thy time."

" Thank you kindly," says Thorstein.

" But," says Asmund, " take a word from one who knows. It is not all of us who have the trick, like thy poor father, of being soft to friends and sour only to foes: and even betwixt brothers things do not always fall as one would. Now, was it quite wise in thee to throw thy brother Orm, think'st thou, those two times ? Was not once enough ? "

" What ! " said he. " I threw him fair."

" Ha ! ha ! " laughed Asmund. " Fair is foul in such matters. Riddle me that, lad. But when thou comest to know Orm a bit better, from serving him a month or two—"

" Serving him ? " cries Thorstein.

" Well, what else ? since he is master of the house, and a masterful man at any time. But when thou hast need of a friend and a friendly roof over thy head, take thy money-bags, if aught be left in them, and hie thy ways over to Asmundar-lea. Say no more, my lad, but bear it in mind."

So they went to supper, and Asdis sat again by Thorstein, daintier than ever, and not a bit put out with him : and he was a deal more at his ease. And while men drank after supper, said she, "Bonny things, master wrestler, I spied among thy goods : and a lucky lad is the getter of them."

"Aye," said he, "they are fine enough, I suppose."

"Would it be asking over much to have a sight of them once again before we go ? There's a stitch in some of thy hangings I would be glad to learn."

So he brought an armful and cleared the table where they sat, and she fingered the embroideries and praised them, and praised him, until he had given her a good half of them in in spite of her nays.

"What," she said at last, "I'll see no more if everything I touch is to be given to me. But in one of thy kists, I saw a fine draught-board. Shall we have a game ? "

"I doubt," said he, "I have forgotten how to play."

"Oh," said she, clapping her hands, "then I'll teach thee, master mountain bear : and that will be fun, for it's dull for us poor lasses if you men do nought but drink till bedtime and aboon."

So he found the draught-board and the carved knaves, and they played fox and geese until he learned something of the trick of it. Then she said, "Nay, thou art fairly my master. I'll teach no more. Let us play rightly as folk do, and stake a trifle on a game or two."

Well, the end was she won a good bit more of Thorstein's fineries, and carried a great heap off to bed with her. And if she was pleased, so was he, at finding any way to please so pretty and dainty a creature.

CHAPTER XXVIII.—WHITE ROSE AND RED.

NOW the third day of the feast had come, when the guests bethought them of going their ways homewards. Thorstein went out with Asdis to catch her nag for her, and to set her on the way with Asmund and his men. But when they got up to the fell-pasture where the horses were, thralls were cutting wood from the stubs in the coppice hard by. And just as Thorstein was laying hold of the nag, what should he see but a poor, thin, gaunt figure in rags, among the wood-cutters, carrying a huge load of sticks, and the red hair hanging down unkempt over her face. One of the men, in rough horseplay, as rude rascals do with a strange new fellow-servant, put out his foot, and let her trip over it, and tumble with the load and all. Then another went up to her and cursed her for a fool and gave her a kick. Thorstein flew at them, and it was right for one and left for t'other, and down they went, heels over head, one with a broken jaw and one with bloody nose. Thorstein picked up the lass, and would have kissed her, but she fought herself loose and struggled away.

"Raineach!" he cried; "Raineach!"

She turned and looked at him in his finery. Then she looked at Asdis who had come up, staring. Then she looked down at her tatters, and black, bare feet and fingers.

Asdis put her hand on Thorstein's shoulder. "Eh, what breaks!" she giggled, and then burst into shrieks of laughter. Thorstein shook off her hand, and darted after the ragged lass, who fled through the wood.

"Oh, Raineach!" he cried after her in her own language, "Raineach my darling! forgive me, forgive me! Listen to me: only hear me! Stay, Raineach, only stay, and hear me!"

Poor little thing, she was too weak and ill to run far: and stopped at bay under a ridge of rock in the wood. But still she kept him off with her hands, while she wept and laughed and wept again.

Thorstein grovelled on the moss before her, and poured out his heartful of passionate words: blaming himself for knave and fool: and excusing himself by telling her what had passed, and how his mother had promised to have her well bestowed in a thrall's cot, out of the way of the stoore of the guests: and how he could not come nigh her till they were gone: and over and over again he said it, till he had no more to say. At last he lay quite still, sobbing bitterly.

"What's all this?" shouted a rough voice through the wood. It was Orm. "Look here, young fellow, don't go knocking my thralls about: I'll thank you to learn manners, if you mean to stay. And who is this ugly goblin, I'd like to know?"

Thorstein was on his feet in a moment, and Raineach in his arms as if they had never been parted.

"She's my sister, kinsman: the child of my foster-father. And I give thee to know, that there's not a lass in the land to match her."

"One would think the giant had fostered thee, barn," said Orm, using the old byword, and laughing scornfully.

"Then beware of the giant's fosterling."

"Well, come and show thy mother what a prize thou hast got."

"Aye, that I will, and all the world," answered Thorstein, as she nestled to him, and clung to him, sobbing no more, but tall and straight and proud, in her rags and dirt.

And then he led her to Greenodd house, whence all the guests had gone away: and speaking in her tongue, told his mother who she was. And his mother answered him, and spoke to her words that she could hear, and that made her weep for gladness. And when she was washed and fed, and dressed in clothes from Thorstein's own store, simple things that Asdis had not cared to take, she sat by the fire while Thorstein told them, far into the night, the story of his wanderings and of her kindness to him.

As the story went on, Unna drew nearer to her the child, that wondered, and understood nought of the tale but what she guessed from their glances: until her head was on the good mother's lap, and from her eyes, half shut, the tears crept out, and through the great red mane, upon the kind hands that petted her.

When Thorstein had done, Hundi kissed him, and Orm came over out of the high-seat he was proud to keep, and held out his hand. "Kinsman," he said, "let bygones be bygones."

"Why," said Thorstein, holding his brother's hand :
"What is there to forgive ? "

But Unna said, in the soft Erse tongue that came back to
her like a dream of childhood, " Many a time have I prayed,
whiles to the Allfather, and whiles to the White Christ, for a
little lass, though I dared tell no soul else of the folly. And
he has heard me, whoever it is hears poor folk's prayers. He
has taken my man to himself, and he has sent me this bonny
maid."

CHAPTER XXIX.—RAINEACH AT GREENODD.

IT was not all plain sailing, though the start was fair.
They tell how, once upon a time, a lad brought home a
wild kitling from the woods, and nursed it up among the
house-cats by the hearth. So it was at Greenodd with
Raineach.

With the best will in the world, she found it hard to learn
their ways, and quite beyond her to follow them. At first
there was the labour of a new speech to get. Thorstein had
picked up her talk with ease : but she could never frame her
lips to the strange sounds, nor force her thoughts into the
words of the Northfolk. She would be eager to chatter, and
brimful of news, or wonderment, or recollection, or explana-
tion : helping herself out with gestures, and the forcefulness
of her native manner, unlike the slow steadiness of the
Northern delivery, and strange to them and disquieting. And
in the midst of it all, a word wrongly spoken, and drolly mis-
interpreting her meaning, would set them all roaring with
laughter. At which she would be vexed and sulk : for her
people were grave and staid, though forceful and rapid in
speech and gesture : while the Northmen, slow of speech and
drawling, were ready with rough jokes and childish fooling.
So she took their laughter in bad part : and they took her
glumping for the sign of a bad heart : and Thorstein had
work enough to come between them all.

And then she could never learn the deft neatness of their
household ways, their cleanliness in kitchen and dairy, and

tidiness of table and chamber, and handy management of needle and shuttle and rock. If there were doubt in their counsels, mishap with beasts or men, or any grave trouble befalling, who but Raineach was run to for help: for she kept her head, while the other women-folk were shrieking and scurrying; and she was dry-eyed while they were weeping; or sober while they giggled like fools. But even for that they thought worse of her, as one who had not the feelings of other folk, and never laughed nor greeted when she ought, nor was shocked like a decent lass, nor disgusted like a dainty one.

And that bush of red hair was never dressed for long; and her kirtle was torn, and cobbled up coarsely; and her kerchief awry; and her work fouled with losing, and leaving in corners, and crumpling in hasty forgetfulness. And if sometimes she was the pride of them all, for her tall, slim strength, and her bright bonny face with the proud high-set cheek and brent brow, and with the earnest friendliness that shone in her eyes; at other whiles she was dismal, and the light faded out of her, and she was no better than a draggle-tailed slut, they said. And then nothing healed her but a run with Thorstein on the fell, and unmaidenly scraffling among the beasts, or rough pulling and hauling at the boat-sheds with Hundi and the ship-wrights. Unna would often say over to herself how much she owed the lass for Thorstein's sake, and how much she might do for the lass to bring her into shape: and so schooled herself to be good to her: but it was not always easy to keep back a sharp word; and a sharp word spoiled everything.

Thorstein too was a puzzle to them. Every indoor business he shirked, and cared only for herding and boating and the rough work of the farm. He had been so long on the fells that quiet life came amiss to him: and often by the fireside at nights, as that winter wore, he would fidget and worry until he found a call for turning out, so that even the shepherds bade him leave them in peace to look after their own job. Then he took to hunting: and they owned he was a famous hunter. He would fish in the firth, day and night and all weathers, as if he had a bear's warmth in him. They were glad of the fish he brought home: but it was irksome to have him bring in his dripping self along with it, to reek and simmer by the hearth, when all was redd up and snug for the evening. "Folk must do as folk do," said they behind his back: but when they said it to his face he looked ugly, and Unna dreaded a fight with Orm one of those days.

So the nights wore on to Yule: and then came a messenger from over the fell to bid the Greenodd folk to Asmundarlea for the feast-tide: and "Over and above that," said he, "my mistress Asdis bade thee in especial, Thorstein Sweinson, and charged thee to bring the young may, for she would fain know her, and make a sister of her."

When Raineach understood that this was the lass that had laughed at her, on that dreadful day which nobody ever named, she said flatly that she would not go. But Unna begged hard, and told her that the lass was good at heart, and meant all kindly, and that it would be a feather in her cap to win such a friend. So Raineach dared say no more, though she loathed the journey.

But Thorstein found her some right bonny fairings and tricked her out as never was: and Raineach was child enough to be proud of her attire, and said in her heart she would be a match for them all. And they took her on a nag like any lady, and rode over the fell, and were received heartily; and all went well at first.

Asdis was a handsome lass in her way: less tall and strong than Raineach, but far more snod and neat and womanlike. Raineach at her best was a wild-wood goddess, and at her worst she was a grey-faced tatterling again: but Asdis was always the same, blithe and bonny, well set up and well seen to. So that one would have thought there need be no strife between them.

But the very next day Asdis was at her tricks: and every one but Thorstein aided and abetted her in showing off poor Raineach in little things, that bit and stung like midges on a wet midsummer eve. She would flatter till Raineach was

led into simpering, and then they chuckled : she would ask
her advice about tapestry stitches, and Raineach, seeing no
malice, would give grave counsels that a body might see were
nought : she would mock her gait and manner of eating, and
entice her to say the words she always said wrong ; and folk
would laugh ; and even Thorstein laughed as one who couldn't
help it.   Then Asdis cast a sheep's eye at him, and as it were
claimed him for her friend and ally, and Raineach was furious,
and paled, and blushed, and wept, and sulked.   Asdis did it
all so cleverly, and was so pretty and innocent over it, that
even Thorstein would take her part and bid Raineach not be
a fool.   She promised to amend, and was bitterly ashamed,
and tried again : and so it went on until they were all glad to
part and get home again.   And Master Asmund at the farewell clapped Thorstein on the back and said " Well, lad,
we'll not forget, and we look to see thee when thou art tired
of Greenodd and all thy folk."   And so the lad was set up
with himself, and vexed with Raineach, thinking that she
had spoiled their sport, and was after all no better than a
pettish child.

One day when Yule was well over, his mother called him
aside and " Lad," she said, " I doubt I am wearying of these
doings.   It's not that I don't love the lass from my heart,
and there's nothing I would not do for her.   But its dreigh
work putting up with her whimsies, and setting things to
right after her.   Never a stitch she sets, but 1 have to unpick
it : never a pat of butter she turns, but I have to wash it :
what, and she was stirring the cream this very day with a
horn spoon when the rowan thival was there at hand.   And
she slaps the servant lasses if they so much as smile, and she
has words with the men, aye, even with Orm himself.   Why,
he said to me this very days, Mother, said he, tell that young
spitfire that I'll have no more of her sauce ; let her know who
is master here, said he."

" Well, mother," said Thorstein, " Raineach is a good lass,
and means well."

" Nay, never doubt it," said his mother.   " But she does

ill, and sets us all by the ears. It's grieved I am to say it, but I would be thankful if one she would hearken to gave her a word and got her to amend."

"You are hard on her, mother. You all said you'd take her for one of us, and make her at home. And it's nothing but tease and worry, till the poor child never knows whether she's on her head or her heels."

"Nay, Thorstein: that's not a fair word to the mother that bore thee. Who brought her here? Who fetched the wild cat into the house?"

Then he was angry, and she was angry, and they had high words, and parted with little peace between them.

He went out to look for Raineach, and "Lass," he said, "what hast thou done to set them all against thee?"

"I?" said she. "Peace for shame, Thorstein!"

"Nay," he answered, moodily. "It's truth. Here's mother can stand it no more, and Orm fit to turn us out of the house."

"Well then, I'll go for one. Thou canst stay if thou wilt."

"Raineach," he said, "hear reason."

"Little reason in you folk," she answered. "And thou, Thorstein, once I thought—." But she burst into weeping, and fled away.

Thorstein turned in again, angry with her, and more angry with his folk, and angry most of all with himself. As he sat and thought it out it seemed to him that this would blow over like other storms, and that Raineach would surely come back to supper. But supper-time came, and no Raineach.

"What's to do with the lass?" said Unn. "Well, hungry folk can't wait, and I'll keep a bite against she comes."

"Nay," said Orm, "sulky dogs go supperless."

But Thorstein was uneasy, for he had never before parted from her in anger. He left his porridge in the bowl and went out. It was starlight, and snowy, and he called her name. But the sound died away over the dim white fields: and he went forward calling for her, and into the fields and up to the ford.

He searched high and low, far into the night: and knocked.

at the thralls' cots to ask for her. At last one said, coming sleepily to the door, that he had seen her in the gloaming making her way to the fell through the bare woods. He knew it was the wild may by the glint of red in the boughs on the snow. Then Thorstein was terribly fleyed, and ran to seek the place where she had been seen. He found her track in the snow and followed it up, leaping with all his might, breathless, and stopping only now and again to call, and to listen for an answer. The late moon rose, and her traces were still there, the little holes where her feet had gone, and the blur where she had stumbled or rested.

It was long before he found her, plodding ahead up the fell, far beyond their bounds.

" Let me go," she cried, " to my own people. Let be, and forget Raineach."

" To thy people ? " he said ; " then I follow." And he tramped onwards by her side.

After a while she said, " They will kill thee. Go back."

" What do I care ? " said he ; and they went on.

Again she said, " Thorstein, thou art a fool."

" No news," said he.

Then it began to dawn : and they were far on the moor, and the mountains stood tall on the rosy sky. She sat down in the snow, and he sat beside her. Suddenly she put her hands before her face and burst out into wild laughing. " Fools we are both," she said. " Look at yon sky, and our own fells, white and still. And we with storm and blackness in our hearts. Oh Thorstein, wouldst thou truly go with me ? "

" To the end of the world," said he.

" And beyond ? "

He took her in his arms, and the sunrise brightened upon them. Long they sat together in the glow, and forgot the night, and the blackness in their hearts, and all the evil of bygone days. They seemed to have grown old, now, and wise. What silly children they had been, once.

It was late in the afternoon when they came into Greenodd

hall, where all went on as ever: but the two were changed, and saw the spot as in a dream.

"Mother," said he, "I have brought her back. Let us rest here awhile: and give us thy blessing. We'll trouble the house no more: give us time, and we'll away to a spot of our own."

"Children," said Unna, "what game is this?"

"I am a man now, mother," said he. "I can fend for myself, with her to help me. Never say nay: we have it all planned, and ask nothing but good-will."

"Good-will, my son, you have: aye, the best. But, barn, hear reason. You are young yet, and little you know of life. Bide awhile; and take your time. Who but guessed what it was coming to? But Thorstein lad, if thou love thy lass, be guided. There's house to build, lad, and gear to get. Will you live in the wood, and eat mast like swine, with a starving brood of piglings running naked in the mire? A man, lad, takes a man's rede: and a woman, lass, must grow womanly. Is it all done in a night?"

CHAPTER XXX.—THORSTEIN GOES ABROAD.

YOUNG they were, but no fools. Raineach was a new creature, anxious to please and amenable to guidance; willing to learn all that Thorstein's wife should know. He on his part acknowledged that there was a deal to do before he could set up house: and when Hundi sometimes joked him about his castle that was to have been on the shore of his mere, he would take it quite soberly, and reply, "Aye lad, I was a bit before-hand: but wait until I have got my gear together, and then."

"Better come for a trip with me this season, and see what skill we make at cheaping. With thy goods on my ship, thou and I might do a conny bit of trade, and see the world: maybe we'd light on luck, and come back able men."

Now it was a saying among these people "Homely wit has homebred barn:" and no lad was thought much of until he had been awhile abroad. There was none but Raineach that

had a word against it; and she was overborne the easier
because she had made up her mind to be good, and think of
her own wishes last. .

So Thorstein busied himself in cleaning all the skins he had
got that winter, and added a good few to his stock: and he
packed up everything he could lay hands on, if only it would
turn him a penny, or barter off against goods that would be
useful to him in his housekeeping. And at last they bade
farewell to all, and taking the shipcarles who had been used
to voyage with Swein, they started merrily on a fine spring
day, down the Leven, and stood over the sea for Ireland.

At that time there was an unwonted peace through the
coasts of England and all round about. These were the last
few years of king Athelstan's life, when he had brought his
neighbours under him, or won their good will. He reigned
in great glory and honour, and his realm prospered : his strong
hand, or the fear of it, kept all the lesser kings and earls of
the North in quiet. Folk were glad of a breathing-space
after an age of struggles and the great fight at Brunanburg ;
and even across the sea there was a lull, so to say, in the
turmoil of the nations. The age of the vikings was over, and
it was now the turn of cooler heads and wiser counsels to set
to rights the new order of things, and to establish the king-
doms and governments which had arisen out of the disorder
and wreck of the old world.

By these days the Northmen had left being nought but
rovers and robbers : they had become settlers and traders and
rulers of realms on the seaboard of all the northern lands.
And not only in the North; for scarce a spot was there
between Greenland and Constantinople where they or their
children were not found, like bees in a garden, at once
gathering honey for themselves, and sowing for others the
seeds of new life and strength ; the busiest and brightest of
all the kindreds of the age.

But the Northern lands were their homes. On salt shores,
where farming alone could never thrive ; on bleak headlands
among the seamews' nests ; on lone islands veiled in the mist

or girdled with the surf,—homes where any but a race of
sailors would have hungered slowly to death, or pined into
dismal savagery,—there they bred and multiplied, and sang
through the winter, and strove through the summer; their
wit and wisdom and valour putting to shame (though little
they knew it) the follies and the vices and the idleness of the
South. It were long to reckon up all that we owe them, in
thought and speech, in law and custom, in arts and crafts;
for without books, they made themselves learned; without
schools, they became artists; without examples, they perfected
laws; and without bigotry, they found freedom. A wonderful
people, and greatly to be gloried in, even yet, by their in-
heritors; still more by their own children in the day of their
strength. For a thousand years ago it might well be said
wherever a Northman's keel strake strand there he found his
kin to hand; be it west-over-sea from old Norway, in Britain
or Ireland and the isles thereabout; or in Greenland or Iceland; or on the Baltic coasts, and thenceaway to the Atlantic,
from Finmark and Denmark to Holland and Valland; everywhere the Northman's tongue was heard and the Northman's
hand feared.

It was no wonder then, if lads of the breed, born in this
corner of no man's land, and nourished up among wild folk
and woodland swine, should long eagerly to see the ways of
the world and the dwellings and the doings of their kindred
far and wide. Over and above the need to eke out the scanty
gift of the earth by sea-going trade, there was the same spell
that had beckoned them up the Crake, as boys,—curiosity,
and the love of adventure,—hailing them now from over sea,
and waving afar off who knows what glittering thing, to which
reach out they must, whether they would or no. " Homely
wit has home-bred barn "—aye, indeed, if his overword is
always " Elsewhere," and his day always " To-morrow."

So it was in the spring of the year, nine hundred winters,
thirty and eight, since our Lord was born, the lads departed
and came into Dublin Bay. And when they were landed,
officers of the king stayed them to know their errand and

whence they came. When they said they were chapmen, they were brought to the palace; for the king's folk had the right to be first buyers, and to fix the prices of wares.

At the gate who should spy them but Olaf Guthferthson himself. He asked the name of the bonny boys, and they told him their names and their father's name, and that they were from Furness way.

"What," said he, "are you the sons of that brave Swein from those parts who fell at Brunanburg? Ah!" said he, "if we had found but a few more such men, it's not in Dublin I'd be sitting now, but holding my court in London town." And when he knew for certain that they were the sons of Swein Biornson the kemp, as he called him, he brought them in to the queen, and bade her treat them well, for they were the sons of a better man than any of his.

So for a day or two they had famous entertainment, and thought themselves made men. But they soon saw ugly looks among the house-carles of Olaf: and one of their folk bade them beware of a shrewd turn; "for these Danes," said he, "there's no trusting; and stranger's praise is the surest doom."

So they came before the queen and told her how their business pressed, for that they had far to go: and then she bade them farewell, but not willingly as it seemed; and a fine gift she gave them. And as they scudded out of Dublin Bay, they thanked their luck, and cursed all kings' houses for downright wolf-traps.

Then, for the wind was in the South, they went up and cruised about the Irish Sea to the Isle of Man and the great bights of Galloway. There they met many of their own people who guested them in one place and another, and gave them good speed: but little trade they did, for their wares were such as all men had in plenty. They sailed from Galloway up the firth of Clyde, and by the Kumreyar or Isles of the Welsh, to Alclyde, which was also called Dun-breton, where was the chief city of king Domhnall: and there Thorstein was somewhat shy of being known lest a grudge might be owing him for his escape and for the death of the red giant. But nobody seemed in those parts to know or care for old stories of wild fell-folk. He asked news of the queen, hoping to hear that his friend Aluinn was by now wedded to Domhnall and advanced to be lady of the land. But folk laughed and wagged their heads, and gave him to understand that there might be a dozen queens up and down for aught they knew: and he asked no more, for pity of the poor beauty away in the Cumberland fells, who had put her trust in the gay raking spark. He said a deal to Hundi, out of the fulness of his heart: what a shame it was that men should be light of love, and how he would like to see the blood-eagle carved on Domhnall's back. To which Hundi Snail answered lazily that he talked like a great guff: and Thorstein was near coming to blows with him.

When they came out of the firth of Clyde they rounded Satiri's muli, the Mull of Cantire: and sailed to the Hebrides, which they called Il-ey and Myl, Tyrwist and Skidh, Iwist and Liodhus; and everywhere they found Northmen and friends settled, and an open market. So then they came to the mainland again, in Sutherland, and looked in at the Lax-fiord, and rounded Cape Hwarf, and so to the Orkneyar.

At this time Turf-Einar the earl was dead, and his sons Arnkel and Erlend and Thorfinn Skull-cleaver had the power. Thorfinn's wife was Grelaug, the daughter of earl Duncan at Duncansby in Caithness, over the Pentland firth: and Grelaug's mother was Groa the daughter of Thorstein the Red. Thus there was even some far-away kinship between her and the lads; and when this was brought forward they were taken as the queen's guests, and they got protection for themselves and their men, and a good market for their wares. And as the season was now far spent, and the Northern seas are stormy when the winter comes on, they asked that they might sit there in Orkney until the bad weather was over, and offered themselves to Thorfinn to serve him. How they wrought for him at ship-smithying, and fought for him in raids on the Scots and on rough neighbours, and how they saw many a roof burnt and many a limb lopped, and how they hunted and drank and quarrelled and escaped,—all this is not in the story : but no doubt they saw life as it was lived, both the good and the ill of it, and hardened into sturdy lads, fit for the give and take of the world they dwelt in.

When the spring was come they took their leave of the Orkney folk, and sailed for Iceland: for they had a great mind to see what was to be seen, and to visit all the homes of their kindred, and never come back until they could give a good account of their voyage.

Now Grelaug of Orkney had a cousin out there, the daughter of her mother's brother, Olaf Feilan. The cousin was named Thora, and she was wedded to Thorstein Codbiter, the son of Thorolf Mostbeard, who built the great temple at Thorsness and was a powerful chief among the Icelanders. So Grelaug gave the lads a message to Thorstein Codbiter and a token to her cousin Thora, nothing doubting that it would get them a good welcome.

When they came to Iceland they asked their way to Helgafell, the homestead near the temple. It was easy to find, for every one knew the name and fame of it : and in a few days they came there, sailing westward and northward round the coast and into Breidafiord : but they learned that Thorstein Codbiter was dead, drowned in fishing, a twelve-month ago come harvest-time. Thora was still there, keeping house for her child Thorgrim ; and her brother Thord Gellir was a great man in the country-side. So the lads were in no lack of friends here as well as heretofore, and made hay while the sun shone.

Their goods were loaded on Thora's beasts, and brought up to her house. Thorstein Swart, who kept the temple, and stood as Godi until Thorgrim the child should grow old enough to take the priesthood of his father, he fixed the prices, according to custom ; and then our lads were free to go about and trade with their neighbours. They sold their wares to such as wanted them ; and those that would not have them at the price fixed, had them not at all.

There was much for a stranger to see in Iceland. At Helgafell there was the new temple, and its high-seats adorned with the old carved pillars that came from Norway, and that showed the way to Thorolf Mostbeard, when first he came off the coast and threw them overboard to drift ashore. And there was the inner house of the temple, rounded like the choir of a church, with the altar-stall, and the great ring lying upon it by which all oaths were sworn, and the blood-bowl and sprinkling-rod for the sacrifices, and the images of Thor and the gods standing round about. And at the Thing-stead, on a low rocky point of land reaching out into the firth, with the islands of Breidafiord all around, and the snow-capped mountains of Bardastrand at the back of the water, there was the doom-ring; and a little way inland, beside the booths of the thing-men who came to the great meeting in summer, was the stone of Thor, where men were sacrificed.

After they had done their business, the lads went with a party of their friends from Helgafell, riding to the Iceland Althing; and they saw the wonderful valley with the precipices around and the deep rifts that seam it, and the throngs that come together year by year making a populous town of that waste and terrible wilderness.

But when they were safe returned and had taken leave of Thora, they made ready for their voyage to Norway: for they had a mind to see the old home of their kin, and to come before king Hakon the good, the fosterling of Athelstan of England. So in the summer, when the days were long and seas were fair, they sailed east, and came safely to Throndheim.

CHAPTER XXXI.—KING HAKON THE GOOD.

IN Throndheim this summer sat the young king Hakon, newly come from the West country where he had wintered. He had been well received by the Throndheimers, for he promised them to get back all those rights which his father Harald Fairhair had taken away threescore winters ago: and over and above that he was a handsome lad and well spoken, every inch a king. Earl Sigurd of Ladir, the lord of the Throndheim country-side, was his great friend, and managed matters for him; so that he came peaceably into the power, when his brother Eric Bloodaxe was once driven out, and away to England. "He was the blithest of all men, and the sweetest spoken and the kindest," say the stories: "and he was a very wise man, and set forth the laws of the people with the help of their wisest men; and in his time there was good peace amidst bonders and chapmen, so that none did hurt to other, nor to other's wealth, and plenteous were the seasons both by land and sea."

So when our lads came over the sea straight from Iceland to Throndheim, they found king Hakon there, and went before him. He was big and strong, and very fair to look on, with long curling hair: and he was only of the age of twenty winters, being a little older than Thorstein Sweinson and somewhat younger than Hundi.

He asked them many things of their voyage, and where they came from, and whither bound. And when they had told all their story and said they settled to go to England, and maybe to see London town, "Then," said he, "you will go to my home: for it was not long ago that I came thence: and ever since I can remember anything I have been bred up there. I reckon it the best of all places, and would gladly live and die there, for the sake of king Athelstan my foster-father."

"King," said earl Sigurd, "that is bad hearing for us Throndheimers, and for all thy people of Norway."

"Nay, good friend," answered Hakon, "thou art hasty. For my mind was to say that I would fain be in England if I were not called hither by the best friends I have."

King Hakon bade the lads to supper in his hall; and afterwards, when they were beginning to drink their cups to Thor and the gods, came a page to Hundi and Thorstein where they sat, and said, "Guests, if you have drunk enough, there is one would speak to you without."

So they followed him, and came into an orchard; and

under the apple trees they found the young king walking alone in the sunset.

"Welcome, friends," said he. "I owe you thanks."

"Thanks, king?" said they.

"Aye: for maybe you had rather sit at table with earls and famous men, drinking to the gods, than walk here with such as me?"

They said that they were glad to walk with him, and thought it no loss to leave their drinking. "Hush," said he, "say nothing over loud; for here in Norway folk must do as folk do. Maybe where you come from, the gods are honoured with drinking after supper, and with sacrifices at the Thing, and so forth?"

They said it was so, among most: "But," said Thorstein, "though I know not if thou, king, wilt take it in good part, many of us are no great sticklers for the old faith, and some of us—"

"What?" said the young king eagerly, but in a whisper, and looking round to see that none were by. "What, lad?"

"I was but saying that some of us think maybe he they call White Christ is a stronger god after all than old Redbeard and the rest of them."

"And thou?" said Hakon, looking earnestly at him.

"King," said Thorstein, "my father was a prime-signed man, and often has he told us the story of king Athelstan and his priest, and the good words they gave him, and how his own mind was one day to forsake the sacrifices. But he was among his neighbours, and it was not easy to be open about it, and then he died in battle."

The young king looked at him sorrowfully, and thought awhile. "It was not easy to be open about it," said he, "—and he died in battle. Where, think you, is he now?"

"Nay, king, who can tell? He was a good neighbour, and gave every one his due, and died like a brave man."

"Ah, but," said Hakon, leaning back against the tree, "I have heard from a book they have in England, Whoso denieth me before men, him will I deny. That was what the Christ

said. Oh lads, it is an awful word. It comes to me in the
night as I lie awake: and then I sleep and seem to hear one
saying to me, Hakon, I died for thee: what wilt thou do for
me in all this realm of Norway that I have given thee? And
then I have spoken to earl Sigurd, and he was angry with
me, and bade me hold my peace, or lose everything. Oh, it
is hard to be open about it, and yet—"

"King," said Thorstein, "I am but a youngster, and I
have never heard sayings spoken out of books, nor even
talked with a mass-priest. But I have a dear friend, and she
had a cross that she prayed to: and one day she sold the
cross for my sake when I was in danger. And when I asked
her how she would pray, seeing she had no cross to pray to,
she said that there was an old man whom she had seen after
she had sold it, who bade her take comfort, for, said he, the
God of the Christians, they call him the Lord, looketh at the
heart. These were the words."

"Aye," said Hakon, "that is in the book."

"Is it?" said Thorstein. "Well, king, and if thy heart is
with that Lord, is not all right?"

The lad Hakon took the lad Thorstein in his arms, and
kissed his cheek. "Brother," he said, "I brought you lads
here to preach to you, and you have preached to me a better
word than any since I was taken away from home to be a
stranger among my own people, and an outcast from all
kindly Christian men among the heathen. You have preached
to me: will you pray with me?"

They understood nothing of what he said: but he knelt in
the twilight on the grass, hidden among the orchard trees,
while the shouting of the Bragi-cup was heard from the
windows of the hall. They knelt beside him, and he said in
a low voice, and as if sobbing, the Lord's Prayer.

Then he stood up radiant and joyful. "Brothers," he said,
"stay by me here, and help me. I will give you all your
heart can wish, only stay and help me in this terrible loneliness. We together will win the realm for the Christ; or, if
we must, die like the blessed saints and martyrs, and go to be
with him in heaven."

Thorstein looked at the beautiful face, aglow with earnestness.

"King," he said, "I will slay thy foes for thee, and spend my heart's blood for thee. And I will take thy faith, and break Thor down from the temple yonder, if thou wilt."

"Hush, dear lad," said Hakon, suddenly bethinking himself, and looking round with the old fear: "Hush, not yet. Oh, it is hard to know what to do. And there is no one to tell me. We must be gentle with them, and win them one by one: we must speak to them the words of life, and pray for them, and teach them."

Thorstein shook his head. "I could fight them, or some of them," said he. "But as to words of life, king, if they be the teaching of priests, I know nothing, for I am not even prime-signed."

"Ah, I forgot," said Hakon. "I am hasty. But you will not betray me. I thank you for your good will, and I love you for your good words: but it is other help I need. You are going to England, lucky lads. Do an errand for me."

They said they would do anything for him.

"Then go to Bishop Ælfheah at Winchester, him they call the Bald; and tell him that his son Hakon remembers his teaching, and that he has sent two brothers of his to be christened. Take this token" (and he gave them a little cross which he drew out from his bosom) "and he will receive you. And then, if your mind is to come hither again, think of me and the work I have to do. Again and again I thank you. Come to-morrow; but not a word to any soul of our speech together, if you love me."

They went to their quarters for the night, and though they saw the king again it was only when others were by. In a few days came some of the king's men with a rare gift for them, and a message bidding them take the fair wind before it fell. So they made ready and sailed out of Throndheim firth, and down the coast: and when they had coasted Norway they stood out West over sea and sailed for England.

CHAPTER XXXII.—AT LONDON.

A T last they were come to Grimsby at the mouth of the Humber, and thence the way is plain, what with river and what with road, to York, and over the Keel into Cumberland, and so home. And indeed the lads had a thought to lay up their ship and take the journey forth and back to see how their folk were getting on, and Thorstein especially to ask after Raineach. But for three reasons they determined to withhold themselves: first that they had resolved to sail all round Britain and never go home until they could tell their tale: and next that king Eric Bloodaxe, the new king of York, who kept the place under king Athelstan, was no friend to Hakon, and awful tales were told about his queen, Gunnhild the witch, so that they had no desire to put themselves in his power: and last, that they could not for shame forego their errand upon which Hakon had sent them.

So they sailed round the coast until they came to the Thames, and up to London. Off Billingsgate they were stopped by the boats of the officers, who brought them before the port-reeve: and when they had told him their names and business, and paid toll in four silver pennies, they were free to dwell there. As it was now late in the year they sought a lodging in the house of a Northman whom they met: and in order that they might buy and sell, and go freely among the Londoners, he brought them to a priest at the door of a church, who made upon them the sign of the cross, so that they should be prime-signed men, until they might find bishop Ælfheah and get christening at his hands.

At Yule was the Witan held at Westminster, and earls and thanes and bishops flocked together; and among them the man they sought. Then they had their desire and did their errand to him, giving him the token of the cross and the message of the young king. The bishop wept over the tale, for joy that Hakon still bore in mind his teaching, and for sorrow that he should be out there alone among the heathen. "And yet," said he, "is it not written, Behold, I send you forth as lambs among wolves? May the Lord grant his young child the wisdom of the serpent and the harmlessness of the dove, and in due time give him to see the travail of his soul."

Then the lads asked that they might be christened : and the bishop gave them in charge to one of his priests, who taught them as much as it was needful to know : and afterwards they were baptised. But when they spoke of going back to Norway, he smiled and said, " It is other help than yours that Hakon needs. You have done well in bringing this message, and no better news could be brought. As for his heart's desire, I take you two as the first-fruits of it. Do you depart in peace, to be shining lights in your own land. Without doubt when Hakon is established in his kingdom he will send for priests fitted to teach his people, and never fear but there will be labourers for the harvest."

And here we may say that old stories tell how the young king spoke first to one and then to another of his own friends and those about him in Norway, and without any other help of man, won them over to the Christian faith : and when many were thus converted he ventured to send for priests, and to hold open worship. But he was overborne by the common people, who would have nothing to do with the new doctrines. So for many a long year it was a struggle between them ; and every man that the king won over he counted gain ; and every time the Throndheimers forced king Hakon to come to their sacrifices and share their feasts they reckoned it gain to their side, even if they had done no more than make him smell the steam of the horse-flesh aboiling in Thor's kettle. But for such backsliding as this the king blamed himself in secret, and went on in life-long fear of the doom of a castaway ; hoping from year to year that things would turn out so that he might lay aside his crown, and become a monk, and end his days in penitence. But his rule was so good that his people would not let him go ; and yet he still found it hard to be open about it, and at last died in battle, and was buried by the heathen with a great burial as if he had been one of them.

Now when spring was come, Hundi and Thorstein took their leave, and sailed out of the Thames and round the South coast, calling as they went at one port and another by the way, and always increasing their store; until they came at last to Bristol, which was the great thrall-market for the Irish trade in those days, and a thriving city. And thence they sailed down the Severn to those settlements of Northmen at Tenby and Milford and Haverford; and so up the coast of Bretland, as they then called Wales, in whose firths, as in those of Morecambe and Solway, many a viking had refuged, betwixt Lund-ey and Orm's Head. From Orm's Head it was but a short passage to the bay of Morecambe: and by now they were wearied of seafaring, and longed for home.

And as they sailed briskly by the shores of Amounderness over the tossing green waves, Thorstein felt himself already in the arms of his lass; and the spray from the bows where he sat, with half-shut eyes, seemed like her hair blown about his face. At last Black Combe rose over the sea-line higher and higher, and then the green woods, and then the yellow sands. There was Ravenside, there was Aldingham, there was the bonny Leven between its dear old hills.

" Eh, mother and Orm and all, it's right good to be home again : " says Thorstein heartily ; " but where is—she ? "

Orm turned on his heel and went out. Unna kissed Thorstein. There were tears in her eyes.

CHAPTER XXXIII.—THORSTEIN'S WELCOME.

SPILT milk, they said. His mother assured him of it. Orm nodded aye, it was so ; and the thralls, men and maids, cried " What, master Thorstein is bad to suit : there's mays in plenty and bonny ones too, for a well-favoured young man like thee to light on."

Raineach had run away, and Orm, the good brother, had followed to fetch her back. He had tracked her with difficulty to the ship-strand near Ulfar's town. There he had seen her aboard a merchant ship, and there he had spoken to her,

and she had laughed and waved her hands. And that very
night a storm had come, and the ship had gone down with all
aboard; not a doubt of it there was; he could ask any one
about the great storm two winters ago was haytime; and as
for this ship, why folk at Ravenside were still using the
wreckage of her for fire-elding, or were doing so in winter.
And the worst of it was that the finest of Thorstein's clothes
and jewels, the things he had saved and left under Raineach's
charge against the wedding, were all awanting, to the amount
that a body might bundle up and carry off without other
hands or help.

Again the mother said " She bade me farewell : " and the
servants said " We spied her start : " and Orm said " I called
to her on board, and she would not come back : " and they
all swore to the storm and the shipwreck as matters of
common knowledge.

" Humph," said Hundi Snail. " I didn't think she'd have
done it."

Thorstein was quite beaten down, and had nothing to say.
He went to Ravenside, and saw folk burning bits of the
wreck that ran upon their sands two years ago last haytime.
They remembered it well, and how the ship folk yelled, and
what a crowd of corpses drifted ashore next morning ; and
oh aye, there was a lass with red hair among them no doubt :
aye, bonny lasses and all.

" She's gone, sure enough, poor thing," said Hundi : " but
I don't understand it, somehow."

" Nor I," said Unna.

" Maybe," said Orm, " she had some notion of meeting
with Thorstein. She was always have inklings of one thing
and another, what with dreams, what with fancies. And
maybe she was taking the gear to make her wedding with
him, for she seemed a bit nicked in the head. I wouldn't call
it stealing : what's mine is thine, the saying is."

" It's kind of thee, Orm, to speak up for her," said Thorstein : " above all, when I think she didn't suit thee over
well."

" Humph," said Hundi, " very kind of Orm."

When the seafarers' tale was told, and all their goods
shown, who but Hundi and Thorstein were the pride of the
place ? Folk came from far and near, and they said that it
was none but their own lads would go up and down the round
world, starting as youngsters with nought to speak of, and
landing home great strapping men who had supped with
kings and fought with earls—

" And courted the kings' daughters, and kissed the earls'
sisters," added a saucy voice.

" And brought home a shipload that would be worth, I
reckon, about twice their father's stock, beasts, thralls, and
all."

" Well, father, we always said Thorstein Sweinson was a
good lad and would turn out well." For here was mistress Asdis
Asmund's daughter of Asmundarlea over the fell, as blithe as
ever, and bonnier, if that could be : anyway more womanly
grown, with a little motherly manner towards Thorstein, as
if she were very sorry for him,—least said soonest mended ;
but she would make him forget it after a while, and then.
There was nobody but was thankful to her : for they had been
dreading the day of his return and fearing how he would take
it. But Asdis was that clever, she twisted them all round
her fingers, and him in particular, as wankle as a wet sark.

If Thorstein was moody and dismal, and he was that,
Hundi was jolly enough for both. To be home again after a
three years' voyage, and to be made much of wherever he
went, and to be master of his half share in that rich cargo,
let alone the ship and boat-stock, all this made him welcome
at every neighbour's. As to his christening, they said he
could suit himself; it seemed that it meant money anyhow.
And so it was no surprise when Hundi begged his brothers
to don their best clothes and come with him to Rolf's seat
awooing ; nor when, after the handfasting, he took land up
the Crake, and began to build him a house against the
wedding.

Thorstein was glad of the job, and worked right hard for

Hundi: and before Yule they had the rearing-supper, and at Yule the wedding-feast; and started housekeeping merrily, with a full larder and the best of good will from all. Thorstein went to live with them as foreman of the farm, and there was a deal to do this winter, clearing land and getting ready a thwaite for tilling. In the spring Hundi meant to buy beasts, and pasture them in the fell; and meanwhile he had plenty to live on.

Halldora Rolf's daughter was the name of the bride. She was a right good sort; and Hundi was that fond of her, and she of him, that Thorstein could not but laugh, many's the time, as they three sat together by the new hearth of nights. But if he laughed, he would fetch a deep sigh, and then take a turn up and down the floor: and Halldora would get off the knees of her good-man and go to Thorstein and bid him pluck up heart: and she would take his arm and walk up and down a bit with him. Then Hundi calls out from the hearth, laughing, "Now, mistress, no carryings on with my brother: it's me is thy man!"

"Never fear," she answers coming back to him. "The poor boy is sore at heart. And pity it is, when the finest lass in the country-side would take him at the first word."

"What? Asdis?"

"Aye would she. Many's the time she has told me that she meant to get him, too. And I am sure there is no cleverer, nor bonnier, nor better bred. He might do a deal worse."

CHAPTER XXXIV.—THE WOOING OF ASDIS.

WHO knows what plots and plans were laid, and all with the best intentions? The upshot of it was, one fine day appears Asdis herself, with men and maids, come to visit her dear friend Halldora in the new house. For three days it was "O Thorstein, how well you boys have managed! what a fine house! what bonny gear! what a sweet spot!" and so forth. And everything was Thorstein's doing, as if he had built the fells and rigged the very sky overhead.

"Heigho!" she sighed, when Hundi and Halldora had left them alone, "it's bad to be illfavoured."

"Who's illfavoured?" said Thorstein.

"Not Halldora, in her own house at home: and with a man of her own fit to kiss the ground she steps on."

"I warrant Hundi is a lucky fellow: but the mistress of Asmundarlea must be ill to suit if she waits a day longer than she likes."

"That's your London talk, Thorstein: thou'st gitten o'er fine for us hereaway."

"Never say so. Nay, Asdis: there's not an earl of the Northmen nor an English thane would be o'er fine for thee."

She rewarded him with a very sweet smile.

"What, we are old friends, lass, are we not?"

"Aye, neighbour Thorstein," and she gave him another smile and a blush.

"And I always spoke well of thee, even to her—to her that's gone."

"Nay, was it so? Poor lass, she's gone. Often have I wished I had managed to make friends with her: it was my fault."

"What was thy fault? That you were not friends? Nay Asdis: it was thou that was good to her, but she, poor thing, she couldn't understand."

"Ah, Thorstein, if there's goodness anywhere it's in thee. And well I know that after her the rest of us are nought."

"My dear, it's years she's gone; and it's months I have greeted for her: and now my heart is like a stone."

"Poor lad."

Her voice was like the cooing of doves in the wood, and the tears were in her eyes: for she was as fond of him as she could be of anyone. And then she was so pretty.

It was a few days after Asdis was gone that Hundi was late in his chamber, though their porridge stood ready for breakfast: and when he came, "What, man," cried Thorstein, "it's no Thing to-day; and thou with thy best clothes donned."

" Well, lad," answered Hundi, "it's a fine morning, and I just thought mayhappen we might be riding over to Asmundarlea, and I might as well be ready first as last."

Thorstein blushed. " I don't care if I do," said he.

" Well said," cried Halldora clapping her hands. " Here, sup thy pottage, Thorstein, good lad : and then don thy red silk kirtle that ye bought in Londonburg. No lass could say nay to thee in that."

So by noon they were at Greenodd door to ask Orm to go with them. For it was the custom when a man went awooing to take all his folk with him ; not only to show that everything was fair and above-board, and to have witnesses of the word given on both sides, but also to show what good friends and kinsfolk he had to back him. For in times when wealth was held only by the strong hand, the best of havings was a good following of friends and friendly neighbours who would see one righted if need was.

But Orm said he was throng and could not come : and when they pressed him, he would not ; and Unna said there was no need, for she warranted the job was no hard one to manage. So Hundi and Thorstein, with all their ship-crew, and all the farm servants that could be spared, rode over the fell, and knocked at Asmund's door.

They sat in the hall, and Asdis served them meat and drink, and Asmund sat in his high seat and talked of this and that, as though nobody knew on what errand they might be bound. It was an open winter : they settled that. And king Athelstan was dead : they talked that over. And folk seemed to take the new king, Eadmund they called him, a deal quieter than was expected. "Aye," said Asmund, "now is the time for decent quiet folk to be setting up house and settling down."

" Well, master," says Hundi, "it is a job of that make brings us hither. My brother Thorstein here has made up his mind seemingly to take land and build house, the same as I have done : and he has the money, and the means, and all he wants is the mistress. And we are just thinking that if thy daughter could be spared, and if she would take to it kindly, she might happen do worse than settle down with my brother: and I am sure there's nought but he would do to make her happy; and as to money matters, ye can suit yourselves."

Then master Asmund put on his sober face, and hemmed, and said, " Well, neighbour, it's a fair offer : but it's not for me to say aye or nay until we have spoken with the lass."

By this time the servants had fetched in Asdis, who had slipped out, as was proper, when things began to look like business. And there she was, blushing and rosy, standing by her father's seat, and plucking at her apron.

" Well lass, and what are we to say ? Wilt thou take the young man Thorstein Sweinson ? For that's the job they have come about."

" Nay, father, it's not for me to say."

" Come, come, lass : that means aye ? "

" As you please, father : and as it pleases Master Thorstein Sweinson. I am sure it is a great honour for the likes of me."

Then Asmund sent out to the neighbours, bidding them to a handfasting or betrothal feast, which should be held next day : and until then Hundi and Thorstein and their company were well entertained at Asmundarlea. In this while they talked over the dowry that Asdis should have from her father, and the settlement she should have from her husband, and when the wedding should be, and so forth.

When the neighbours were come, they bade them listen to the business on hand, and told them what had been done on both sides. Then Thorstein went over to where Asmund sat, and Asmund put his daughter's hand into the hand of Thorstein, who said aloud " We call upon all to witness that thou Asdis Asmund's daughter dost lawfully pledge thyself to me Thorstein Sweinson, with dowry due and holden hands, to finish and fulfil our whole agreement both trusted and true. This handfasting is fairly done."

And so the wooing of Asdis was accomplished.

CHAPTER XXXV.—HOW THORSTEIN TOOK LAND.

HUNDI sat on his own howe, and Thorstein with him. They were looking out for neighbours who were to come by the old path from Broughton beck to Lowick, and to the new household where Hundi and Halldora were master and mistress.

"Dost thou mind when we were barnes, brother, how we sat here and parted hence ? Six winters have gone since we planned to keep house away yonder " ; and he pointed up-bank, where the Crake came down between the crags on the right and the Blawith, the blue wood as they called it, of dark firs mantling the long slopes of the lower banks, on the left. And far beyond were the great fells that surrounded the head of Thorstein's water, this Coniston lake that he, first of Northmen, had found.

The neighbours for whom they waited were coming to be witnesses to Thorstein's land-taking. It was the custom for settlers of uninhabited land to go round a tract of country, as much as they could encompass in a day, carrying fire, and lighting from point to point beacons which might be seen one from another. And when this was done with proper wit-nesses like any other deed of law, the land became the possession of that landtaker and his heirs for ever. Now up the Crake valley, above Lowick where Hundi had settled, there were no inhabitants at this time : the fell-folk, who used to hunt in the woods and fish in the waters, dwelt upon the moors on either hand. It was Thorstein's mind to take all that upper valley between Lowick and the water-foot ; and he had bidden his neighbours, from Asmundarlea especially, and from Rosset, and round about, to come and bear witness, so that there might be no dispute thenceforward, and that he and Asdis and his heirs might dwell there undisturbed in lawful freehold.

It was early in the morning of a bright frosty day, when the days were already a good bit longer than at Yule, that Thorstein and Hundi and his neighbours were already out, and at the bounds of Hundi's land before the sun was up.

There was a company of half a score or so, dressed in their woodland dress of rough homespun, with axes in their hands; and Thorstein himself carrying an iron pot with burning peat in it. They stood by the brink of the stream a little above Lowick force, and stamped their feet on the crispy sedges of the marsh-ground, until the sun should be up; munching the remains of the hasty breakfast they had left, in order to be in good time and to make the most of the winter day. When the edge of the fell to the eastward blazed, and the sun began to get above the silver fringe of trees, a shapeless point of fire, "Away with us, friends," cried Thorstein; and they made a move for the fell where the sun was standing, and started upbank through the trees that clothed it, and over the scree that lay between. Here and there they had to hew their way through the underwood, and where that was not needed, they marked the trees with great notches, in order to leave no doubt of the boundary they had beaten.

As they passed along through the forest, where every leaf was laced with rime, and the frozen twigs crackled underfoot, beast and bird fled before the noise of their axes and the loud talk and laughter of the merry company. "A grand hunting-spot for Thorstein the hunter," says one. "Oh, man," says another, "there went somewhat I'd be fain to follow." "Never heed it, friend," said Thorstein; "business is business. Wait till my house is built, and then I'll show thee a day's hunting, and the tricks I learned with the fell-folk."

When they came out on the ridge, they could overlook the whole valley, and down into the next where Colton stands, and southward away to Legbarrow. Here some of them began to cut elding and logs to build a balefire, and others rolled up a huge boulder to be planted on end for a meer-stone or land-mark. And when the fire blazed up, they lost no time, but set out again along the ridge, up and down, until at last they came to a high place overlooking the foot of Thorstein's water. To most of them the sight was wholly strange, well known as it was to him. The mere was just as he had seen it years before; just as quiet and as wild; only now it lay dark blue between its white promontories; the shores were disguised with shelves of ice that stood far out into the ripple, and countless birds flew screaming about over the open spaces, or dived and settled in flocks.

On this high point, for the morning was beginning to wear, they built another balefire, and set up another meer-stone; and then picked their way down to the water-foot, where they came about mid-day, travelling but slowly, for the way was hard to find, and rough.   At the crossing of the Crake, where mere ends and beck begins, they ate hastily the bannocks they had brought with them ; and Thorstein, wading into the shallows with his fire-pot in one hand and a brand lighted at it in the other, cast the brand into the water ; and as it floated hissing, cried out, " I take you to witness that this water and all its shores, oyce and ere, dub and deep, are hereby in my holding."

Then they started again along the western bank, and so up into the moor, where they built another beacon and set another meer-stone.   But here Thorstein bade them turn, for he said that thence-beyond he reckoned he would be within the bounds of old friends, namely the fell-folk of the moor. And he would have no disputes with them.   " For we North-men," said he, " have land enough in the wooded bottoms, and can well afford to leave the moor-tops to the wild folk who dwell there."

So they came round in a great half-moon under the brow of the moor, leaving the heather and enclosing the woods : and at last by sunsetting they were back again where they started from.   Thorstein took them to witness that he had lawfully carried fire around untenanted land, and the land was thenceforth his and his only.   And so after due feasting at Hundi's, the neighbours went their ways : and Thorstein, with such as were in his service, began the building of his house.

On the slope of the great blue fir-wood, that rose to a howe behind and fell to the Crake in front, beside a little beck, they cleared a thwaite, and made the timber of it into a house. It was no long job to skilled wood-wrights, and with plenty of hands; for Thorstein's wealth got him all he wanted, what with buying thralls, and hiring free men who lay by the fire for the most part in winter. The house was like the Greenodd house; a great hall with little chambers built along each side of it for bed-chambers; high roofed and thatched with broom; and the walls, where the roughly squared logs left chinks open to the wind, daubed with clay and roughcast. A few outbuildings, byres and sheds, were put up to begin with; and round about the whole a turf wall was raised, to keep out wild beasts and to make some stand against enemies, if such should ever appear. But who would expect foes in so lone and peaceful a spot?

By cuckoo-tide, or Gowk-month as the Northmen called it, the house was standing, and wanted but little; and that chiefly what a body might do after the flitting. And on the right flitting-days, that is to say about Whitsuntide as we should call it, they began to move goods into the house, carrying in first of all the salt and meal, and starting a fire upon the hearth. Since beds and benches were built there as fixtures, there was little to carry in the way of moveable furniture, and what there was came in kists on horseback. And when all was flitted, there was nought to hinder the wedding.

CHAPTER XXXVI.—THE WEDDING OF THOR-STEIN.

ON the day appointed, Thorstein and his men, dressed in their best, to make all the show they could, and carrying food and drink, rode out a good way from the house to meet the bride, who came riding with her father and kins-folk and bridesmaids by the old path to Lowick. At the border of Thorstein's land they met, and alighting from their horses ate and drank to the good luck of the place they were come to. Then they made their procession, two and two on horseback, by the woodland path that led them through the Blawith. The bride and bridegroom rode together at the head of the procession, and right glad was Thorstein to think that at last he would have house and wife of his own.

" Well, sweetheart," said he, " and now it's home."

" Is it always like this?" said she. " One would say it does nought but rain in your fells."

" No such thing," said he; " whiles it snows. But never mind; there's a warm hearth hard by. Thy riding cape will soon dry on the rannalbalk."

" Like a man! to put my cape in the soot indeed. And what for a road call you this? Who will ever come to visit one, away here?"

" Oh, there's Halldora; she's a good neighbour, and no pleasanter visitor could we have."

" I'm thinking there's been a deal of Halldora lately."

" Well," said he, " come, Asdis, it'll be all right when we get there. See, yonder's the little house."

If the day was dull and cheerless, bright lights were shining through the windows that evening, and a plentiful feast was made in Blawith hall. In the chief high-seat was set Master Asmund, and beside him the neighbours who had been bidden to the wedding. Over against him the bridegroom sat in his high-seat, with his men on either hand : and on the bride-bench, set across the hall at the upper end, was the bride, all dressed in white linen, with a white veil hanging down her back, with a silver brooch on her brow, a gold necklace at her throat, and housewife's keys clattering at her girdle. Beside her sat the bridesmaids and her friends, with Unna and Halldora on the right hand and the left.

After they were set and the feast was well begun, Thorstein rose and went across the hall to his bride, and gave her for a bench-gift a cloak lined with rare furs and richly embroidered. Then they drank to him and his bride, wishing them luck and long life, and with all the lights lit saw them to their lock-bed; at the door of which her father Asmund gave her with a fitting word into her husband's keeping.

The next morning, as the custom was, the marriage settle-ments were finished. Thorstein made over to Asmund the gifts that had been agreed upon, and Asmund put them in the keeping of the bride, to be her own property. And folk said that Thorstein had done well by Asmund's daughter, and that no lass of those parts could wish for a better husband. Then they went on to keep the wedding for three days with feasting and games and every pleasure that could be got for them. But still it rained, and they took to playing indoors, mating men, and wrestling in the hall, and skin-pulling across the fire spot, and draught-playing, and story-telling, and song-singing, and all that a body might do to pass the time.

But before the three days of the feast were well over, came a loud rapping at the door, and there stood a man holding the arrow to bid them to the midsummer Althing, which was to be in some three weeks. They made him welcome to the wedding, for they were fain of somewhat new.

"Nay," said he, "I reckon you will think twice of your welcome when you hear me out."

"Why so?" cried they all.

"For the reason that our bonny bridegroom here will have to choose between a far journey and a fair bride, unless he stands out of the play, and I doubt he will never do that. At last, neighbours, there is a chance of some ado, and that speedily, if you take the counsel of them that sent me. You must know that when king Athelstan died, no hand was raised against him that followed, Eadmund etheling that was, king that is: and all things seemed to be even as they had been. But why or how I know not, Eadmund could never abide Northmen, and in especial he hates king Eric, him they call Bloodaxe, whom Athelstan had set over York. So when the word came to York that Eric was like to be turned out of his place, he never waited for Eadmund, but went forth and sailed away out of the Humber: and men say that he has gone north to Orkney where Arnkell and Erlend Einarsons are his friends."

"Like to like," says Thorstein; "and a good riddance too."

"That's as it turns out. For it's ill mending bad with worse. The York folk seemingly think any change lightsome, if its nobut out of bed into beck, as the old body said. What have they done but send to Dublin bidding Olaf Guthferthson—"

" Plague on it," says Thorstein: " if it had been old Thor-finn, or young Hakon, but a Dane ! "

" Hear me, I say. Olaf the Dane, being of the old stock of Ivarsons, is bidden to take the power: and that speedily, before the young king can step in. And as Eadmund is but a lad of eighteen winters and no more, it is thought the Danes will have a chance of setting up once again in England. Now the Cumberland Welsh mislike it, and our friends thereaway mislike it : but they look to see the whole job done in the twinkling of an eye. And for you, if you have anything to say about it, now is your time."

So they asked what was to be done: and he said that it was likely Olaf would come in with no very great following, by the old road from Ellenburg through Cumberland ; and Domhnall was to be there to meet him, but whether as friend or foe was yet to be seen. And if the Northmen wished to have a hand in the matter, they should be at their Thing-stead at once, to take counsel with themselves and their neighbours, and to be ready for Olaf by the time he came into the defensible road among the fells.

" What, Thorstein," said Asdis, " you are never going on this fool's errand, and me nought but half wed ? "

" Why, lass, it is but a three days' run, and I'll be back again in a hop, skip and jump."

Something seemed to come before him as he spoke: as when in a dream one says, " All this I have dreamt before." Then he remembered ; and turned away.

CHAPTER XXXVII.—THORSTEIN SEES GHOSTS.

" AND so, friends," said King Domhnall, ending his speech, " we betake ourselves to the great road under Blen-cathra, and if the men of Athacliath come in peace, it shall be peace : but if in war, war let it be."

Then all the Northmen took their weapons and shouted aye to what he had said : and the meeting broke up, and men moved away in groups toward the deep dale that led north-ward from Legburthwaite. Some sought their horses, and some were for lading their gear : and everything was in hurry and turmoil.

"Hundi," said Thorstein, leaning on his brother's shoulder, "Seest thou yon fell? they call it Benn in their tongue, the fell-folk: and up yonder are the houses where the. beauty lives : and behind it is the giant's castle, where I was with— with her that's gone. Little did I think when we fled away over the fells and dells and mountain moors, how it would end with all of us."

"Leave thy maundering, man, and come to see what uproar is yonder," said Hundi; for among the men left behind by the main guard there were shrieks and shouts, that seemed to mean no good. It was but a step, and they found among the rough followers of Domhnall, struggling and crying, who but Aluinn? whom they rescued, not without hard knocks. But still she went on like one wild, and it was long before they could get reasonable speech out of her. As they led her away, sore against her will it seemed, in spite of the mishandling she had got, they heard her story bit by bit.

What came out was this;—that she had gone like any other to the camp where the Welsh king lay, and coming to his tent door was for marching in. Who but she had the right, indeed? But within was another woman, with two sturdy lads at her knees, and a fair woman too. "Who is this?" says the woman. "Who is this?" says Aluinn, and shows the collar of gold that certain lover once gave her. With that the wife bids her begone for a slut; and then Aluinn gives her words, and gets to blows: when in comes Domhnall with little love in his looks, and to make short work of it, turns her out to his rascals.

"The nithing!" cries Hundi. Thorstein said little, but set his teeth and growled, remembering what was heard and said at Alclyde.

But when the fell-folk that dwelt about Armboth heard the tale, Aluinn's own neighbours whose pet and pride she was, you may guess if they vowed vows and threatened threats. As they shook their weapons Hundi plucked his brother by the sleeve. " We do no good here," said he, " and may come to harm. Hie thy ways along with me, or we are shamed men at the tryst." So they got off without leavetaking, and footed it down the dale that now we call the vale of St. John : for their nags were gone in the tumult, and not a soul in sight.

Along the old road they passed, bemired as it was with the trampling of man and horse in that foul weather, and at every wath the beck was a torrent. But since the track lay fairly high on the fell-side it lay dry, if aught was dry, and was not lost in swamp like the flats in mid dale. In the space of an hour or two they spied a great flickering of weapons waving under Blencathra, and guessed that the kings had already met, and spoken each other fair, and were now settling down for the night : for they could spy tents going up and smoke starting. And so in a while they were among their friends, supping and singing round a fire in the open, until men dropped off one by one to sleep where they sat.

But Thorstein slept little for thinking of Aluinn and her wrongs. She was as it were a ghost of his old life come back from the dead, and little ease it was to think of those times, and then again of these. For, thinking of Aluinn, he could not but think of Raineach who was dead : and how he had loved her, and how fain he would be if he could but get the sight of her face once more. " Ah my dear," he cried, half aloud, and opened his arms and turned over on his side, for his heart was sore within him. But only the heap of snoring soldiers lay around, under Blencathra and the lowering cloud. And yet, what was that face that flitted over the heap, gleaming in the red glow ?

His blood ran cold to the finger-tips, and he clenched his hands. He had wished, and his wish had come to pass. It was her ghost, he thought : for ghosts come when they are called. The hair tingled on his head, he was so terrified. Then he shut his eyes tight, and drew up his knees, and doubled his arms over his face, and lay there for a while, still as a hedgehog when it is scared, and curls itself up.

At last the terror began to die away. He said to himself that it was but his own thoughts his eyes had seen; and he could not help looking again. There was a gap in the clouds, and a star. The fire was not so bright. Nothing did he see beyond the men who lay around, though he fixed his eyes on the spot where the vision had been, as if he dared it to come again. But it came not. By and by there was a stir behind him, as of the wind rising in the trees. He turned sharply round, and there!

But it was gone again: and once more he lay quaking, with cold in all his limbs, and in his heart an agony which he could not understand, like a child when it is beaten for something it has not done, and cannot tell the truth : blank misery as when one is utterly spent with sickness. He lay staring at the black cloud overhead, and it was an ugly thing coiling upon him. He shut his eyes and dreamed over the days of long ago: of the wild, proud slip of a girl that hunted and fished with him at Greenodd: of the poor little ugly, blubbered face that leaned over his, when he was a child captive in the giant's hut on the fells; the tears that made dirty water-courses among the freckles,—how he remembered them, and every eager feature he had loathed at first and loved ever after. He brought to mind how he had opened his eyes after his sickness, wearily and lazily ; and then!

CHAPTER XXXVIII.—RAINEACH'S STORY.

"HUSH," she said, "don't crush me, or we shall stumble over yon snoring swine. Hither, lad: away with me. Into the wood. It was always our hiding-place,—dost thou mind, Thorstein? Why, what a man thou hast grown! But I knew I should tell thee among them all, wolf-dark as it was. Kiss me, Thorstein? Am I woman enough for thee now? Am I bonny? Folk say so; but I'd have none but thee, heart of mine. Thorstein, Thorstein: my boy, my little hurt beaten boy! Ah, but I will comfort thee. Laugh lad, never greet: kiss me. Oh Thorstein, kill me not: I am only a woman, and thou art a great strong man.

'The queen told me about thee. They say she wept for a day and a night when thou wast gone, until Olaf the carle gave her a slap and bade her be merry. If thou could'st but have stayed until I got there;—it was but a few days. Silly lad to run away from friends! And yet thou would'st have loved the bonny queen, and poor Raineach was but her bower-may: but fain, ah, fain to serve thee and her, anywhere, any way. But it was so long a-coming, lad!

"Oh me, I am losing my wits. Only have patience, and I will tell thee all as it happened. There, loose me awhile, and let me think.

"Orm, it was. Orm said I must tell nobody, but I'll tell thee, sweetheart. Orm said thou wast oversea, and bade me come. So I went. I took all our bravest things to make a show at the wedding. He set me on shipboard, and bade the skipper have a care of me, and signed farewell off the shore. And then the waves beat and the wind blew, and eh, my head worked, and the eyes came out of their pits. They thrust me down among the bulk, and among poor wretches that howled and groaned in the bilgewater, and I could see nothing for sickness. The ship whirled, and flew, and fell into the depths of the sea. Oh, lad, I was sorry for thee in those terrible ships; and I prayed and prayed to have thee safe on dry land. And there were poor Welsh lasses and a two or three Saxon ones, worse off than I, with hands tied: and I loosed them, I did. And then came the skipper and clouted me over the head, and tied us all up again, and I was mad with him, and begged and shouted; but he laughed, like Orm when he kicks his thralls, and bade me be at peace, or he would throw me to the fishes. Eh, it did hurt to have one's hands tied. Did'st thou ever have thy hands tied, Thorstein? and kick and scream at people? The other poor wretches laughed at me, and said things, but I could make nothing of their talk. And so I was still, for anger and weariness, all that night.

"Well, when it was day, I was no more sick, the water was lound, and the men were rowing us to shore. Then they

gave us food, and the skipper said I was to look bonny, or I
would fetch nothing on Dublin strand, and shame it were if
all his labour and all the money he had spent and the care
he had taken of me should be thrown away.   He said we
should be very thankful to be there at all, for in the storm of
that night other ships had gone to the bottom of the sea.   I
could not hit him, for my hands were tied, so I spat out the
food they put in my mouth, and I looked as ugly as I could;
and he beat me.   Oh man, I was angry.

"Then they shoved us over the side of the ship and set us
down in a great crowd of people, but I was too dazed to take
notice.   At last came a fine lady; that was the queen, understand.   King's folk have first weel of the wares in Dublin
town.   I was the wares, Thorstein: think of that, lad.   I
couldn't think: but I cried to her in my own tongue, I am
not a thrall, I am not a thrall: I am Thorstein Sweinson's
sister.

"'What girl?' said she: and I said it again.

"Then there was a deal of talking with the skipper, and
my hands were untied, and they tingled all over, and I could
feel nothing with them.   But I made shift to creep after the
queen: and she led me to the king's house, and oh she was
good to me: and it was a bonny spot, if it had not been for
the men-folk plaguing.   There's none of them like thee, lad.
I could tell thee things about yon Olaf—but what's the good?
I am woman grown now, and bonny; and I can sew and bake
and brew and everything.   Thy mother will be pleased with
me now, and Orm, won't he be surprised?   Are they all
hearty, Thorstein?   And that young lass, does she still play
her tricks on folk? how did they call her—Asdis?"

Thorstein's arms fell and his knees smote together.

"What's to do, lad?"

"Three days since—I wedded her."

"Thorstein!" she cried in a terrible voice, and thrust him
away from her, and fled.   He fell backward, like one that
has got his death-stroke.

CHAPTER XXXIX.—ORM PAYS.

IT was high day, and he lay there slowly coming to himself; and recalling that dreadful nightmare, as it seemed, bitter-sweet. At last he staggered to his legs, and drank at a beck that ran through the wood. Every one was gone from the spot where the camp had been: and whither? He only knew that Orm would be with the Northmen faring homeward. He loosened his sword and thrust it back again, and stumbled forth along the road he had come but yesterday.

At Legburthwaite the Northmen had halted, to hold their Thing once more, to talk over the business that had passed, and finish the work they had on hand. On the mound the chiefs were assembled, within the hallowed ring that no man might profane.

Thorstein leaned on the hazel rods, that stood as bars from stake to stake to encompass the place. Some one was speaking in slow, steady tones, and men were listening, in the rain, with grave faces, intent upon the speech.

"Orm Sweinson, come forth. News for thee: ha! ha!" cried a voice, breaking the quiet of the assembly: and there was a haggard man with bloodshot eyes, beckoning strangely.

Forth stepped Orm: "What now, youngster?" said he.

"Raineach is come again, and that's for thee!" screamed Thorstein, lashing his sword through the throat of his brother, where the coat of mail left it unshielded.

"A wolf, a wolf in the temple!" they shouted, and rushed forth. But he was gone headlong down the bank and across the lake-foot and into the woods on the other side, on the rugged slopes of the Benn.

CHAPTER XL.—A DOOR-DOOM.

UNDER Blawith roof-tree sat dame Asdis, fresh and fair as a daisy: and when she had broken her fast she looked to her outdoor servants and set them their tasks: and when she had put them all in order, she came in, at the time folk take their drinkings: and she drank a horn of ale, and ate sweet cakes, one after another: and then she washed her hands at the trough by the porch and got her a clean apron and sat down in her high seat, and took to her sewing; and and if the day was hot, and she dropped off to sleep while one might count two score, it was no shame to her, now she was wedded woman and ever a house-wife of the most notable. And then she wished Halldora would come to pay her a visit. For it was nought but dull in these backwoods, and news was worth whittlegate. So she went to the door to see if the weather was holding up: and sure enough it had brightened, as it does sometimes at mid-day after stormy weather, and the lift was lighter than heretofore. The rain had stopped, and the beck was roaring white.

"Who comes tramping over the lea land? Hey lads, a stranger. Run for your weapons. What, not Thorstein, surely? and all so draggled and dabbled? Wenches, here's the master, and a pretty pickle he is in. A bath is the next thing; but fetch me the ale-tub and the biggest horn first."

For you see she knew the ways of menfolk to a tittle, to treat them high and low as they should be treated.

"Well, Thorstein," says she, as he came up to the door, "here's a conny mess. Sit in the porch, man, and the ale will be here gey soon. Thou art not fit to touch before a bath and a shift of clothes: and I can't have that filthment of a kirtle on thy new high-seat bolster, thou know'st. Eh, these men, they are nought but great barnes. Now, Thorstein, what hast thou been doing?"

He leaned back and drank off the ale, and looked at her strangely.

"I have killed Orm," said he.

"None of thy jokes, lad. Say a better word. How is this? That the bonny bridegroom could wait no longer, eh, lad? and made more haste worse speed homeward?"

"But it's truth," said he.

"What's truth? Gods forbid. And when, and where?"

"At the Thing," said he.

"Killed Orm at the Thing?" she cried. "Is he daft? It's outlawing!"

"Then I'm outlawed," said he, drinking again.

"Thorstein! how darest thou! and me but new wed. Man this caps aught. Unsay it, lad, and never torment me."

"There is nought to unsay; it was his due: and I'd kill him again if he came to life."

"Came to life? Folk never come to life," said she, scornfully.

"They do, though."

Asdis was pale as grass, staring like a stone woman for a while. Then she was red as blood, and looked this way and that, and at last muttered something about the ale being over strong on an empty belly. Thorstein looked at her in wonder. Then she burst out:—"Who has come, then? Nay, I care not for thy hints nor thy threats, thou false thing that never was true to me. Away with thee! who will believe a word from a wolf's head? Who dare say I had a hand in it? What have I done, tell me that? What did Orm say, the liar?"

"Orm said nought. Maybe Asdis has said a word over much," answered Thorstein, rising from his seat and going into the house.

"Thorstein, my dear, Thorstein!" said she, "I meant nought: I said nought."

But he slammed the door of his lockbed in her face, and shot the heavy bars, and would not come out for all she cried.

It was late in the afternoon that horses clattered into the garth, and there were Asmund and Hundi and a dozen of neighbours, who three days ago had been the wedding guests, and had ridden away from Blawith to the Althing. Asdis came out to meet them, with the smile she always had ready, and ale was standing in the porch. But they would not drink, and she was outfaced and browbeaten by their stern looks.

"My poor child, it's ill news we bring," said Asmund. "Is Thorstein Sweinson within?"

"And what's to do with Thorstein Sweinson, father?"

"I fear me he will be man of thine no more, if peace-

breaking gets its due. We are here,—thou knowest, child,
it is sore against our wills,—to summon him for breaking the
peace of the Thing by slaying his brother Orm ; and we
would know, in all kindness to himself, for what cause he did
the deed."

"What, father ? this caps aught ! It cannot be."

"Nay ; as to the deed we were all in a way to witness ;
for it was done hard by the Thing-bounds. But what was
said none heard."

She clasped her hands until her fingers cracked, and caught
her breath : then she broke out, "The villain to kill his
brother. Oh me that I am wedded to such a man : a wolf's
head that is to be. Oh father, take me away and get me free
of him."

"What, is he here ? "

She pointed to the door of the lockbed : but no man stirred,
for they might not enter with the strong hand until doom had
been given. So they cried out to him, but got no answer.

Then stood forth Asmund, for he was chief man amongst
them, after Orm who was gone, and after Hundi who might
happen inherit, but now hung back. Said Asmund :—

"Neighbours, a foul thing has been done, no less than the
breaking of the Thing-peace. Ye know our old use and
wont : for how could we have law or counsel else, unless the
Thing were hallowed from all violence and the peace-breaker
put out of the peace of all true men. And this is doubly foul,
for he that was slain was our chief: and trebly, for it was his
brother slew him unoffending, so far as we know, and un-
prepared as you all saw. Now stand we here over against
the door of his house, and give doom."

So they drew a few paces back to give room for the accused
to stand with his friends at his door, if he would appear : and
for a loaded wain, so the old custom was, to pass between the
two parties. And they named Asmund their lawman, and he
named six to give judgment, who took oaths that they would
judge right. Then he stated the case, and shouted aloud to
Thorstein to come forth, and speak up for himself.

But when no answer was given, Hundi stood up and said " Friends, you are too hasty. It is never our way to doom a man unheard : and if any has the right to speak it is I, who stand here between brother and brother. Of him that is dead, I would speak no ill : but ye knew him. Of him that lives I have no ill to speak. Ye know him not as I do : and here I say that against all seeming I hold him sackless and sinless."

With that there was a shouting against Hundi, that he was always in a tale with Thorstein, and both were runagates and had turned Christians abroad, and there was no trusting them. Shame it was to Hundi that he would not take up the vengeance for his brother, and do right by the laws. Some cried out that he should be charged with abetting the manslaughter.

" Nay," said Asmund, " peace, friends. Hear me. This let us do. Put Hundi in keeping, and harm him not ; but let the jury give doom."

So they made a ring round Hundi and bore him down with their shields, and took his weapons, and led him out and bound him ; while the six men gave their doom that Thorstein Sweinson had broken the Thing-peace, and slain his brother their chief, and for that he was put out of law.

Then Asmund gave out their finding, and said moreover that he put the wonted price of a hundred of silver on the wolf's head, dead or alive. And then, for the sun was nigh its setting, they pressed into the house, no man withstanding them, and made for the door where he lay, to kill him, as the law was, while it was still day. They brought a great beam of wood and battered it against the panels, swinging it between them ; while others ran round to keep the back of the house.

All this while Thorstein lay whist, and gave no sign, like a fox in its bield while folk twine the screws to draw him out : and still they battered, for the door was new built, and strong. And still Hundi lay in bonds without, struggle and shout as he might.

" And thou, Asdis," he cried, " shame on thee to leave thy

husband to his slayers—shame and evil on thee ! Ill befall
the finger that betrayed him, and the tongue that spoke never
a word while they doomed him ; and mischance on the gear
that thou art shifting from his house.   I see thee, woman, and
thy tricks : thou robbing and thy kin murdering.   Shame and
scathe on the scrow of ye ! ''

For Asdis had bidden her servants carry out all her goods,
seeing very clearly what was forward, because she was a
wise woman.   By this time she had loaded horse and man
with bales and arks, and away down the road homeward,
saying nothing to Hundi's curses ; which was the easier, for
by now the door was battered in amid great tumult, and
Thorstein was standing there, at blows with his pursuers.
One lay on the ground at his feet among the wreckage : a
couple more sat in the hall, out of the fray, nursing ugly
wounds.

" Hold, boys," shouted Asmund, " we are but spending
good stuff."   They drew back, seemingly as eager to keep
Thorstein in, now, as they were to get him out before.   They
began to drag tables and benches to block the passage and
pin him down, and then they got fire from the hearth and all
the elding they could compass, and cast it among the splinters
of the burst panelling and the lockbed-door.   And soon the
bed was ablaze, with such a smoke that they were glad to
get out of the house : and there they stood in the twilight,
watching the flames catch the roof, and grimly waiting for
Thorstein to rush out and get his death wound, or to hear
his last cry in the fire.

The wind had shifted to the north-west, now that the
weather was holding up ; and it drove the smoke of the new
green wood in a great whirl by the door of the house, which
was set, as always, to catch the morning sun.   The men were
forced to give it a wide berth ; but sure they were that he
could not escape, and so fierce against him that not one of
them had a thought but burn and kill.   They got victuals
from the out-bowers, remnants of the wedding feast, and
emptied the ale-tub from the porch, and rubbed their hands

while the long tongues of flame wavered into the air against the stars, and the forest behind showed every branch and leaf in the glow : the crackling and spitting dinned in their ears, and the smoke was red in coils against the black sky.

There they watched until the fire died down : and said Asmund, " Lads, we have done a good deed, for to ash he will be burnt in yon cinder heap. As for the price, as we have all shared the work, let us share the pay. Come home with me and see if I keep my word. And thou, Hundi Snail, never show thy face again, unless to thank thy best friends for ridding thee of thy worst foe. I take all to witness that justice has been done, and nought but justice."

CHAPTER XLI.—WOLF'S HEAD.

FOREDONE with his anger, Hundi crept home to Lowick by the dawn of the day, and told the grewsome tale to Halldora. She, good soul, wept bitterly for Thorstein, and most of all for the part she had taken in mating him with that false and heartless minx. When she had taken her fill of weeping, she looked up and ran forth of the house as she was, like one bewitched.

The day was far spent when she came back, queer to look at.

" Is there any quarrel between thee, Hundi Sweinson, and thy brother ? "

" Nay," said he. " Would not I have saved him, but I was bound ? "

" And if he had fled ? " says she, between laughing and crying.

Aye, there he was, at the door, bemired and bloody with wounds, and the hair of his head singed off him, and his eyes nigh bleared away with the fire through which he had fled. But she had found him in the woods, and comforted him, and wormed a true tale out of him, and led him home. There he was and there he stayed in safe hiding, for Lowick was an outlying spot, with no passing : so they nursed him for weeks until he was whole again.

But if his body was whole, his heart was hardened, and never a word would he speak of good or ill, after that first talk in the wood with kind Halldora.

Now Halldora's one hope was to see this wrong righted; all the rather because she could not help blaming herself for the hasty wedding. But it was not easy. For there sat Thorstein like a log, and if he showed his face it would be death to him and shame to them. Hundi was a good boy and no fool, but he was not to be sent on ticklish errands, she knew that. And now she was tied, for there was a lusty urchin, Thorstein Hundason by name, in her arms, with a face as round as the harvest moon that rose up night after night over Colton fell.

So one fine day came to Greenodd door the Lowick folk, with a led horse, bidding Unna to visit her first grandchild, which she could not refuse. And when Halldora had got her as pleased with all as she could be, out came the story of Thorstein: not easily, for at first Unna was woe and wrath at her son's death, and would hear nothing to excuse the slayer. But who can say nay to a mother with her first babe newborn? and Thorstein was ever the best loved and longest lost of the three. Unna's eyes were opened, and when she came upon her boy, so beaten down and disheartened that he scarce knew her, she could do nothing but weep over him. And going home she sent for her brother Raud and set the case before him, and made him a promise of the chieftain's place, which had now fallen into her hands to bestow as she liked. And so he was brought into the business.

And then Halldora sent for her father, Rolf, and won him over likewise. And they plotted that when the autumn Thing was held, Raud should be made chief, and be there with a great following. Then Rolf should come with all he could bring, and a round sum of money, which Unna would find, to get Thorstein's outlawry taken off; and Hundi should confirm the true tale, and back up the suit.

But in the meanwhile, what with all this going and coming, and the tattling of thralls, it leaked out that Thorstein was not dead after all : and that the men who had burnt Blawith were but fools for their pains. Asmund sent a furious message to Hundi to warn him of the danger of harbouring an outlaw : and bade him look for visitors some night when he did not want them. Hundi was greatly put about, but Halldora laughed, and said that she knew Asdis would never forgive Thorstein for finding her out. Rolf sent some of his biggest men to bide at Lowick, in case they might be wanted : and they slept with one eye open.

Well, the day came for the Thing : and folk were there from far and wide in their feast array, and everyone that could be spared of Thorstein's kin together with their people. Before the meeting, Unna feasted the elders and householders at Greenodd, and sat among them in her widow's weeds ; and after the tables were cleared she bade them to witness that through her son's death the chieftaincy had fallen to her : that, alas, one of her sons was outlawed, and the other was ill looked upon by neighbours, so that she could name neither of them to the office : whereupon she would give the place to her brother Raud, who lived hard by, and was an able man, and would see that the Thing was kept up with due offerings to the gods, and entertainment to all comers, and so forth.

Now this was not just what the other party would have liked, but they could not gainsay it. Then Raud, as the custom was, killed a ram, and reddened his hands in the blood of it ; taking at the same time the oath of a chief : and so after due hallowing of the spot, sat him down on the topmost seat.

Then stood Asmund on the one side and Rolf on the other, each claiming to be heard. The new chief ruled that Asmund should have the first word : for he thought it wise to let them talk it well out. So Asmund set forth that his daughter Asdis being wedded to a man who had been outlawed, claimed to be released from him, and to take all that belonged to her, namely the third of land and goods.

For you must know that in those heathen days, among the Northmen, the wife was master. She had her own goods and

land to herself, and could sell them for her own use : even
against the husband's will she could make away with the full
half. And yet he had to manage it all, and to manage it
well; and to defend it and her in every way. They were
grand times for the women-folk. A wife could turn off her
husband like a hired servant, for almost anything that dis-
pleased her. And there was nothing a man could do in law
that the woman could not do as well, or better. Now Asdis
might have just turned off her husband, with a word, when
she left him : but she would not then have had a claim on his
land. So being a wise woman she held her tongue, and now
brought this suit against him.

There were witnesses to the outlawing at the door-doom,
and there was little defence made ; for nobody of Thorstein's
friends wished to bind him to the woman ; and as for land,
there was plenty more to be taken, if she made a point of
holding to a bit of uncleared timber.

This business being done, the other put in his plea. He
was a hearty carle, was Rolf. With his great grey beard,
and his tall figure somewhat barrowbacked, he was well
listened to at meetings, and much respected by high and low,
but no great hand at cunning and trickery. When he began
to speak of Thorstein there was a disturbance. At last Raud
got peace, and the suit went forward. Rolf told how Thorstein had not been heard in his defence,—how could he,
standing alone and all his foes about him ? And then he
went on to tell the other side of the story ; how Raineach had
saved Thorstein as a lad, and had been received by his people
as a sister : how Orm had been a rough kinsman to all his
house, and a hard master to his folk : and how he had tricked
Raineach into thralldom, and made up a lying tale about it.

So far so good ; though it was no new story for a stranger,
man or wench, to be sold off as useless or troublesome rubbish.
But then he went on to complain that the doom of outlawry
had been unlawfully given; for the crime was done at the
Althing, said he, and to the Althing the case should be taken.
He said moreover that so great a penalty as full outlawry

should not have been laid at a door-doom, which was meant for little cases, such as the distraint of goods from a refractory debtor, and the like. Then he said that the attack had been continued after sunset, and therefore if they had killed Thorstein it would have been murder. " And all this," said he, "comes of the folly of men I see sitting over yonder, who have let themselves be led on from bad to worse by a wicked woman."

Then there was a terrible to-do. Men ran for their weapons; and the only way of saving the Thing-stead from blood was for Raud to break up the meeting, and draw off his men, begging them to be guided and to save their strength for another chance.

Thorstein at Blawith heard the news as one who heeds little. He thanked them for their kindness, and said he must be going, for he would not bring them into straits. And so Hundi set him on his way across the Leven to Raud's-ey, and Raud kept him for a night, and asked him whither bound. Thorstein said he had a mind to go far. It was in his heart to go in search of Raineach, even if he had to lait her at York and in the house of King Olaf: but after her anger and the falsehood of one he had trusted, he feared and doubted, though he said nothing.

" Kinsman," said Raud, "take my counsel. Things have gone against thee, but the tide will turn. Thou hast friends, and good ones, at Rosset and at Greenodd, at Lowick and here ; and when the truth gets ground and springs up, it will bear fruit, never fear. We were in error to open the case anywhere but at the Althing ; but we shall try again and get thee cleared at last, in spite of that woman and her witch-face. It is only a fool that throws his oars overboard because his tiller snaps. Now go not far. Over yonder in Cartmel is out of our bounds. None of our Northmen will touch thee there : but when good news is to be sent, thou wilt not be hard to seek."

CHAPTER XLII.—CARTMEL CHURCH.

CARTMEL was a queer spot, thenadays. It was a little village of wattled huts, heavily thatched above, and daubed with clay, round the miry green where children played in the sunset. On one side of the green a beck ran up, and on the other side a beck ran down; and between the becks was a big house, not unlike the rest except that it was big and they were little. That was where the Reeve of the York priests dwelt. In the midmost of the green was another house, daub and wattle and thatch, standing all alone, with a cross on the gable-end of it, and a wooden tower of open work wherein a bell hung.

A man in a long gown was pulling at a rope and ringing the bell. It tinkled in the quiet air, above the shouts of the children on the green, with a pleasant music that seemed to well over the fields of the broad valley, and their quickset hedges and flagged walls, to the brown woods of the hills that lay around, and up into the golden evening sky.

It was but a twelvemonth ago that Thorstein had been christened and taught the faith: but since then, what things had happened? Dare he now enter the church, he who had kept no day holy nor heard mass, nor even latterly said the prayers he used to say night and morning? It had come to this that his stony heart was shut to man and God alike. When Hundi and Halldora knelt, for she had learned her husband's faith,—when they knelt to their cross, he would walk out of the way dowly enough. If his brother's blood was on his hands, that was little in an age when few men's hands were white: but there came over him a vague and terrible fear that he could not name to himself,—the conscience of backsliding, the haunting of Hakon; and the words of the applegarth at Ladir rose up in his mind, " Whoso denieth me." He could not say what he had then said to Hakon, nor take the answer. " You have preached to me," said the poor young king: and here he was, a castaway.

The bell stayed ringing, and there was a voice within, the sound that he knew well, of evensong. He sat down by the

church door, rudely pillared in wood with some rough notching
on it to imitate the carving of the great churches he had
seen: and sitting without, listened while Amen followed
Amen like the noise of a beck in a gill. The children left
playing, and stood round him out of arm's reach, to stare.

By and by the droning within stopped. A hand was laid
on his shoulder.

"Who art thou, son?" said an English voice. But there
was no answer.

"Who art thou, son?" it said again in Welsh.

"A wanderer."

"Returned?" said the priest.

Thorstein knelt before him and burst into sobs. The
children had crept up behind the priest, and two or three
were holding by his gown.

"Children, run home: it is supper-time for all of you,"
said the priest, making the sign of blessing over their rough
white heads. "And thou, son, give me thy heart. It shall
be in safe keeping."

He led Thorstein into his dwelling and set food before him,
and bade him rest. In due time the lad's heart was opened,
and he told his tale, or somewhat of it; so much as let it be
known that he was born a heathen and baptised a Christian,
but had fallen back; and that all was wrong with him now.

"Aye," said the priest, "for thy sin's sake. I spare thee
not, for it is written, Whom the Lord loveth he chasteneth.
But I smite thee not, for it is written again, Him that cometh
to me I will in no wise cast out."

"Father," said Thorstein, "I have learned enough to know
that a man may be made clean with penance from many a
crime. Is there a penance strong enough for such as me?"

"Son," said he, "for every sin the church has penance,
and for every sinner she has room. To confess thy sin is the
first thing; to weep for it is the next; and what more is there
but to bring forth fruits worthy of repentance? For thy
backsliding I bid thee dwell henceforward with Christians,
and forsake the heathen and their ways. Fast and pray as

it is commanded. And for the man-slaying thou hast done, if thou have told the truth about it, God alone will be thy judge: It is not for me to bind or loose."

Thorstein slept that night, and awoke with a new heart. After matins were done the priest brought him to the Reeve, praying that something might be given to put him in a way of living among Christian folk, for he was a penitent and a brand plucked from the burning.

The Reeve, a burly Englishman from York, and to all purpose lord of Cartmel, looked the stranger up and down.

"Well, my penitent," said he, "this is church land, and churchman's word is law here," said he. "But by thy looks I should name thee a church-robber, and no lamb of our flock. However," said he, "since father John there stands for thee, knowing the risks, I'll see to it. What can'st thou do, man?"

Thorstein said, very humbly for him, that he would put his hand to anything to earn his victuals : that he knew something about beasts, and smithying, and suchlike.

"In a word," said the Reeve, "man of all trades and master of none, or thou would'st not be here. But come thy ways, and I'll prove thee."

Sure enough he set him one job and another : and if Thorstein was willing at the muck-heap, he was clever at the stithy : until the Reeve laughed again, and clapped him on the back saying, "Good lad. I never knew yon thieving, murdering rascals could turn out such a fellow!"

So he guested him in his house that winter, and took on with him as never was. And to cap all, when the spring was come, "Young man," said he, "folk can't be always on hand," said he.

"That they can't," said Thorstein wondering.

"And when they are gone they would like to lie easy, by the church yonder, and see things done right by the land?"

"That they would," said Thorstein.

"Well," said he, "I am but the servant of the blessed Minster of York, and of the abbot yonder : but I think they

owe me somewhat ; and what with father John's good word
and all we might manage it. Now, look here. There's none
of these fellows fit to hold a candle to me and you, and none
knows the land as they that live on it. Reason is when I
drop off the best man should follow me : and the abbot, he
would say aye to that, if we got the soft side of him. Now,
Master Thurstan, I've a daughter. She is a fine girl, though
I say it who shouldn't : and a right good one, and the apple
of my eye. But what, lad, thou hast set eyes on her. What
then ? "

Thorstein thanked him kindly, and said it was more than
he deserved.

"Not a bit, lad. There, think it over, and I'll answer for
the wench."

Thorstein went to father John, for he was very thick with
him, and never missed his church, fast-day or feast-day.

"Father," said he, "I would go on pilgrimage to York.
Maybe a sight of the blessed Minster would do me good."

"Well said, my son : go in peace."

CHAPTER XLIII.—AT YORK.

YORK city was a wonderful place as one came upon it
by the old North Road. From afar its towers rose
up above the green tillage of the plain, beyond the winding
Ouse : and as the traveller drew nearer, he saw the great
high mound that encompassed the garth of houses, set with
its bristling stockade above, and parted from the fields by a
water-ditch as broad as a broad river. In the midst of this
great wall was the North gate, through which the road ran ;
and within were houses and houses, some high, some low,
some mean like cottages at Cartmel, some grand with painting
and carving : but all cheek by jowl, as one may say, along
the narrow winding streets, thronged with people and wares
set out to sell, and foul with the refuse and rubbish of a
thickly inhabited town.

Above the house-roofs rose a great building, the famous
Minster : with its towers standing high over gable and

pinnacle, graceful and slender. Up there the bells clanged
above the din and hurry of the town in those dark deep
streets, that were like roaring gills and whirling torrents
below.

But it was not for the Minster that Thorstein was bound,
as he elbowed through the crowd, and picked his steps over
the unpaved lane that was more gutter than path. He
hardly dared question the wayfarers, such a stoore and a stir
there seemed to be. But he knew that somewhere in the
heart of the houses he should find Olaf's palace, the new
castle that had been built after Athelstan destroyed the old
Danish stronghold,—the great hall where King Eric had sat
with his witch-wife, and skald Egil the swart had sung the
lay that won him his head.

So he went forward along the streets, with a beatiug heart
and pale lips, towards the midmost of the city where the
great towers rose. When he came before the castle there
was an open space, and the houses fell back like trees from a
green glade in the forest. But instead of coneys skipping
in the grass, here was a great crowd gathered and a tumult
going on. Out of every window round the place was a head
thrust, and folk fringed the house-roofs a-straddle on the
thatch-rigging, and all shouting at once. Stones were flying ;
and the shopkeepers at the corner, where Thorstein came
into the square, where scrambling their goods under cover
and shutting their shutters. It seemed as if the townfolk of
the baser sort were trying to force the castle doors : and whoever came out of the narrow streets, like rats out of their
holes, thrust themselves on their fellows in front and shoved
and shouted ; and ill luck it would have been to have tripped
in the midst of that scrimmage. Over heads and fists many
a stick was waving ; and here and there an axe, and here and
there a sword, flashing in the sun-gleam, that now and then
broke on the square through the rain-showers. On they came
by hundreds ; aye, by thousands, swarming : for the old books
say that in those days no less than thirty thousand souls were
crammed within the narrow walls that girt the city of York.

so you may well believe there was no lack of hands in a townsfolk mote, whether for peace or for fighting.

"What's to do, friend?" says Thorstein to a neighbour, who by the look of him was no Saxon, but a Dane; and a right hearty, well-to-do looking merchant man he seemed, now that he had got his goods shifted, and shutters up, and stood there with one hand holding his door ajar, and with the other gripping his axe.

"What's to do?" repeated the Dane; "why, it's the old story. A stranger, eh? none of the Saxon folk anyhow." For Danes and Northmen talked the same tongue, and fore-gathered among strangers.

"Nay," said Thorstein, "no Saxon, though a traveller from over the fells."

"No offence," said the Dane: "but one can't be too careful, with Southron spies all about. Our kinsmen, thou knowest, friend, have no bed of roses in this bonny burg."

"I know nought," said Thorstein. "What is forward?"

"What thou seest, and I hope they may break the castle. For if the great doors yonder hold, they will sack the shops for want of a job. Thou hast heard, maybe, rumour that king Olaf is dead. To-day it is assured. It was somewhere in the North, Tyningaham I think they called the spot. Look out, man!"

There was a rush towards the door, and stones flew. The Dane plucked Thorstein into the house, slammed the door, and made it fast with stout bars. Then he cast an eye on the bolts of his window, and laughed as they stood in the shop, lit only through the cracks in the shutters.

"It is a pretty stiff bit of oak," he said. "We shall hold out awhile, unless they take to fire-raising, and that would risk their own kennels. Well, as I was saying, Olaf being gone we must have a new king. Some of these Saxon rubbish would be glad to see the Southrons in here: and anyhow they mean to make hay while the sun shines."

"So they are trying to plunder the king's house?" said Thorstein.

"That's it: but never heed them. I have seen three or four such ados in the last few months, and one gets hardened. Though indeed if it were not for business, I should be glad to be safe again over the seas. It's a fine town is Dublin. Thou wilt not be from thereaway I reckon?"

"Nay," said Thorstein: "but I was there a while when Olaf Guthferthson was king, and indeed I was guested in the king's house, and it is now for nought else but to have speech with the queen that I am in York."

"Then, my lad, thou art a bit late: and a good job for thee too, if those rascals—how they shout!—get into the castle."

"She is gone then? What, is she dead, poor thing?"

"Nay, not so bad as all that. You see it was something o' this way. Olaf owed a deal to Earl Orm, for without him he would never have halved England with Eadmund. And Orm is a good business man, and looks ahead. Says he to Olaf, If anything happens now to Eadmund, thou wilt be king of all England: and what shall I get that helped thee thereto? Says Olaf, What wilt thou have, friend? Says Orm, There's my Aldith should be wed: queen of York is not bad, and queen of England is better. Says Olaf, Well, says he, king Harald Fairhair had more wives than one. Nay, nay, says the Earl, that's out of fashion nowadays, and I doubt if the Minster-folk would stand it: the king of York is a good Christian now, my lord, and behaves as such: eh? So Olaf he goes to the Irish queen and My dear, says he, a sad unhealthy spot is York city; better go back to Ireland. Says my dame to me,—but come in man, and make thyself at home. Any news from Dublin will be welcome to the mistress."

So he brought Thorstein into the living-room behind the shop. It was crowded up with their goods, and looked like a poor place after the great halls of the Northmen: but everything was rich and rare. Such hangings to the beds, such carved work in the tables and stools, such shining copper pots and pans! And the merchant's wife was dressed as grand as a queen, Thorstein thought, with brooches and rings for a dozen. The children even were finely clothed, though they would have looked but blue and wan alongside of the apple-cheeked rogues from the Northmen's homesteads.

"Dame, it's all right; the doors are well barred, and if they break them there is the earth-house to hide in. But see, here's a young man has been in Dublin."

"Welcome, friend," said she, "and what news of the old country?" Thorstein could see with half an eye that the Dane's wife was Irish, and so he replied in the language he had learnt among the fell-folk, saying that it was a good while since he was in Ireland, but he was now come to speak to the queen, who had been friendly with him once. At which Master Dane screwed up half his face and winked, and his wife shook her head at him, and said the queen was a good body, and sorry she was for her, and pity it was they had not gone back together with her to Ireland.

"Nay, nay," said the Dane: "business is business. Keep your shop, say I, and your shop will keep you."

"Well then," said the wife, "keep thy shop, my lad, and this young man will take a bite, and be the readier to lend a hand if needed."

So she set food before him, and he ate. And while he ate he turned over in his mind the chances about Raineach. Soon he burst out, "Mistress, is it true, as the master says, that all the queen's folk are clean away and out of the castle?"

"Aye," she said, "and a burning shame it was: but better for them maybe. They got a good ship to sail in, and good pickings. They were stinted of nothing."

"They would be a deal about the town before leaving York, and well known to all?"

"Oh aye, it was always in and out; they coming to our shop and we at the castle. Not so bad to do with, they weren't, for king's folk."

"And did you happen to know a great lass, a bonny one with red hair, a bower-may that the queen made much of, Raineach by name?"

"And what of her?" asked the dame.

"Oh, she was just one of them in Dublin."

"Was she that? Ah, she was a sad one if ever there was. Hey, man, hark here! The young man would have news of that great, strapping, red-haired wench, her that the castle-folk were always fighting about."

"The minx!" shouted the merchant from the shop. "Never heed her, lad, wherever she is."

"All the men were after her," went on the dame, "and never a one would she take. And that proud with folk, she might have been a king's daughter. I'll be bound she was no good, though the queen was always abetting her. Olaf would have let them stone her for a witch, one time, but the queen got her off. She'll be gone with the rest."

It was little help he would find there, Thorstein said to himself: but angered as he was, spoke fair: and said he would take a turn at the look-out while the master came to his supper. But the tumult had died down, and the rabble was dwindling as speedily as it had gathered. The stir was over like a summer storm, and evening had come. Thorstein asked where he could find a lodging for that night, and said he was not penniless. The Dane merchant said he would be glad to board him, but one might see there was little room for guests in house or shop. Nevertheless there was close at hand a house of priests called St. Peter's, where travellers were lodged, and he would set the stranger on the way when all was quiet.

So Thorstein came to St. Peter's, which Athelstan had founded not long before, giving to the Minster priests a thrave, that is twenty sheaves, from every plough-land in the bishopric, that they might entertain strangers and do good to the poor and sick. There he was received, and no questions asked: and they gave him supper in the great hall, and a place to lie down for the night among other wanderers and wayfarers. Some of them were decent folk, some ugly-looking enough to make Thorstein feel for the few silver pennies he carried, and tuck his poke well into his sleeve, and loosen his weapon in its sheath, before shutting his eyes.

But he slept safely, still seeking even in his dreams for Raineach, who was now farther away than ever.

When day was come, and the doors were opened, the priests' officer gave each wayfarer a cake of bread and bade him God speed. Thorstein stood there in the doorway with his dole in his hand, and sore doubt in his heart which way he should turn. East or West was all one to him. The Minster bells broke out into a chime, and pealed through the air. Sweet and sunny it was after last night's riot and unrest. He bethought him that this was the Lord's day; he could not leave York without at least hearing a service, now that he was a Christian man once more.

People were going all one way in the streets, but quietly now, and very unlike the crowds of yestereven. He followed them and went with the stream into the shadow of the Minster tower and up the great steps, gaining one at a time in the throng at the porch. Presently he was carried through the dark door, and inside as into some sudden astonishing turn of a dream. For it was wonderful broad and lofty in there; the walls betwixt the arches and above the ranks of columns were inlaid with polished marbles, painted with long processions of deep-robed saints and emblems of glory, lit with glimmering, flower-like windows of glass, and ceiled with canopies of carven work, with beams and bosses wrought curiously. It was the foundation of archbishop Aelberht not long since finished; the new church risen on the ruins of the old church that Halfdan's Danes had burnt; witness to the life and might of the faith, a noble monument of craftsmanship. Its gilding was yet untarnished and its rich colours were as if fresh from the hands of the artist; a marvel to behold, even for a traveller who had been in many lands and had seen the dwellings of great kings, and temples both of the old faith and the new.

Thorstein knelt on the paved floor, and beside him and around him knelt the people, men and women, rich and poor: maybe among them many who last night had been foremost in the tumult, side by side with those they had attacked to

rob and slaughter. Far off, in the twilight of the choir,
re-echoed from roof and aisles, came the sound of the singing
and the solemn voices of the priests: the very psalms and
prayers that were heard in little Cartmel church among the
mountains, and in every church of Christian folk from thence
throughout the round world.   Everywhere the same, and in
every age. For to think of the abidingness of it all ! Kings
came and went, nations rose and fell, but the church drooped
its head only to raise it more gloriously.   Year by year, while
battle and plague were raging without, within the Minster
there welled, as from a healing spring, the same unending
litany for peace from poor folk to the poor folk's God.

No prayer said Thorstein as he knelt thus, while the voices
from the choir rolled forth like gathering thunder, or mur-
mured through the aisles uncomprehended like the wind in
winter trees.   It was enough for him that he was in a holy
place, in the palace of God, in the very presence of the King
of Heaven.   Surely the Lord Christ there, somewhere in the
dim bewilderment of gold and gloom, amid those cloudy
odours and mysterious answerings of music, surely He was
looking forth.   And what was the word ?   The Lord looketh
at the heart.   Peace, then.

CHAPTER XLIV.—WOOD-BIDERS.

VERY home-sickness, and nothing else, drew Thorstein
back to Furness. He stayed awhile in York, hoping
for news; but the only news was of Olaf's death, sudden and
strange,—the hand of God manifest, folk said, and St.
Balthere's vengeance on the church-burner.   So all was fear
and flight in the old city and throughout Deira.

Then Thorstein took leave of his friend the Dane merchant,
and shirking talk with the Minster-priests, won his way back
over the Keel, and wandered homewards.

Out of the Northmen's land he was free from their laws.
But in those days a stranger was a stranger, in whatever
land he abode.   If he had no strong friends he was nought.
So that between wandering abroad and wood-biding at home
there was little to choose.

Now the way of the wood-biders was this. When a man was utterly outlawed no friend might receive him, under pains and penalties; every enemy had the right to hunt him like a wild beast, and to get the reward for killing him, if reward were offered. So there was nothing for it but to stay in the forests, hiding in some cave or secret hut of tree-boughs and turf, and living on what he could hunt, or maybe rob from the neighbours who had put him out of law. In this manner, afterwards, William Cloudeslea and Robin Hood fled to the greenwood, where the king's sheriffs could not take them. And even to these days, men who have been in trouble with the law have been known to hide themselves in the wide woods that cover the Furness fells, skulking by day and prowling by night; sometimes friendly enough with the poorer sort, and troublesome only to the gentlefolk and greater farmers of the neighbourhood, whose stock they pilfered: and their hiding-places are well known to those that know the country well. In the end these wood-biders either got their peace with the law, or were hunted down, or died like wild beasts in the wood.

Thorstein was not without hope that his business might be done by his friends, whom he never doubted. But when he came one morning to Lowick, risking his neck for the sake of news, heard that things were no forwarder.

"But," said Halldora, "hark to this. Two days ago, as I was sitting in the sun—it was bright autumn weather—and the child was kicking about on the grass, I heard him crowing and chuckling; and I looked up from my sewing, and there he was, staring at somewhat, and laughing. Then I was ware of one among the trees hard by,—for it was on the edge of the wood,—looking eagerly at us through the branches. I could see nothing but the gleam of an eye, and a white hand. I made no stay, but caught up the barn and ran for it. And yet by the white hand, I reckon yon was a woman; and none of the folk hereabouts, be they fell-folk or farm-folk, by the same token. But by the gleam of eyelight, I reckon she was gradely tall for a woman. What dost make of that, lad?"

He went straight to Greenodd, caring nought who might meet him. Into the hall he strode, and " Mother," said he, " where is Raineach ? "

She was not very far to seek after that; nor so very hard to suit when he found her. The true tale had come out on both sides. Unna had told her of Orm, and of Asdis, and of Thorstein's beguiling; and Raineach had given her own story,—how she was carried to York, after finding that Thorstein had left thinking of her; and then of her adventures at Olaf's castle there; and then how they were sent away, and sailed round by Pictland and Orkney and the South-isles; and then how the wind had brought them to the Cumberland coast, and how she wept at the sight of her fells again ; and how the queen was sorry for her, and said at last, " There, wench ; hie away with thee, and have better luck than to be a king's castaway."—" And maybe," said Raineach, reddening, " she was a bit weary of me, for there was always some stir forward, and she had no man now to keep her folk under. Any way, by dint of this and that, I made shift to get clear of them all ; and short was the way hither, for fells are easier to pass than foes."

O but Raineach was grown great and strong, and more than womanly, for she was such a one as a giant's daughter should be ; but as fine spoken and as fair-skinned as a princess, with three winters of court and castle-biding. She had got used to outlandish doings and unkid havings, one could see that by the very way she supped her porridge. But when Thorstein told her to think twice before she took him,—and he did so,—how she laughed ! The rose-red came and went, up and down the bonny slim cheeks. She reached out both her hands, and held his. It was good to feel that firm grasp.

" How many times dost thou reckon I have thought of it, lad, before now ? "

They walked together over the fells by woodland paths where none could spy them, to a little village near the shore of Duddon firth. There they found the priest whom Raineach had known of old, he who had given that counsel to her when she sold her cross to the wood-wrights. He was a strange figure, with the hair hanging matted round his bald crown; the beard thick above his mouth, and cropped below. And his little church was more like a hut of the fell-folk than the clay daubing at Cartmel: for he was one of the old sort, and of the rule of those Irish priests who came over sea and settled up and down the Cumberland coasts, building them cells, and there serving those Irish saints, like Patrick and Sanctan and Bega, whose names are still known hereabouts, and were known long before the York Minster-priests came to that land.

There was no grand wedding, with neighbours to feast and gifts to scatter. They knelt alone in the bare little cell before the priest, and in his own speech he blessed them in the name of the Father and Son and Holy Ghost, and bade them be one heart and soul, world without end. It was no wedding at all, the heathen Northmen would have said, this of the outlaw to the stranger, unwitnessed and unwarranted. But then, to the Christians the bridals of the Northmen were nothing, no more than a manner of partnership in trade, that could be on and off like any other bargain in worldly matters.

It was Thorstein's hope to rebuild his own house at Blawith, if he had to do it with his own hands, none aiding him. And if he could but settle there again and hold his own, far away as it was from the neighbours and buried in the woods, he thought the turn of the tide would come, and after a while he would be once more a free man among his own people. So he knocked up a shed among the ruins, and gathered together such trifles as he could save out of the wreck. But they had not been a week at work on the new home, when before daylight one morning the dogs awakened them, and they fled into the wood, only just in time. Their little cot was ablaze, and a band of armed men was slashing about, and hunting for them up and down.

But they would not leave hope, so fully persuaded as they were that better days were coming. It was the back-end of

the summer by now, and winter was upon them. It would
not do to risk another door-doom; and as they cowered in
hiding—wood-biders well skilled in the craft—they talked out
a plan to put more than dry land between themselves and
their enemies, until the time should come when they might
get peace.

In the midst of Thurston-water there is a little island, lying
all alone. When you see it from the fells, it looks like a ship
in the blue ripples; but a ship at anchor, while all the mere
moves upbank or downbank, as the wind may be. The little
island is ship-like also because its shape is long, and its sides
are steep, with no flat and shelving shores; but a high short
nab there is to the northward, for a prow, so to speak; and a
high sharp ness to the southward, for a poop. And to make
the likeness better still, a long narrow calf-rock lies in the
water, as if it were the cockboat at the stern; while tall trees
stand for masts and sails.

The island is not so far in the water but that one can swim
to shore, nor so near that it would be easy to attack it without
a boat: and at that time boats there were none on these
lakes, except maybe a coracle or two of the fell-folk. For
fishing, no spot could be better, nor for hunting, if one wanted
a safe home and hunting-tower. And if need were to run
down Crake to Lowick for news or victuals, that could be
done with little risk. This should be their hold and their
home, they planned. Here they would make themselves
secure, and let the storm drift over their heads.

So said so done. By nightfall they were on the island,
with little goods indeed, but with a fire alight, and a rough
lair of branches wreathed to shelter them. Into it they crept,
and cuddled together as when they were children, laughing
at their makeshifts and eager over their designs. Through
the shivering, falling leaves the moon shone, patterning the
grass of the glade in their dell, and dying out as the clouds
raked by; flashing again, and fading. The woof of the waves
against the rock-wall of their castle, and the voice of the
wind flying past, booming in the great forest that rose steep

over against them on the eastern shore, and then shrieking
in the branches overhead,—all these touched them not in
their shelter, and only made their peace more peaceful, and
their security more secure.   It was the old time come again
for both of them, and they were as lightsome as children in
their new happiness.

"Hark to the wind," said Raineach, "afar and away
there: it will be down at the waterfoot now, ruffling the great
oak trees as if they were barnes' curly heads.   It is coming
upbank.   Ah, it is catching the nab end: hark to the dash of
the waves on the shore and on the rock in the water.   Here
it comes.   That was a big one, Thorstein: it made the
ground shake, like a ship-deck.   I had liefer be here than on
shipboard, though.   Shall we hold, thinkst thou?"

"Oh aye; the trees sway a bit and the roots jar in the
mould: but we are snug enough here.   It's not the wind will
harm us."

"Nay, the wind is bonny.   It sings.   They used to sing a
deal in Dublin, the bards, and there were your skalds, they
called them, in York: whiles they sang me songs all to
myself.   They were fools.   It was like this:—The red fern is
tall and fair.   She sways in the autumn breeze.   Swords
flash; blood flows.   The red fern heed them not.—Nay, nor
I didn't.   Not I.   They sang nought.   But yon wind, what
does it sing?   Home again, child: home again, old playfellow:
home!—Make a hole, lad, through the bield to spy at.   There's
no window in our island palace: and I want to see the fells,
and count them.   Nay, then; it's no use: we are all umbered
up with trees.   Aigh! it's wolf dark: pull the boughs again,
Thorstein; the wind blows at me through the spy-hole."

"The pet of Dublin and the pride of York has got over
nice and nesh with her queens and earls and such like, I
doubt, for a bield in the wood.   Nay, don't nip like that,
Raineach: it hurts, thou great rough minx!"

"I'll be named no names then.   Did I hurt thee?   Truly?
Beat me.   But thou, Thorstein, never cast up against me
what was none of my doing.   I did no wrong to thee, of all

people. None. The wind knows. Hark, it begins again. What is it saying?—The red fern grows round the tall great stone, out on the fell: on the fell. And it grows and grows, and it hides it, and it smothers it, and it chokes it, all in its red, red hair!"

"Oh let be lass; I am that weary. What is the night for but to sleep? It will be up and doing, over soon."

"There, then, shut eyes. Bad lad, they are not shut. I can see them, I can see them in the dark, shining.—Dost thou mind the wild cat, Thorstein, and how angry we were? Now we are never to be angry again, are we? Shut eyes and snore, I say, or I'll beat thee."

CHAPTER XLV.—ON THE ISLAND.

HERE as the days went on they made their home. It was no great job to build a cot in the gap between the two ridges, the twin backbone of the island: for the rock on either hand is steep like a solid house-wall for more than a man's height, and runs thus maybe two hundred feet, now choked with ruins of the old building that once stood there: but formerly a deep and sheltered trough.

They had only to roof it over with poles, which they cut from the trees growing on the spot, and to thatch it with boughs and turfs like one of those huts the woodcutters and bark peelers make themselves even nowadays in the woods. Then they built up the ends, leaving doors and windows, and there was as snug a home as might be in all Lakeland. Nor so long a task was it, either, for a lad like Thorstein, who many a day before had enterprised to build a house for the folk on the fell.

And then he bethought him of a bit of a boat, to make the shoreward journey easy. For himself, he could swim like a duck: but to ferry another, and to fetch such things as kind friends might give, not to say for fishing and fowling, and for watching the shores of his mere, something more was needful than swimming-strokes and a wet sark.

The fell-folk had their own old way of boat building, which

was this. They cut a tree, and trimmed its ends with the axe; and then, heating cobbles in the fire, they burnt out the heart of the log and hollowed their canoe. But a Northman born, who was no mean woodsmith, thought scorn of that ancient makeshift. And yet to save time, he was content with bent boughs, and withys to bind them into a framework, and skins stretched around all: making a coracle light to lift and easy to drive, even when the water was none so lound. For our lake-waves never run high like sea-billows, though the strength of the breeze and its sudden gusts sometimes give a rower hard work to keep head to wind. And the many sharp rocks and cobbly shoals upstanding beneath the water-line are somewhat dangerous for a heavy boat under way: but with a light craft it is light work. And no sweeter life could be dreamt by one to the manner bred than this fishing and fowling on a teeming mere, aboard of a handy little tub that answers every touch and wish of the rower.

So thus they lived as if life were one holiday: safe from prowling beasts and far from mankind. Now and again Thorstein would travel down Crake to his friends, who helped him willingly with goods and tools and porridge-meal for housekeeping. And yet it was little they lacked, to be as well off as they used to be in early days among the fell-folk. There was the same hunting ground: firewood and the sweetest of water in plenty; and well they knew, if any did, how to make the most of the wilderness and all it held, and when that was done to be content.

For a long while nobody meddled with them. It seemed as though they had been forgotten. And just to be let alone, and to be together, was enough to make the morning bright and the evening merry. Winter was not so sharp, down there by the water, as it was on the fells. The lake freezes over but seldom, and even the hard weather was friendly to them, for it sent beasts and birds down from the high lands to milder grounds, and so to their larder; and the warm feathers and furs were welcome for clothes and bedding.

When the spring came, and lilies made the shores all

golden, and the snow on the great fells dwindled into delicate
lacework, white in the blue air, then Raineach was glad of
the sunshine to sit in, at the land-locked harbour, plying her
needle, while Thorstein was away in the boat fishing. He
was never so far but she could climb upon a rock and spy
him out, a speck upon the broad water-line. Then she would
wave to him, and if he was not busy with a fish he would
wave back. So it was not lonely. After the worry and
weariness of the court, where there was no true friend to
count on, it was the merriest company. The loneliness was
when she was lost in the crowd.

But when the bluebells lay thick upon every rock ledge of
the island, sweet smelling and bluest blue in their fresh
green leaves; when the cuckoos called loud from shore to
shore, and the sun was strong, looking down into the depths
of the still water and counting every different stone, laid clear
and fair in its crystal bed, and the minnows flickered over
them; then sometimes she would weep a little to herself as
she sat. She could not tell why, if it were not that she was
in dread of the time when he would be again among his own
people, and hers the less: when she would have to be as any
other house-mistress, and his the less: judged by their words
and fettered by their ways. Then life would no longer be so
free and so loving as it was to the wood-biders.

But when the spring flowers were all gone and the nights
were sultry and dark again, she wept no more: for she had
new company: a little thing that reached out its hands to
her from the bundle of furs where it lay, and that made such
quaint faces as were a wonder and a lasting gazing-stock.
There was time now for nothing but to watch it, and fondle
it, and feed it: and if at first the island was a sweet home to
her, now it was more lovely than ever, to be there with her
big man, and her little man, and none to let or hinder.

After a while they made a great journey over the fells, and
came to Duddon side again, to the strange old priest, that he
might christen the child. They called it Swein after Thorstein's father, as in duty bound, though the priest halted

somewhat at the name, so outlandish and unchristian as it seemed to his way of thinking. However he blessed the child, and bade it prosper, and they took their way home without mishap: and the journey gave them talk for many a day to follow.

So they won through the second winter, with never a thought of wearying either of one another or of their home. Now they cleared a little thwaite of land over against the island, and kept a goat or two, and sowed a patch of oats, so that their porridge-stuff need not be so far to seek, and milk for the barn should be plenty. And the summer went by in game and glee, and they had no fears for the winter.

For a Yule-gift they got another guestling, whom they carried in a while to the priest, tripping through the woods with him in his mother's arms, and the sturdy Swein on his father's shoulder. They called the baby Thorstein: and when they saw him and his brother wax and thrive, they laughed a bit sometimes to think of the day when they should take their piglings that Unna had foretold, to show the grandame at Greenodd.

Yet with all this well-being there was somewhat wrong. What with his own labour and his strong friends, Thorstein got all he wanted for bed or board: and with a sweet wife and bonny barnes he was set up with the best of company. Over and above which, he knew in his heart that he was now no outcast of holy church, though seldom he saw priest or heard those words of life he had stumbled at long since. Nowadays, what talks he had with Raineach, and reasonings of unknown things, piecing together his scraps of learning with her, as an old wife plans patchwork: for all the bits must fit into the pattern, whether or no they matched.

And some bits would not fit, such words as told folk to be at one among themselves, and that promised peace between mankind. There was he, out of law and no man's neighbour. Peace with God his heart told him he had; but peace with man was still far to seek: and if all he had done, and all his friends had done, gave him not that peace, how could God command it? how would God provide it?

And being no dreamer, but a man with his eyes open, he knew right well that, if to-day was fair, to-morrow might be foul. So far his foes had given him a wide berth; but says he "When I am gone, who will take my lads by the hand, and give them their place among their fellows, and assure them land and living?"

"Heed it not," Raineach would answer. "Are not they as well as thou in God's hand?"

"Who heeds it?" he would say. "Not I. And yet!"

"Oh man, speak fair and be thankful."

"I do speak fair, and I am thankful," said he: "and yet!"

CHAPTER XLVI.—UNBIDDEN GUESTS.

BUT what about Asdis, all this while? She was never the worse off, whatever happened. She was too wise to spoil her looks with weeping, and too pretty to sit long at Asmundarlea waiting for a new husband. She lighted on her feet, like a cat, wherever she fell: and before many months was purring by another fireside, with the cream of the milk to lap. But as she blinked in the fireglow, she was only watching her mouse.

The land was not so bare of people as it had been twenty winters since. Bit by bit, as the days went on, the dales were cleared and inhabited. From the low country one after another went up to take land among the fells. For the Northmen could never abide close quarters. They hated towns, and loved a free life: a spot to themselves, with elbow-room; a seat on a howe overlooking broad fields and fell-pastures, with the smoke of the next neighbour's hall rising far away through the green wood. It was one thing to have good friends within hail and call, but another to be thrust among folk in one of those stinking swine-styes, said they, where Southrons herded. And so their biggings crept up from the shore of Leven and Duddon, and from nook to nook the house-reek rose, like bale-fires lighted to tell the world that this Lakeland was the land-take of the Northmen.

Therefore all the coming and going of Thorstein could not fail to be spied, and the tale sped from mouth to mouth, time and again, and lost little in its travels. In a while it came to dame Asdis, where she sat with black anger in her heart against Thorstein, and against the wild she-wolf of the fells who had stolen him out of her arms. And in all this she blamed herself never one whit, and folk came to look on her as a fair woman with great wrongs to avenge.

In a time of quiet, when ill men are aweary of peace, and stirring men hanker after the adventures of old days, no great work was needed to egg on rough fellows to the job she had on hand. A gang of lads and louts was drawn together, and some silly vow got out of them that they would rid the land of the wood-biders: and all as if it had been some great deed.

Now the island was but very little known to the North-folk at the back of the fells; but one thing they knew, and this was that they could not come at it without boats: and if they stayed boat-building they would be spied and foreset. But said Asdis, "Wait until the apple drops. Why build a boat to cross a bridge?" At which they gaped, but she bade them watch the birds and the bushes.

For that third winter began to be a hard winter. The swallows went early, and the wild swans came in flocks from the north. Choups and holly-berries reddened the hedges; and after Yule the fells were creamed over and the becks dwindled. As the days lengthened so the cold strengthened, until even the sunny shores of Leven and Duddon were frozen fast; and when a high tide came, it burst the floe, and left the sands and mosses strewn for many a mile with huge blocks and tables of ice, piled one upon another like peats to dry. Then Asdis rubbed her hands said, "Now, lads, your bridge will be built."

So they set out and away through the snowy woods until they came to the waterside of Thurston-mere; and there was a sight. Still as death the white fells stood around. Still as death the lake spread, white and black; white where the snow hid it, and black in great reaches that could hardly be

known from standing water, but that its soft ripples stirred
not, and the picture of wood and fell lay upon them clearer
and quieter than the shapes in a tarn on a summer day, for
all the north-wind's blowing. The only thing that moved
was a wreath of smoke in front of the fell-side over against
them, and the likeness of the same wreath in the glassy field
below. And where the two wreaths met was a crag, standing
up from the flat; an island no longer.

They adventured from the snowy shore, hardly knowing
when they were on land and when on lake, until suddenly,
beneath their feet, deep down, they saw the stones lying at
the bottom, clear in the sunlight, through the wonderful floor,
such as the floor of Heaven may be to them that walk upon
it, and look down upon us thence. Slowly now and warily
the men went, for the ice was smooth and slape; and if it was
roughened at all, it was not with waves, but as if stars and
arrow-heads of crystal had been inlaid in glass, like the silver
a smith inlays in steel.

Then as they walked there arose a strange turmoil in the
stillness. Far and wide the ice began to crack and settle,
with groanings and thunderings that roared and muttered
from shore to shore. Across the black, clear deep there flew
white, ragged lightnings, on either hand, before and behind,
as when one watches a thunderstorm in the valley beneath a
lofty mountain. Then a great crack flitted screaming right
under their feet, and half the company turned and scattered,
crying out there was witch-work in it, and they were lost.
But as they staggered and slid and fell others cursed them
for fools, and kicked them up again, and egged them on;
showing them how to set feet together and shove themselves
along with their spears thrust hard behind them upon the ice.
And so they won a mile or so to the island.

But before they were half way over, the smoke shot up
into a thick cloud, and flames flickered; and over the waste
of white and black, above the moaning and groaning of the
ice field, arose the deep note of a horn, stifled and quivering
at first, and strengthening into a hollow peal, that suddenly

stayed.   As suddenly it was answered from the fell ; and then
again from the Beacon hill behind ; and then again far up the
lake ; until the sky was ringing with it.   They stood in amaze
to listen ; and the flame blazed higher, and the smoke rolled
in coils, brown against the white moorland.   Again the war-
horn pealed, and the answers came ; and when the last had
died away, another answer, over and above the echoes, a faint
clang, far down the Crake.   And then there was only the
groaning of the ice to hear ; and the island, when they came
to it, was nothing but a snowy rock, untenanted, for aught
they could see, and lifeless, but for the great fire.

All round the brink the slape ice shelved away, by the
settling of the lake, so that footing was bad to get.   The rock
went down sheer into the smooth floor, grey and bare beneath
and heaped with pillowy snow above, from which hung
fringes of icicles, like teeth of a dragon in northern deeps.
They scrambled up the shelving slide, and grasped at the
rocks to break away the icicles and beat down the snow, for
hand-hold and foot-hold.   But as they strove up the lower
rocks, half smothered with the mealy drift, two heads came
out upon the top of the crag, and two great stones rolled
among them.   And those they fell upon cried but once.

Then began a storm of stones from above, to which they
could make no reply, for the defenders were hidden behind
the highest ridge, and safe from shot.   Even if the attackers
could make a shift to use bow and dart, and that they could
seldom in their eagerness to win upward, and in their un-
steady footing, their weapons only rattled down among them
again from the icebound rock.   And so this went on for a
while, until many had been maimed, and some killed outright.
The nearer they got, the steeper and more dangerous were
the battlements of that castle built without hands : a long
wall, high enough and steep enough to be dangerous any day,
but hopeless in this snow and frost, with the great stones
plunging down, well aimed from above.

They drew off to the open and held council.   In a while
they broke into two bands, and went round the island to try

for scaling spots, and to break in on both hands at once.
Now the ends of the island are less steep than its sides, for
there is a way up between the ridges, both to north and
south. But nobody who meant to hold the place would fail
to stop those doors with some stockading at least, if not a
good stone wall: and so they were brought to a standstill
here as heretofore. The north end was not only well blocked,
but the rocks there are stiff and steep for this work; and of
the two defenders one followed each company round about,
never leaving them alone, what with stones, what with hand-
strokes when they tried the wooden palings. And if fire was
hot within the hold, it was all frost without, and never a
spark to set the doors alight.

So now they met together at the south end, where the twin
harbour lies between the calf and the crag. They began to
swarm up a buttress that makes a narrow ladder to the top,
easy enough to climb if it were not for the ice that sheeted it,
and for the rough welcome that awaited the first man on the
sharp and dangerous crest. By this the far-away fells stood
rosy red and dim around; the sky was like fire behind Beacon
fell, and the cold floor of ice seemed to be all one lake of
blood. The bale on the crag reeked and roared, and out of
the smoke came a sword that lopped the first comer like a
bough, and sent him rolling down the unbroken rock for
many an ell. Then they were aware of the wood-biders
standing over them, each with a weapon. They took heart
and shuffled up the harder, shouting curses, and what they
would do when they won to the top. But the next comer
rolled into the bay with his brains knocked out. That was
the doing of a big stick that swung round and about in the
hands of Raineach.

"Well done, lass," shouted Thorstein, who kept his distance
from her, however. "It's not for nothing she's a giant's
daughter," he laughed, for he was warming to his work.

But then the children waked behind them, stirred by the
noise; and they screamed. Raineach was scared lest some
of the rascals had got in the back way, and she flew to seek

them. The carles below set up a jeer, and three or four flung in at once. One was down, and another was down; but Thorstein's sword bent; and as he kneeled on it to straighten it, the others were at him. They had him on his back, and a stroke would have done their job; but out came Raineach with such a swingeing batt of her club on the one of them, as broke his backbone like a rotten stick; and she gripped the other by the throat and hauled him off. She lugged and tugged, and fairly lifted him off his feet, and bundled him over the edge among his fellows. Up springs Thorstein with a great shout, and she beside him; and every mother's son that could stir a limb scattered off the edge in a flock. The weight of them all coming down together broke the ice where it was rotten from the warmth of the flat rock, that caught and kept the morning sun; and they went into the hole like corn into the miller's hopper. It was deep there: the rock goes down at once into the lake, and rises again in ugly teeth, bound to cut a swimmer's knees, let alone the edges of the broken ice. He with lopped arm, their leader in the assault, after a few wild strokes went down in a red spot. The rest struggled out, to the nearest shore, and shouted themselves hoarse with their anger.

Thorstein and Raineach went up to look at the man whose back was broken. He cried for water, and she gave him to drink. Thorstein stood over him, fierce and stern.

"Who sent thee, man?" he said.

But they got nothing out of him, and in a while he died.

And, then, when all was over, Raineach burst into a blurt of weeping. "What, lass! what, lass!" said Thorstein, as she shook and sobbed in his arms; "hold up, my little one; all's right now. I warrant we see no more of them. There's not a scratch on thee, and I am none the worse but for a bruise or two. What's there to greet for?"

"It's not that," she sobbed.

"Here, then; take the barn: hark how he is crying on his mother." Then as the sobs shook her, and the baby at her breast, said Thorstein, staring at them, and biting a twig

"Eh, queer things women are. Aye, and," says he, "there's women and women."

And so Asdis goes out of the story.

When the stars were shining, they had more guests, not unbidden, though late to the play.

"Kinsman," said Hundi, as he panted and caught his breath, between draughts of milk in the cot on the island; "Kinsman, no more of this. To the Althing thou goest this midsummer, if I drag thee yonder by the scruff of the neck." And "Aye, goes he," said the half score of men that had come hot-foot from Lowick.

"Never saw I woman more scared than Halldora when thy horn sounded."

"Scared was she," said one of them: "but for a scare, oh boys, the master capped all. Snail? says I, as I peltered after him. Hare! says I,—Hundi Harefoot's the word!"

Hundi caught him by the hand, laughing. "A forfeit," he cried, "to fasten the name! But Thorstein, my man, get thy peace, and let us share it. Life is not worth living, with this horn-blowing to look for."

So when mid-summer was come, Thorstein set forth alone, sorely as Raineach grudged his leaving her. She said it was for no good he was going. But he kissed her, and said she should be mistress of Blawith before the summer was out. "That may be," she said, "but never so happy as here."

CHAPTER XLVII.—THE HOST OF WEIRD.

THORSTEIN travelled over the fells to the waterhead of the great lake we call Windermere, meaning to stay there for the night, and so to come upon the Althing when folk were at their meeting about mid-day. But when he was at the door of the Welshmen's cots, in that old ruin of the Romans, there was a great noise within; and he spied a many Northmen sitting there at drink, and among them some faces he knew and misliked. They too were on their way to Legburthwaite: and no sooner did he darken the door but they leapt up and ran at him. He had no mind to redden his hands with them, just when he was going to sue for his peace; and away he went, out of the great road and into the woods again.

This was a part he knew but little, and yet he found a track that led him up a steep dell and over a hause where was a wonderful big stone, like a kirk, by the way side, with high fells running up on either hand. Before him lay the great deep valley, reaching away northward, and all its forests and crags purple and golden in the summer afternoon. Here and there was a gleam of water; and far in the distance, smoke rising as if from the houses of men. The path led onward and downward, rough and steep. He followed it for a good while, and came to a tarn which afterwards the Northmen called Brotherwater, from the ancient road that passed by. Then he was on the floor of the valley, with the steep heights all around and above: and it was but an hour or so to the village of Patrickdale.

This was another of those few spots in the fell country where people were found before the Northmen came into Lakeland. The dwellers were mostly like the rougher sort of fell-folk, and their cots were of the poorest, scattered, and buried in wood. And yet they had a church in their midst, if it were no more than a cell; where a kind of hermit priest lived, and in one little chamber slept upon the ground, and ate his crust, and performed the holy service, with nothing but a rough stone for his altar and another for his pillow.

Thorstein sat down weary and hungered at the church door, and knocked upon it. Presently in the quiet village there was a barking of dogs that echoed from crag to crag around: and then the church door opened, and the priest came out with a thumping big stick upheld in one hand, while he unbarred the iron-hasped door with the other.

Thorstein bade him have peace, for it was a Christian and a wayfarer who begged for alms. He spoke in the fell-folk's tongue, reckoning that whether the priest were English or Irish he must speak so in his cracks with the country-folk hereabouts. So the priest let him into the church and from

an ark brought out a bowl of sour milk and a cake of rye
bread.

"Maybe now," said Thorstein, "this is all thou hast."

"All I have here," said the priest. "But there are good
neighbours."

So Thorstein drank the milk at a draught, and ate the cake
in two mouthfuls.

"I am no stranger in these parts," said he, "but I never
was here before."

"Like enough not," said the priest. "We call this St.
Patrick's church, for on this spot many a lifetime back the
glorious and blessed Patrick preached: and in the well hard
by christened both men and women that heard him. And
here in this desert, unworthy as I am, I strive to keep the
lamp alight, as those that watch for their Lord."

They talked together awhile, for the priest seemed right
glad of a friendly face other than those of his rough flock,—
goats he called them, "for lambs they be not indeed, but
very mountain goats. And yet God forgive me for saying an
ill word of them," added he: "for I mind me of the days
when I was in the world. There was as much hardness of
heart and stiffneckedness among our townsfolk yonder at
Dacor—"

But now there was a noise without, and the dogs barking
again. More than that, eager voices. Out stepped the priest
to hear what the news might be, bidding Thorstein stay
where he was, or he would not answer for him.

There was a couple of men,—fighting-men of Domhnall's
they seemed by their weapons; but no great champions, by
their faces. Around them a knot of rough villagers, half
clothed in skins, and shaggy-headed, with staves in their
hands. They all talked long and loud. Thorstein could just
hear something about an army and flight and slaughter; but
he deemed it wise to do as the priest bade him, lest he should
be mis-kenned and mauled by that rabble.

"Lord help us," said the priest coming back into the
church: "God and all blessed Saints protect us. Ill tidings,

young man. Awful tidings. But as the mountains stand round about Jerusalem, even so the Lord stands round us who fear him."

Then between prayers and sighs he told the news. These were two men of the dale who had gone to fight in Domhnall's army, called out but lately. It seemed that Eadmund the English king had been warring in the North against Domhnall's people in Strathclyde, and against the vikings in Galloway : and having wasted far and wide, he was entered into Cumberland where Domhnall, though he had fled from place to place, thought to make another stand : and so had called out every man he could levy. But still he got the worst of it, and fled before the Saxons : and no wonder, for with the Saxons there were Malcolm king of Scots and a host of his, and Llewelyn of Wales with his men, a terrible great multitude. Last night they lay at· Penrith, and Domhnall was pressing his men forward towards the fell-country, hoping either to escape into the mountain fastnesses, or to entangle his enemies in some strait pass among rocks and swamps, and so destroy them. But before these men fled from his army, it had been given out that he aimed at the mountain road to the city of Helvellyn.

" What," cried Thorstein, " near our Northmen's meeting place ? Aye, father, though I am Christian, I am a Northman born, and neither Dane nor Saxon. Tell me, oh man, tell me how I may come to them and give them warning. Is there a way over yon crags ? It cannot be far : and yet the rocks stand up like walls of heaven."

The priest took him to the door and pointed out a deep dale that runs up into the fells : Grisedale we call it now. When he was at the head of that dale he would find a tarn : then he was to take the valley to his right hand, and it would bring him to the hause above the city of Helvellyn. " But," said he, " it is trackless forest : none rougher in our mountains. And it teems with wild swine. If it were for a boar-hunt with a party of stout fellows, no place could be fitter. But for a lone traveller, at speed, and a stranger, I doubt the end of the journey might be nearer than its goal."

"Path or no path, boars or bears," cried Thorstein running back into the church for his weapons, "I must try it and that hastily."

"Stay," said the priest. "There is another way, if thou canst climb the rocks like a wild cat, and keep a cool head while the eagles scream around thee. I know this only by report: but men have climbed above the woods where all is open grass or naked rock, and so across over Helvellyn. They say it is a fearful place: no otherwise than when one mounts a ladder against a castle-wall: but that this is terrible in its loftiness and horror beyond any high tower or deep sea-crag. And the night is at hand."

"The night," said Thorstein, "is fair, and never wholly dark at this season. As for crags and the danger of the fells, I have fared through a many before now. Point me out the way, father."

It was the clear gloaming of summer midnight when he had forced his way through the woods that clothed the valley side, and that crept up the crags like moss on a stone. He was on Striding-edge: forest and fell around him were black, a tossing surge of darkness; in which gleamed ugly and strange the great lake, that reached away into distance of slaty gloom. On the ridge there was light from the north, a brown light, no more than enough to see footing and hand-hold. But when his foot slipped, and a great stone rolled from under it, there was a crash and a roar that raised the echoes all round the cove, as the stone whirled and leapt towards the round tarn that he could hardly discern in the darkness,—how far below he could not reckon. And on the other hand it was no less steep. Pinnacles of rock stood up along the abyss, and in front a great mass, a wall it seemed in the uncertain gloom, unapproachable. With the falling stones the eagles were roused, and sailed screaming about him: so that he clung to the ridge, and drew his sword.

Then he came to a place where the rock fell away into darkness: and he sat doubting the priest's guidance, and scanning the black wall that rose over-head before him: for he was weary by now and began to be faint with hunger. He cast overboard his shield that he had carried so far, and it fell down the rock but a little way, and then caught. He followed it and found it, and then scrambled up the wall; which turned out to be no more than a scree-slope, though it was one of the stiffest.

From Helvellyn top he saw the arch of light in the north again, sunset and dawn in one, streaked with black bars of cloud. But underneath them, strong against the meshes of faint daffodil colour, and the lowest band of dusky red, stood out the lines of Skiddaw and Blencathra, the shapes he knew right well of old, and welcomed joyfully. He ran along the brown and rounded grassy summit, forgetting his weariness, until Thirlmere gleamed beneath him,—the winding lake with its steep shores, and the crags where he had first met Aluinn and Domhnall. Then, how high that mountain eyrie of theirs had seemed : but now it was nought but a heave in the dark land that was spread out before him like an embroidered garment cast upon the floor.

Then, as he went forward, wary of the swamps that lie among the grass of those great mountain-backs, he saw a man come up on the moorland, but from some point farther north; and run, as he had run, across towards Thirlmere. " He will be another of the fleers," said Thorstein to himself. " He is bound for Northmen's camp, like me." And he shouted, and tried to overtake him, but in vain. Then came up two or three others : they were dimly seen and grey in that twilight : but he could make them out enough to know that they carried weapons, and fled in haste. He shouted again ; but no answer. Then more followed ; and he could see that among the new comers were pursuers as well as pursued : and now one fell, and was killed outright before his eyes. But there was no sound of shouting : and as he ran towards them he seemed to come no nearer, whether it was that the twilight put him out of his reckoning, or what. And then came a flock of men marching forward with banner and spear, aye, and horses among them, and chariots, on the bare mountain-top, with pathless crags behind and in front, where no army could have marched in order, nor waggon gone upon wheels. But still they crossed over, a very great multitude, under the broken light that held his eyes fixed to northward. He stayed running, and listened. The waterfalls roared beneath : but not a sound was there of living men ; neither tramp nor shout : and still they passed.

Terror was upon him now, and his knees shook. He looked behind him, and out of the deep blackness a few great stars shone, and around was the moorland with its strange forms, and he knew not what else, crowding upon him. With a cry he fled down the grassy slope. It fell away steeper and steeper. He stumbled among the hidden stones : but he could not stay his feet ; and down he rolled from rock to rock, into the thunder of Helvellyn gill.

CHAPTER XLVIII.—THE STORM OF THE LAW-BURG.

AT Legburthwaite the morning was wild. The wind had risen in the night and brought rain. The clouds were low, raking along the fell sides, and one could hardly see the crags across the valley for greyness.

The Althing was not yet hallowed, for the Northmen were not met together. Some early comers had arrived and spent the night in their booths,—rough hut-walls, unroofed, put up of old to serve for lodging at these summer meetings, and covered, when the time was, with tent-cloths cast over them. A group of elder men sat talking in the rain : others were setting up the bounds of the doom-ring, driving in the posts with pick and mallet, and cutting hazel poles in the copse hard by, to lay across from stake to stake. Others were repairing the winter's damage to the turf seats within the ring, where the chiefs and the jurymen were to sit.

Down from Helvellyn side, though the driving rain, crept a battered man, slowly working his way among the boulders of the slope. He dragged himself up to the group of elders, and they saw that he was newly wounded, and foredone with toil and travel.

Then said one, " This is Thorstein Sweinson of the Mere: he that slew his brother. Away, fellow: the place is not hallowed yet ; there is no peace to be got now for such as thee."

Said another, " Let be : the wood-bider is not here for nought, and maybe has a story to tell."

But he gaped upon them and could not speak. So they gave him to drink.

" Thanks, friend," he said. " Neighbours, do with me as you will, but hear me. Domhnall is fleeing before the Saxons. He is upon us even now. Last night I saw two of his men : they had fled to their home in the fells. They said Eadmund the English king was at Domhnall's heels, and with him Malcolm the Scot and Llewelyn of Wales with a great multitude. Domhnall was for leading them hither, to entrap them if he could ; or to escape into the mountains. I have seen them. On the top of the mountains I saw the hosts pursuing and pursued. Whether it was a vision I cannot tell : but the tidings are truth."

" Here be fine dreams," said the first speaker, " and midsummer madness."

" Dreams or no dreams, the man is spent with travel and battered, and he gives his head into our hands for the sake of the tidings. We shall soon see whether they be true. Meanwhile, my lad, come into my booth and be fed."

Thorstein had hardly brought hand to mouth, when there was a stir without, and the foremost flyers of Domhnall's army came by. They were the guard of the king's wife and children, and a troop of pack-horses with them, heavily laden, maybe with treasure. They made no stay, but for a hasty word, and away towards the city of Helvellyn.

The Northmen, taking short counsel together, agreed to draw out of their booths, and to make a stand upon the Thingmount, and so abide what might happen. Why they should thus meddle, when they might have escaped with the foremost flyers, or easily hidden in the woods, who can say ?—except that they were bred fighting men, and thought

scorn to leave their own Thing-stead without so much as a
stroke.

So there in battle array they stood, on their mound where
the four dales met, and the great crags around.   Over
against them the path crept by the skirts of the fells; on this
side the Greta and on that Helvellyn beck : and the clouds
flying low, and the rain driving.

Out of the mist came the flyers, horse galloping and foot
running; whoever was sound and unwounded outpacing his
fellows, as they streamed up the road and into the mist again.
Then came the wearied men, some scant of breath and half
blind with toil and with watching under arms, pushing and
pressing along the narrow path ; here and there one falling
with a groan, and kicked out of the way into the river, or
screaming as the horses stamped the life out of him.   And so
they swept past, while the Northmen cried to them across
the dale to turn and stand by their friends.

Then there was a pause, and the sound of the pursuers
shouting along the vale of St. John ; and presently their
vanguard was seen pressing along the road,—Welsh they
were of Llewelyn's company, to whom the foremost place
had been given in this enterprise because they were
mountain men, and led where the Lowlanders, with all the
fire of the chase, sometimes held back from following.

When they came to the place where they could see the
Northmen in array on the howe, they were brought to a
standstill : and fresh comers behind them crowded at their
rear, like the wreckage of a streaming flood, when one great
bough is held fast at a force-head.   Then they crossed the flat
field, and stood on the bank of Helvellyn beck, and cried to
the Northmen to come down and yield themselves.   But
the Northmen shouted in answer, and gave them a flight of
spears: and when spears were spent, stones and the turf of
the Thing seats, and everything that was handy.   Soon the
Welshmen, seeing how few they had to deal with, and how
many of their own men had come up by this time, took
heart, and rushed up the bank shoulder to shoulder.   But

along the bank top it was shield to shield, and a line of whirling blades : and down the wave rolled again.

By this time the main army was coming up, and the cry was for bowmen. For in those days it was not as it was in later times, when every English foot-soldier carried his long-bow. Spear to throw and axe to hew with, were their main weapons. The Welsh stood aside, and a file of archers passed through the host, and formed in a line on the Thing-field, while the rest ransacked the booths. Together the bowmen drew their bows, and at a shout of command to let fly, the Northmen fell flat under their shields, and the flight of arrows hurtled over them.

But while this was going forward, behind the line of archers other companies crept this way and that ; and through the cover of the wood on Great Howe other bowmen climbed up to take advantage of the higher ground, and to get the Northmen below them. And soon there was a rattling on shield and helm and coat of mail. When the enemy saw that they were beginning to be discomfited, spears were levelled, and up they rushed in a thick throng on all sides at once, man pressing man from behind, so that there was no turning nor fleeing. Down went the first comers all round the line of red blades : but the shield that Thorstein had carried, and lost, and saved again, was burst through, and a broken shaft left in it, and the strap was riven. He took it in both hands and hurled it edgewise : and shouted when it caught a big fellow in the teeth and drove him backwards into the thick of the crowd below.

"Well thrown, wood-bider," said his next neighbour. "I'll be thy shield-man this holmgang :" as he caught a stroke on his target, and Thorstein leapt out from behind him and cut down the man who had given it. So it was hand to hand and sword to spear for a while, over the ring of fallen bodies. But the Northmen shook them off, and thrust them down the brink again.

Then one upon the Thing-stead began to sing, and then another, in staves of verse that seemed to set their fellows' hearts on fire. They shouted at their foes, giving them every ill name and stinging jest that might prick them to a new attack. But the only answer was the hail of arrows from above: and if the rain washed the Northmen white, there was red enough running to need it. Hardly one among them but had some hurt. Thorstein, who was no whole man to start with, and ill clad for this play, was the worse for more than a scratch.

"Neighbours," said he, "why are we standing still to be shot down like deer?"

Then forth he leapt, and down the slope, hewing right and left, and leaving a lane through the crowd. His friends followed close in a band, and the enemy drew back before them, and closed behind them. The Northmen were like a wild beast in a net.

"Look you there," said Thorstein, holding out a bladeless hilt: "was ever such rotten iron?"

"It has done a day's work," said his friend with the shield.

"Nay, not a forenoon's."

He sat down upon a stone. His friend took him under the shoulder to lift him on. "We shall win through yet," said he.

But Thorstein fell over on the red grass.

"Let be," said the elder who had known him at first. "He has got his peace. Forward all!"

CHAPTER XLIX.—DUNMAIL RAISE.

KING Eadmund stood upon the brink of Thirlmere, and scanned the shore on either side. His enemies had vanished as if by art magic. There lay the path, running down to the ford, and up again on the farther side, and it could be traced winding under the terrible crags whose tops were lost in clouds, and away into huge headlands and shaggy promontories plunging into the water, one beyond another, until they faded afar in the rain and mist.

On this hand king Malcolm, and on that hand king Llewelyn, were instant to go forward and follow the road:

but the Lowland king, brave as he was in fight and bold in counsel, hung back from the attempt and from following unseen foes into unknown fastnesses.

While they talked, across the wath came two or three men, gaunt and red-bearded and clothed in skins. They waved their hands above their heads as if to signify that they came in peace: and the king bade bring them before him. At their first words, "King," said Malcolm, "these are folk of mine, or should be: for it is our tongue they have. Let me be interpreter."

Then the fell-folk told the kings that Domhnall and his men were lurking in the woods, ready to roll rocks on their enemies. But they could show the Saxons how to get the better of the ambush.

Asked by what device, the said that fell-climbers could reach the top of the brow under which Domhnall lay ; and once there, a few men could roll rocks on him as he had ment to roll rocks on the Saxons : and then the main army could pursue them along the road, which was no worse than that by which they had come.

"And a good counsel it is, king," said Malcolm, when he had interpreted : "and one that we use often in our mountain warfare. Give the business into my hand, and you shall see them swarm out of the woods like ants out of a stirred ant-hill."

"But what faith can we put in the word of these savages ? " asked Eadmund.

They said proudly that it was so as they had spoken, and they were in the hand of the kings to reward or to slay. "And beside that," said one of them with a scowl, "we have an old grudge of our own to settle with Domhnall."

So the army moved over the wath, and the main body halted on the road, ready for the chase when the game was beaten out of cover. Malcolm with a band of mountain men, guided by the red folk, climbed the brow of Armboth fell : and when they were at the top, set to work heaving rocks over the edge. There was a crashing among trees, and shouts

and shrieks; and presently men were beheld fleeing down
the screes among the woods, and the great stones whirling
down after them.   Such as got away, streamed out into the
road, and fled along it up and down, like worms out of a
dunghill when it is beaten to get baits.   Then the trumpets
were blown that should signal to the men above to leave their
work: and forth marched the army in hot pursuit, along the
path and along the low foreshore of the lake, and then mounting over the crags where they were high, and descending
again among rocks, and cliffs, and wild wood, that overhung
the length of the lake.   And at last they looked down upon
the city of Helvellyn.

Here for a while they were brought to a stand: the walls
of great stones, and the swampy flats on one side of it,
threatened to hold them longer than they liked.   The day
was wearing, and if the nut were cracked the kernel was not
eaten yet.   So they took up their stand on the high ground
between the city and the fell, and the trumpets sounded an
assault.

Then was there shouting, and a terrible cry that rose to
Helvellyn top, as the Saxons clambered up the rugged wall
in throngs, and leapt over, bearing down the defenders and
slaughtering all before them.   Domhnall's wife and his two
children were taken; but for the rest it was kill and slay, as
men ransacked the rude cots within the walls for their
enemies, and hewed them down where they found them.

But while all this was going forward, a band of men was
spied making away along the fell side.   They had escaped
by the farther gate and along the road; and the freshest of
the Saxons who were still outside the walls, and the fleetest
of the horsemen, were sent in pursuit.   But the road was
rugged and difficult as ever, and if they came up with one
party, and brought it to bay, it was but to waste time, and the
rest had the better start of them.   And so the battle went
on, at every beck to be forded, and every rock to be passed;
and especially where the great tongue of land at the foot of
Steel fell stands across the valley, like a twin wall of huge
earth-works cast up by giants long ago.

The foremost of the flyers was Domhnall himself, running for dear life up the long slope of the pass. He was alone now, and on foot. One horse after another had fallen under him, and of all the army he had led out to its ruin not one was there to stand by him. This man had come between him and the spear that threatened him : that one had turned back to keep the hunters in play. They were gone now : but he was still a king, if the crown on his helmet could make him one. And he bethought him of hiding among the moors and rocks, anywhere, like a wild beast : and he peered this way and that through the rain as he ran, with none following, escaped, he hoped, at last. He neared the brow of the hill : soon it would be down-bank and away ; surely some woodland dweller would harbour him.

Under a hawthorn tree at the summit sat a woman, with long golden hair lank in the rain, and green gown wet, and clinging to her sides : hard featured, and fierce she looked : strange, as she rose and stood before him in the way. He dashed at her blindly with his sword, but she caught his hand ; and as he stumbled at her feet, the crown fell from his helmet, clattering on the stones of the path. She took it up, and weighed it in her hand.

" Domhnall," she said, " it is mine at last, then."

" Oh, Aluinn," he cried, " save me, hide me ! "

She led him by a roaring stream and up a steep narrow gill, away from the valley and the shouts of the pursuers, aloft into the cloud. It was but a step, and they came to a black water, shoreless, beyond, for the rain-mist. As he sank down, out-wearied, she flung the golden thing into the dark tarn.

" It is safe, there," she said.

And there they say the crown of Cumbria lies to this hour, in the depths of Grisedale tarn.

Domhnall passed away into the cloud and was seen no more in these parts. Folk might well believe him to be dead, or gone to fairyland. Whether his flight was spied by some of the Northmen coming by Dunmail raise toward the

Althing which they never held, or howsoever it might have been told, the place kept his name, changed but a little in alien mouths ; and still haunted, they say, by the fleeing king and the fairy maid flitting before him.

CHAPTER L.—THE PEACE OF THORSTEIN.

TERRIBLE was the tale they brought to Furness about the storm of the Lawburg and the death of Thorstein and his fellows. Though indeed not all of them perished. Hopeless as it seemed, some of that band had cut their way through the Saxon army and escaped into hiding among the rocks and woods on Brackmere bank : and some that had been left for dead had been found by their friends when the storm was over, and taken up and healed of their wounds. But not Thorstein. He lay where he fell, within a step of the spot where he had slain his brother. They gave him his peace, late as it was : for it was not too late to let his children inherit the land around Thurston water.

Hundi and Raud, Rolf and the rest of their kinsmen and neighbours came together and rebuilt the homestead at Blawith, freely giving their labour as the custom was ; and over and above their labour, each comer gave a share toward the things that were needed to keep house and farm. So that with what she had and what she got, Raineach lacked neither servants nor stock, furniture within nor gear without. They brought her from the island, and bade her dwell in peace on the land that was hers and her children's. Many a time came to her one or another who would gladly have cast in his lot with them for her sake : but she said nay to all. After a while she sent for a priest, and built him a church at Blawith, that she might bring up her household in the right faith and fear of God. And before Yule she was the mother of a third son to Thorstein, one that favoured her father, for he was red-haired and long limbed.

" Thorstein of the Mere will not want for sons to avenge him," said folk, when they came to see her.

" Nay," she said. " He has found his peace. Let us keep it."

But a twelvemonth had not gone by after the battle, and midsummer was not yet come, when they heard tidings of the death of Eadmund in his own hall at a feast, by the hands of an outlaw. The North-folk looked at one another, as much as to say it was but his due ; vengeance had come upon him already for the strife he had stirred up, and especially for the sackless and innocent men who had fallen with Thorstein Sweinson in the war upon Cumberland.

The Northmen continued in their homes by firth and fell, spite of York earls and Scottish kings. For yet two hundred years they kept their freedom. Even when the Normans brought all this border country under the feudal yoke, still for many a hundred years the dalesmen, children of the vikings, used to meet at the Steading-stone by Thirlmere, and kept alive some smouldering memory of their birthright in the country Parliament of Wythburn. And everywhere they held to their old manners and their old speech, changing little of either, and that but slowly.

For in these dales the dream of Unna came true, that saw love abiding and labour continuing, heedless of glory and fearless of death.

SO ENDS THE STORY OF THORSTEIN.

Also published by
LLANERCH:

NORTHUMBRIAN CROSSES
W. G. Collingwood.

LIVES OF THE
NORTHUMBRIAN SAINTS
S. Baring-Gould.

A HISTORY OF THE KINGS
OF ENGLAND
Simeon of Durham.

SYMBOLISM OF THE
CELTIC CROSS
Derek Bryce.

TALIESIN POEMS
Meirion Pennar.

WARKWORTH'S CHRONICLE
John of Warkworth.

BARDS AND HEROES
Carl Lofmark.

For a complete list,
write to:
Llanerch Enterprises,
Felinfach, Lampeter,
Dyfed, SA48 8PJ.